Lily White

CHRISTIAN SCHÜNEMANN, born in 1968, is a journalist who has worked in Moscow and Bosnia-Herzegovina. He received the Helmut Stegmann Prize for Journalism in 2001.

JELENA VOLIĆ is an academic, lecturing in modern German literature. She divides her time between Belgrade and Berlin.

Lily White

A Case for Milena Lukin

CHRISTIAN SCHÜNEMANN AND JELENA VOLIĆ

Translated by Baida Dar

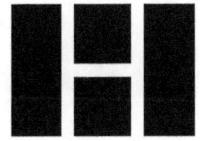

First published in English in 2021 by
Haus Publishing Ltd
4 Cinnamon Row, London SW11 3TW
www.hauspublishing.com
@HausPublishing

Originally published in German as
Maiglöckchenweiß: Ein Fall für Milena Lukin
Copyright © 2017 by Diogenes Verlag AG Zürich

Translation Copyright © 2021 by Baida Dar

A full CIP record for this book is available from the British Library

The moral right of the authors has been asserted

ISBN: 978-1-912208-65-4
eISBN: 978-1-912208-66-1

Typeset in Garamond by MacGuru Ltd
Printed in the United Kingdom

This novel is inspired by two real cases. The plot and characters that appear in this novel, however, are entirely fictitious. Any similarities between them and actual events or characters are entirely coincidental.

In the mid-1990s, a Serbian Roma boy was attacked on the street by two youths in the centre of Belgrade and beaten to death. Investigators found the murder weapon, a section of drainpipe, near the crime scene.

On 12 March 2003, the Serbian prime minister was murdered on the way to his office in Belgrade. It was an ambush: shots were fired from a distance and he died of his injuries.

1

The head of celery had been a gift from the stallholder in the market, and the bones came from the butcher, who had passed them out to her through the back door. Svetlana scrubbed carrots, added some marjoram to the pot, and turned down the flame, so the soup would simmer but the lid wouldn't start rattling. The soup would last for several days, maybe even a whole week. Since she'd come to her decision, life felt better. Not good, but at least a bit easier – as if a great burden had been lifted from her shoulders.

She felt around in the paper wrapper and found two small potatoes left inside. The darkness didn't bother her – quite the contrary. Darkness was good. She gathered up the peelings and wiped her hands on her apron. Jovan was fast asleep, breathing deeply and unsuspectingly. The two bottles he had drained over the course of the afternoon and evening stood next to the waste bin; despite being drunk, he had been conscientious enough to take out the rubbish. Her beloved Jovan. The dreams they'd had: to go out into the world, to make it on their own without the clan, to be free and beholden to no one. What crazy ideas. Of course, it wasn't meant to be.

Svetlana took off her apron. She hadn't managed to make it, but her daughter would. One day Anna would live in a beautiful house, and the laughter of her children would fill the rooms and make her forget what had happened to her in these months – enough suffering to last a lifetime. For Anna, hopefully, the good times would one day dawn. And maybe then everything would make sense after all.

Svetlana took out the small metal box from beneath the kitchen bench. From under the mending yarn, which she had used the other day to reinforce and tighten the buttons on her pockets, just in case, she pulled out a small piece of paper, which she had purposefully set aside a few weeks ago. She opened the curtains to let in the moonlight. One day, Anna would understand what her mother had done. Until then, she'd follow the advice her mother was giving her now to guide her on her way, because Anna was not only a clever girl but obedient too. Svetlana wrote:

Learn.
Work hard.
Hold your head up high.
Don't do anything you'd later be ashamed of.
Be happy.

She folded the piece of paper and took it with her into the room behind the curtain. Anna was sleeping soundly and breathing deeply. Svetlana brushed a lock of hair out of her daughter's face and pressed her lips to her warm forehead, breathing in her aroma. Then she slipped the piece of paper under the pillow, stepped back, and took her cardigan from the hook.

Anna would make her way in the world. Of that Svetlana was certain, and she wouldn't do anything to hinder her. All was well, all was as it should be, and the Almighty would watch over her daughter. Svetlana extinguished the flame under the pot, pulled on her rubber boots, and opened the door. She didn't look back.

From beneath the water butt, she retrieved the bricks she'd hidden there a few days before. Shoving one in the left and one in the right pocket of her cardigan, she buttoned up the pockets and straightened the knitted garment. In Jovan's shed, the glass jar with the lilies of the valley in it stood between pots of paint and glue. She picked up the jar and scooped a little more water into it from the butt.

At this time of night, hardly any cars were on the road, and she encountered no one. She walked along the dark streets in her Wellington boots, work apron, and woolly cardigan as if she were the only person in the world, clutching the jar with the lilies of the valley. Exactly the same roads, the same route, that Dušan had taken, holding in his fist the loose change that his father Jovan had, despite the late hour, allowed him to take to the kiosk specially to buy himself a bag of fruit drops. After all, Dušan had brought home a good school report – top marks in mathematics. He'd been so proud, and she had too. She still was.

'Run along,' she'd told him, as she propelled him out of the door. 'And hurry back.'

Her route took her uphill to Belgrade Street – quite a climb with the bricks in her pockets. Who knows what would have become of Dušan? Maybe a teacher or – his idea of a career – a tram driver. He would surely have succeeded and overcome the disadvantages he'd been saddled with.

She noticed that the kiosk was already closed, but she didn't mind. All those people who'd been there, and who'd either turned a blind eye to the incident or looked on impassively – she'd have looked them straight in the eye, including the kiosk owner. Would she have felt hatred? She didn't know. She had no more tears to shed. Svetlana set the jar with the lilies of the valley down at the spot where it had happened.

At the big intersection, she bore right and crossed the park, paying no attention to the drunks and lovers in the darkness.

Branko's Bridge was bathed in a yellow light. Although she hadn't expected it to be so well lit, it seemed like a welcoming omen. There was only the odd car on the road. The night had something special about it. Svetlana walked on without hurrying, until she reckoned she'd reached the middle of the bridge. She couldn't see the river, but she could smell it. A deep feeling of peace and determination came over her.

Though the railing was at chest height, it seemed lower than she had imagined. She took hold of the cold cast iron with both hands. The tips of her boots fitted comfortably between the vertical bars, as if it were a small stepladder. She hauled herself up, rested her midriff on the top of the railings, and then pulled up her other leg. Down below, she could hear the river flowing by. It sounded like a whisper, and the cool air that wafted up to her had a comforting feel.

She wrapped her arms around her body as if she were hugging her little boy, closed her eyes, and stepped forward into emptiness.

2

Driving down Prince Miloš Street, heading out of town, Milena abruptly switched to the left-hand lane, paying no heed to the symphony of car horns behind her, and drew up a mental shopping list for the way home: 1,500 grams of butter for the buttercream icing, two bags of praline, and some small cake candles – eleven of them. For Adam's birthday, Vera was planning to bake both a crown cake and a snow tart. That meant sixteen eggs in all. No, better get twenty. Her mobile started buzzing.

Milena groped around on the passenger seat, looked at the screen, and took the call.

'Hey there,' came Siniša's booming voice. 'I couldn't get hold of anyone at the hotel. When exactly is your ex supposed to be arriving?'

'Philip's coming next week, on Thursday. Adam's already totally beside himself. Is there a problem?'

'I'm en route to Sarajevo right now, so I was going to suggest you swung by the place yourself – Hotel Amsterdam, Little Sava Street. They were planning to open on Monday. I guess it's a bit of an imposition on you, but I know this young couple; they've put so much effort and love into the project, and I think we ought to give them our support.'

'All right then,' Milena replied, flicking on her indicator.

'And have you managed to have a word with your ambassador-boss yet?'

'About your contract? No, not yet.'

'There's no hurry. Really.'

'Thanks for reminding me. I'll take it up with him ASAP,' Milena promised.

'By the way, I've got a wonderful present for Adam. The little tyke will be thrilled.'

'That little tyke's growing bigger by the day.'

'Exactly!'

'See you later.' Milena hung up, placed the handset on the dashboard, and wound down her window.

The gate guard, a young man, emerged from his booth and straightened the jacket of his blue uniform. 'Can I see your ID, please?'

'I work here – you know that!'

'Don't take it personally. I'm only following orders.'

'Of course.' Milena pulled her handbag off the passenger seat and began rooting around in it. Amongst a variety of items including her purse, some jelly bananas, and other stuff, she lighted upon the small plastic-coated card faster than she had expected.

'A little tip,' the young man said as he handed the card back. 'You could wear the ID on a lanyard round your neck, like a necklace. Then you wouldn't have to search for it every time.' He saluted her and disappeared back into his booth.

A moment later, the gate opened, and Milena rolled into the compound of the embassy. Legally speaking, she was now on the territory of the Federal Republic of Germany. Whenever she turned into her reserved parking space here and switched off her engine, she found herself totally at ease with this foreign country, its strict rules and regulations, and the people who conscientiously made sure the rules were followed. All she needed to appreciate this fully was to tot up all the time she had wasted trying to find a parking space uptown, near her institute.

Sandra, the ambassador's PA, was standing at her desk

in the outer office and checking the contents of a package, a pile of white shirts in a flat box. As ever, she was wearing a suit with a broad belt accentuating her wasp waist, and her make-up was as immaculate as if she'd just returned from an appointment with a stylist.

'Good morning,' said Milena, knocking gently on the door. 'Is Mr Kronburg in his office?'

'*Count* Kronburg,' Sandra responded without looking up, 'is in a meeting.' She replaced the tissue paper covering the shirts and closed the lid. The coat of arms on the laminated box indicated it was from a very upmarket outfitter. In all likelihood, the shirts had come from a London tailor.

'Could you let me know when I could talk to Mr Kronburg?' Milena adjusted the strap of her bag over her shoulder. 'And I wanted to ask you–'

Sandra countersigned a delivery note and placed it on top of the box, before depositing it on the top of the filing cabinet. 'The meeting's scheduled to end at 4 p.m.'

'Did Mr Kronburg mention anything about a consultancy agreement with Mr Stojković?'

'Mr Stojković?' Sandra gazed challengingly at Milena. 'You mean your friend, the lawyer? Sorry, I don't know anything about that.'

'Thank you.' Milena turned on her heel and crossed the hall to her office.

She would have loved to slam the door. It was inconceivable that Sandra was oblivious. She spoke three languages fluently, left nothing to chance, and supervised everything. She even arranged for her boss, Count Alexander Kronburg, to be served dill with his fish on evenings out, rather than the parsley that was customary in Serbia. Milena flung her bag down on the leather couch, followed by her denim jacket.

But what most irritated her was that a young woman

– who at twenty, was less than half her age – could get under her skin so easily. A condescending tone and a raised eyebrow from her were enough. In short, Milena was irked because she felt like she'd been caught trying to wangle a well-paid consultancy agreement for a friend. But nobody knew their way around the jungle of Serbian paragraphs and legal texts better than Siniša and, by the same token, no one was more qualified to advise and support her in expediting Serbia's integration into the EU.

Milena slumped into her comfortable desk chair, which, being well-sprung, easily absorbed the sudden impact of her weight. The resubmissions folder was lying on the desk, perfectly squared with the edge; the flowers in the vase were fresh, and there wasn't a speck of dust to be seen anywhere. Milena popped a jelly banana into her mouth and opened her email.

The minutes of a meeting last Wednesday. The new staff list, petty cash receipts, lots of useless stuff. And a note from Philip, already two weeks old, which curiously had fetched up in her spam folder. *We'll be arriving on Thursday 5 May, at 1 p.m.,* he wrote, *at Nikola Tesla Airport in Belgrade. Are we meeting Adam at the airport or should we go straight to our hotel? Incidentally, which hotel is it? Can you send me the location? All the best, Philip. PS. Jutta's really looking forward to finally meeting you.*

'Of course she is,' muttered Milena to herself. 'So am I. In fact, I can hardly wait. Why don't we roll out the red carpet for you while we're at it?' But the business with the hotel – that really needed to be sorted urgently.

She opened the search engine and typed in *Hotel Amsterdam Little Sava Street*, and a message appeared on the screen: *Website under construction.* No telephone number, nothing. What if she simply booked a different hotel?

'Hope I'm not disturbing you?' Alexander Kronburg, the German ambassador, was leaning in the doorway, one hand in his trouser pocket.

'Do come in.' Milena brushed a stray lock from her forehead, hoping that by some miracle her hair was going to arrange itself into a well-ordered wave.

'Please, don't get up on my account.' Alexander appeared strangely nervous. 'Sandra told me you wanted to speak to me.'

'That's right.' As Milena was still pondering how best to clear away the mess on the sofa, Alexander had already taken a seat on the armrest.

'You look upset,' he said.

'I was at the American embassy yesterday.'

'And?'

'The Americans are thinking of withdrawing from the project.'

Alexander sighed. 'I feared that might happen.'

'Really?'

'Because our Serbian partners are cheating with their emissions figures, and the Americans aren't very patient when it comes to those kinds of shenanigans.'

'But we're in the middle of negotiations.'

'What would you suggest, then?' Alexander stretched out his legs.

'Division of labour,' Milena said. 'I'll try and secure a meeting with the Serbian energy minister. Or at least the parliamentary private secretary.'

'What about me?'

'You'll need to soft-soap the Americans and buy us some time.'

'Agreed.' Alexander smiled, causing the little laugh lines that Milena liked so much to appear around his eyes.

'How long have you been with us now?' he suddenly asked.

Milena thought for a moment. 'Almost three months.'

'And you're not finding this double workload too much, what with your job at the institute, working with detectives and criminologists?'

Milena made a non-committal gesture. 'As long as I'm free to organise my own time, I'll be fine. And integration into the EU is very dear to my heart.'

'Glad to hear it.' He stood up. 'Even so, I've a small suggestion to make.'

'Which is?'

'Why don't you bring in a few personal items? A photo of your son, for example.'

Milena glanced round in astonishment.

'And next week,' he turned to go, 'we'll finally have time to talk over a few things.'

'What things?'

'Well, for instance, what to do about your friend Mr Stojković.'

'Let me just make one thing clear,' Milena smiled. 'He's only a colleague.'

Alexander held up his hands disarmingly and disappeared, leaving Milena in a state of bewilderment.

Next week. Plenty of time. Alarmed, she clicked on her appointments calendar. *5–8 May: Donor Conference for the Western Balkan States, Foreign Ministry, Berlin.*

Milena leant back. That was the first she'd ever seen of that entry. The sixth was Adam's birthday; his father was arriving from Hamburg with his partner on the fifth; Vera was baking a crown cake and a snow tart; and Siniša had a brilliant present – there was no way she'd have agreed to attend the meeting.

She picked up the phone, hesitated, replaced the receiver, and strode over to the anteroom.

Sandra was typing, and the door to Alexander's office was closed.

Milena stepped closer to Sandra's desk. 'The meeting next week in Berlin,' she said. 'There's no way I can go.'

Sandra removed two little earphones. 'We have a problem, then.'

'When did you put the appointment in my diary? Just recently? Why wasn't I told about it?'

'I don't keep a record of such things, but I'll happily call the IT department and get them to look into it for you.'

'I need to speak to Mr Kronburg this instant.'

'Count Kronburg is in the middle of a telephone conference.' Sandra leant across the table and gazed up at Milena with her large doe-like eyes. 'Ms Lukin,' she said, 'if it'll make you happy, I'll take full responsibility in this matter. No problem. Really no problem at all. But if you could excuse me now...' She replaced her earphones, and in the next moment a muffled, rhythmic clatter pervaded the room once more.

Milena crossed the hallway again to her office. She really had to get in the habit of checking her diary more regularly, and dealing with things she'd been tasked with in a more timely fashion, not to mention following Siniša's example and – wherever possible – delegating jobs to others.

In the car, as she drove back into town, her phone rang. It was her mother, Vera. 'Dinner's on the table,' she said. 'We're waiting for you.'

'I'm on my way,' Milena replied. 'I've just got to make a quick detour to reserve a room for Philip and Jutta.'

3

'When's he supposed to arrive?' Cecilia asked.

'At four.'

'Are you nervous?'

Luca looked at his watch. 'Why would I be nervous?'

'Tell me one more time.' She moved closer to him, took his arm, and put it round her shoulder. 'You saw him yesterday, you say?'

'The day before yesterday.'

'The day before yesterday,' she repeated. 'And that was the first time after how long?'

Luca stroked her cheek. 'Twenty-five years.'

'Twenty-five years.' From Cecilia's lips, it sounded almost like a prayer. 'You were only seventeen back then.'

'Exactly.'

'And how about him?'

'A year younger.'

'And you were best mates.'

'Bosom buddies.'

'But you've had no contact with him since? No letter, no postcard, no phone call?'

'Nothing. Complete radio silence.'

Cecilia turned her head to look at him. 'And when you met him the other day, how was it?'

Luca shrugged. 'How do you think? It was nice.'

'Nice?' Cecilia laughed. 'Come on. I mean, is he still like he used to be? Did you recognise him straight away?'

'He's aged, of course,' said Luca. 'And... how shall I put it? He's not as carefree as he was.'

'Carefree? So, was he, like, the joker in the pack back then?'

Luca shook his head. 'No, more of a daredevil. One of those guys who just goes for it and asks questions later. Like, if you said, "Shall we blow this joint?" he'd say, "Okay!" And he'd get up and walk off, just like that, and then turn around and ask, "What's up with you? What are you waiting for?"'

'So, what happened, then? Did you really blow the joint?'

'Jurij always gave the impression he had nothing to lose.'

'And you?'

'Now, don't get mad at me,' Luca kissed her forehead, 'but shouldn't you be leaving?'

She uncurled her legs from the sofa and put on her shoes. All of a sudden, a look of melancholy came into her green eyes. 'One day,' she said, 'I'd really like to meet him, this Jurij of yours.'

He pushed a loose strand of hair behind her ear. 'Really, don't concern yourself,' he said. 'First I have to deal with this on my own.'

'I'll be back Sunday,' she called, without turning to look at him.

He heard the click of her heels on the marble floor. 'Drive carefully!' he called after her, though by then she'd most likely left.

The garage door opened, and he heard the deep purr of the Lancia's engine as it disappeared down the driveway.

He stood up and found himself sighing – a deep sigh, like he'd just pulled off a tricky mission. Strange, given that the actual event was still to come. He stepped through the French windows onto the terrace.

How quiet it was out here. The blackbirds, which could really get on your nerves sometimes, were totally silent. He breathed in the fragrant air, as if he had to prove to himself that everything was just fine. He genuinely wasn't nervous. At most, a bit tense. Or, rather, excited. In less than an hour, his old friend Jurij would enter this house, for the first time after all these years, and would see how he lived and what had become of him.

He took a few paces to the edge of the lawn. It wasn't that he wanted to boast. Far from it, actually. He'd tell Jurij how it had all come about: how Cecilia had found and bought this house, and that it had been a complete wreck. The winter garden didn't warrant the name, and the movie theatre and the sauna downstairs in the cellar had been entirely Cecilia's idea. The garden was his thing, and it was smaller than you'd think from up here. When the foliage on the trees grew denser, you couldn't see the Danube down below any more.

He looked up at the elm tree. The views from up there must be panoramic, he thought. Maybe one day he'd build a tree house at the top, a real one, with a rope ladder you could pull up. He'd always dreamt of such a thing as a child.

Jurij made fun of his childish plans, calling him 'Luca the allotment gardener'.

Jurij Pichler. He'd remembered him as slimmer and some-what taller. They'd spoken on the phone twice, but when he showed up at the restaurant out of the blue, swaggering in his typical manner, he'd given Luca quite a shock.

Despite Jurij's greying temples, he knew it was him straight away, and he had taken a good long look at him before break-ing cover. Then came his biggest problem: how to say hello after all that time, and after everything that had happened.

They'd shaken hands, all very formal. Luca had reserved a table in the corner at the back of the restaurant, where it was quieter, and had ordered appetisers. Wine? Jurij declined, which had surprised him, but he'd immediately gone along with it. A bit of small talk; Jurij praised his restaurant as 'the best in town', and Luca replied that it was all to do with location. Just the sort of idle chit-chat people indulge in.

He hoped he hadn't said too much. But he couldn't help but sense that Jurij was genuinely interested. System catering was the future, he'd explained to Jurij. People wanted to know exactly what they were getting for their money – whether they were in a branch of a restaurant in London, Milan, or Belgrade. And Cecilia and he made a good team. She was half Italian, an estate agent with a certain lifestyle. Oh, God, all the rubbish he'd spouted! Cecilia was cool and elegant – pure and simple. As for children – well, they'd met one another ten years too late for that.

'Right, then,' Jurij had joked, 'if everything goes pear-shaped for me, I can come to you for a job.'

And then they'd ordered some red wine after all. The Chianti, what's more.

Jurij told him that he was in the process of converting his parents' home into a small hotel. The area around the harbour, Little Sava Street, was on the way up. What a strange coincidence that they were now both in the hospitality business. Jurij had been back in Belgrade for half a year now, was married to a Dutch woman, also had no children, and by this time was almost more fluent in English and Dutch than his Serbian mother tongue. Amsterdam – that was what the hotel was going to be called.

Luca pricked up his ears. Had he just heard the door go? 'Hello?' he called out.

He took two small logs from the woodpile, one in each hand, and went back into the house. 'Cecilia?' he called. 'Did you forget something?'

No answer. Maybe somebody had forgotten to fasten one of the shutters again.

If Jurij stayed longer tonight, he'd build up the fire later and chuck a steak in the pan for himself.

They hadn't discussed the past at their first meeting, or wallowed in reminiscences, or asked one another, 'Do you remember when...?' And he'd preferred it that way. The past was the past. They'd both moved on with their lives and were grown men now, not foolish boys any longer. But Jurij had let one remark slip all the same. Back then, his family had packed him off to Argentina. He'd spent seven years gluing soles onto shoes in his uncle's factory. Seven damned years. The same amount of time Luca had been in prison and in the camps.

Luca glanced at his watch. Jurij should be here any minute now. Would they talk this evening about what had occurred that night, twenty-five years ago? Why shouldn't they? He'd made peace with himself and his past. And no matter how tragic, stupid, and unnecessary this story had been, something good had come of it after all: for instance, he wouldn't be standing here now and wouldn't be the person he was if things hadn't turned out the way they had.

He ambled into the hallway. Did Jurij really only want to talk about old times? Or did he have something else in mind? Maybe he needed money. A cheap loan for his little hotel.

At 4 p.m. on the dot, the doorbell rang. Before pressing the entry buzzer, Luca looked at the monitor of the security camera covering the street.

Jurij was standing there with his customary wide-legged stance. Jurij Pichler, the only friend he'd ever had.

He pressed the entry buzzer and watched Jurij stride purposefully up the driveway.

4

Little Sava Street was one of the gently rising lanes that connected the harbour with the old town above. To the right and left stood a succession of narrow houses, two or three storeys high, and narrow pavements. Milena drove at a walking pace, reflecting on whether Philip, her ex, even knew this area. He had only come to Belgrade once. She remembered it well. It had been shortly before their wedding – his maiden visit, so to speak. She'd given him a guided tour of the city, shown him all the places of significance in her life: where she'd been born and where she'd gone to kindergarten, her school, and where she'd been a student. Where she'd had her first kiss on the River Sava Promenade, and the station restaurant where she'd drunk her last coffee before leaving for Germany, where Philip had come into her life.

The evening of that first day in Belgrade, he'd sat with Vera in the kitchen, with blisters on his feet and totally exhausted, while his prospective mother-in-law served up *gibanica,* goulash, and semolina cakes. Milena translated, though there'd been precious little to translate; of the few comments that Philip did make, she let some pass and instead inserted some embellishments of her own. Even nowadays, Vera claimed, 'The fact that he hardly ate anything that evening was a bad omen.'

All these thoughts ran through Milena's mind as she drove her Lada up Little Sava Street searching for the Hotel Amsterdam, where her ex and his partner were due to stay.

The narrow hotel was situated at a slight bend in the road and was set apart from the surrounding buildings by its new plasterwork and fresh paint. The red-brick pilasters and the wall area surrounding the transom windows had been lovingly restored and repainted. Milena switched on her hazard lights and wondered whether this was where the hat shop had once been. No, that had been two houses further down the road, and it now looked even more grubby and forlorn in comparison to this renovated and redeveloped building. The hotel was a little gem, and Siniša was right: it would be the ideal place for Philip and Jutta.

Milena switched off the engine and got out of the car.

The tall glass entrance door was locked.

She pressed the bell but heard nothing. Maybe the mechanism was broken.

The interior was shrouded in darkness. Peering in, she could make out various little tables and a motley assortment of chairs. Behind them was a reception desk that clearly doubled as a bar in the evening. The side walls were occupied by several easy chairs and a fireplace. But there was no one in sight.

'I'm afraid it's all over before it's begun,' a voice behind her said.

An elderly man in a cap stood there, staring up sullenly at the facade. 'Someone bit off more than they could chew – financially, I mean.'

Milena followed his gaze. In one of the building's high-up windows, a curtain twitched.

'Do you know the owners?' she asked.

The man shook his head. 'This was my local for more than thirty years. But nowadays everything has to be turned upside down. Big windows and everything new. Makes you sick, it does.'

'I think the hotel looks nice.'

'And I don't recognise my own city any more. Did you see

the people who were milling about here over the weekend? From God knows where.'

Muttering to himself, he moved on. No sooner had he gone than Milena caught sight of a woman, about her age or a little younger and laden with shopping bags, who approached along the alley and turned down a small path that ran alongside the hotel.

'Excuse me!' she called out.

The woman stopped. She had a loose checked blouse over her T-shirt and was wearing a pair of black horn-rimmed glasses.

'Do you have anything to do with the hotel, by any chance?' Milena asked. 'Or do you know what's going on there? I wanted to book a room.'

'The opening's been delayed indefinitely.'

'Are you the owner?'

Her hands full with shopping bags, the woman pursed her lips and blew a strand of hair out of her face. Then she took a step back. 'May I ask who you are?'

'My name's Milena Lukin. I need to find accommodation for guests from Germany who'll be arriving next week. I was recommended this hotel by Siniša Stojković.'

'Mr Stojković?' The woman's face brightened a little. She had to put down her bags to shake Milena's hand. 'I'm really sorry,' she said, 'but we've got some technical problems at the moment.'

'Siniša couldn't get hold of you on the phone, and your website is down, so I thought I'd better come by in person.'

'I'm sorry you've had a wasted journey. As I said...' She delved into the shoulder bag she was carrying. 'I can give you this, though,' she said, handing Milena a flyer. She stooped to pick up her shopping.

'Hang on.' Milena rummaged around in her bag and fished

out her purse. 'If the opening does happen in time,' she said, giving the woman her business card, 'could you let me know?'

The woman took her card and slipped it into her trouser pocket. Then she turned around, continued down the rough path, and disappeared behind the house. Rubble and other debris were heaped up there, including some old sanitary fittings – probably all the stuff they'd stripped out of the house during the renovation.

*

Milena got home and was busy perusing the graffiti in the lift as she ascended to the fifth floor, when she suddenly recalled how Vera had announced that morning that she was going to wash the curtains. Hopefully the old washing machine hadn't given up the ghost; that was the last thing she needed right now.

'Hello!' Milena called out, pulling the apartment door closed behind her. She put down her shopping bag and hung her key on the board. There was a strong smell of cheese and breadcrumbs in the flat, which made her realise how hungry she was. She eased into her slippers.

The service charge invoice had arrived and was propped up decoratively against a straw hat on the sideboard, together with a voucher from the newly opened pedicure parlour in Carnegie Street. The curtains in the living room smelled fresh and looked like new.

Fiona, the cat, was sitting in Milena's chair in the kitchen between Vera and Adam, who had already started to eat.

'You're late,' said Vera. 'Take a seat.'

Milena opened the fridge to put away the groceries she'd bought. 'How's your cold?' she asked, pressing her hand against Adam's forehead.

'Gran and I packed away the winter duvets today and got out the summer ones,' he said.

Milena stroked his hair. 'Great stuff.'

'And the pillows too.'

'Well done, you two!' Milena gave the cat a gentle shove as Vera heaped an ample portion of gratin onto her plate. It contained the leftover turkey escalope from yesterday, finely sliced, along with ceps and fresh tarragon.

'Is there some white wine left?' Milena asked.

Before Vera could utter a word, Adam had leapt up and fetched the bottle from the fridge.

Milena looked at her son in astonishment. 'Did you get your French test results?'

'Why?'

'Just asking. Have you got a guilty conscience, maybe?'

'Leave the boy be,' Vera said. 'Everything's fine.'

After putting Adam to bed – with his teeth brushed and his arms and legs smeared with the good Pavlović ointment – Milena returned to the kitchen. Vera put down her crossword. Milena poured herself the rest of the cold coffee and sat down beside her mother at the kitchen table.

'What's up?' she asked.

Vera took off her glasses. 'I'm worried,' she said.

'Has he done something wrong?'

'I think he's coming down with something.'

'What makes you say that? He helped you with the beds today, didn't he?'

'And the curtains.'

'So?'

'He's not meant to do that. He's supposed to learn how to behave like a man.'

'But I'm not especially keen on the idea of him standing up to take a pee.'

Vera shook her head. 'You're being deliberately obtuse... you know what I mean. We're two women, and we've got to take care that we don't mollycoddle him.'

'What nonsense!'

'Siniša agrees with me.'

'Siniša? What's he got to do with it?'

'He called. In fact, he was looking for you.'

'Go to bed, Mum.' Milena put her mug in the sink. 'And don't worry.'

She kissed her mother, retired to her room, and turned on the light above her desk. She stopped for a second or two to listen for any noise in the hallway and then closed the door, but not before Fiona had managed to slip inside at the very last moment.

Milena took a cigarillo from the box and half-opened the window. She sat there smoking, stroking the cat, and staring vacantly at the house opposite – the grey concrete wall. For the first time ever, Philip was coming to visit, and the whole family was freaking out. For weeks now, Adam had been looking forward to his birthday and his father's visit with almost feverish anticipation. Milena was no psychologist, but maybe that was why her son had a guilty conscience. She tapped the ash off the end of her cigarillo.

She didn't know whether she had done everything right in his upbringing, whether she was spending too little time with her child, whether she indulged him too much, wasn't consistent enough, or had shuffled off too much responsibility onto Vera. But Adam was a beloved child. And if he was a bit different from other boys, too sensitive, effeminate, or whatever – so be it. She didn't have a problem with that.

Or maybe she did. She stubbed out the cigarillo, sat down at her desk, and pulled out the green folder with the material for the next meeting: Chapter 27 of the EU treaty. The law regarding carbon monoxide reduction.

She tried to concentrate. The Serbs were cheating on the emissions by declaring that the consumption of fuel for heating was a form of renewable energy production, which was of course nonsense. Biomass was needed to generate electricity, and biomass was required to fulfil the EU treaty requirements and finally release the funds they badly needed to rebuild the country. The minister for energy had recently summed it up: 'There's no end of bullshit here in Serbia – but cow shit, which we're badly in need of, is in short supply.'

Her telephone lit up. Milena looked at the screen. A Belgrade number. She pressed the green button. 'Hello?'

'Is that Ms Lukin?'

'Speaking.'

'Please excuse the late call. My name's Pichler. Karen. We spoke briefly this afternoon, if you remember.'

'The Hotel Amsterdam – of course. What can I do for you?'

'I probably made rather an odd impression on you.'

'Not at all.'

'You said Mr Stojković tried to call us.'

'That's right.'

'Could you possibly give me his number?'

'Don't you have a note of it?' Milena opened her address book.

'Unfortunately not.'

'Have you got something to write with?' Milena dictated the number. 'And what about your hotel?' she enquired. 'Any change there? Is the opening still postponed, or have you reconsidered?'

'Don't get me wrong, but I'd like to talk to Mr Stojković first.'

'Of course. Give him a call. He'll certainly help you.'
Silence at the other end.
'Hello?' Milena asked. 'Are you still there?'
But the woman had hung up.

5

With the tip of his index finger, he traced the line of one of her eyebrows, those elegant arches with each individual hair looking like it had been painted, and finally alighted on the bridge of her nose, a soft, bare surface. If only Anna and her beautician hadn't been constantly engaged in a battle against nature, he would have been able to glide smoothly from there across a silky black carpet to her other brow, where, in a mirror image, the hairs grew in the opposite direction.

'Hey,' Steven whispered, 'can you hear me?'

Her eyelashes twitched, but she hadn't the slightest intention of opening her eyes.

So, he continued moving his finger, taking a right turn down the ridge of the nose, a really long stretch with steep drops on either side, before finally reaching the summit. He kissed the tip of her nose once, twice, and asked quietly, 'Are you still here?'

Now she opened her lips, as if she were about to speak to him, but he was wrong, for she said nothing.

At the very first sight of those lips, he had immersed himself in them. And she had let him sink, even though her thoughts were already elsewhere. She opened her eyes.

Those eyes revealed nothing to him. It was as if there were a silent question in her gaze. Or was it contempt? No, it was love; what else could it be? The longer he stared into her eyes, the greener they became.

'Anna', he whispered, reaching for her hand.

'I have to go,' she said.

Wearily, he rested his head on her shoulder, all the while clutching her hand.

She pushed his head aside – gently, almost indulgently, as if it were some object that, while attractive, could sometimes be rather tiresome. He watched her getting dressed, gradually transforming herself. By the time she put her earrings on, there wasn't much left of his Anna, his mysterious Anna, whom he loved and longed to touch and kiss. By now, she'd become Anna the lawyer. The woman who was always leaving him.

'When will you be back?' He held out his arm to her.

His question only seemed to prompt her to stop and think whether she'd forgotten anything. But she never left anything at his place. When she was gone, he never found a thing to indicate that she had ever been there. And the longer her absence lasted, the more convinced he was that he must surely have dreamt the whole thing.

He heard her wash up a glass in the kitchen. Then she returned once more, sat down next to him on the edge of the bed, and lifted her hair from the back of her neck. It was not that she wouldn't have been able to pull the little zip up herself, but she left that privilege to him – maybe she thought he liked it that way, or that this was the done thing when you slept with someone, because it suggested a certain intimacy and closeness. Or maybe just because it was convenient.

Before the last centimetre of her skin disappeared beneath the fabric of her dress, he tried to kiss the bare patch.

She stood up abruptly. 'I'll call you,' she announced, in the same tone of voice she would have used to say 'goodbye'. She plucked a long black hair from the pillow and disposed of it, picked up her suitcase, which she had unlocked but not opened for the entire fifteen hours she'd been there, and left. Once the door had shut behind her, silence reigned. The only sound was that of the lift descending.

He could have gone over to the window and watched her hand her suitcase to the taxi driver. Observed her getting into the cab while he stowed the luggage. But then he'd only have noticed once again that she didn't look back up at him, and that there was no last little smile, no wave. All he'd have seen was the taxi with her inside disappearing around the corner at the end of the street.

He rolled onto his stomach and buried his face where Anna had lain just a short while ago, where there were still vestiges of her warmth and her scent, and where he wished he could remain until the door opened once more and she was back. But when would that be?

∗

'To the airport', she said.

'JFK?' The driver looked enquiringly in his rear-view mirror.

Anna nodded. She looked at the shops passing by, the oyster bar on the corner where she'd sat yesterday evening with Steven. He'd talked so much. She hadn't been able to concentrate or follow him, so she simply resorted to looking at him, like you'd look at a beautiful painting. And with every kilometre that she put between herself and him, that image grew progressively fainter.

How dramatic that all sounded. As if it hadn't always been that way when she travelled. But unlike those many other trips she made for her law firm, this one was a purely private affair, and she was afraid, even though she didn't dare admit it to herself. And the driver now taking 17th Avenue rather than 20th mystified her. She didn't see the advantage, but he must have his reasons. She liked this area.

On the freeway, the traffic was nose to tail, but she'd

factored this in and still arrived with plenty of time to spare. She paid the driver, and he fetched her luggage from the trunk.

'Have a safe trip.'

She made straight for the fast-lane check-in. Scanner, green light, hand-baggage check.

No, she wasn't in possession of any weapons, not even pepper spray. Until recently, the thought of owning one hadn't even crossed her mind.

In the departure lounge, she drank a glass of water. Would she be a changed person on her return? Maybe. The sky above New York looked really bleached out, though that might just have been an effect of the tinted terminal windows. Boarding. What a mass of people there were milling about down there in cabin class. Hundreds of them. Whereas here, on the upper deck, it was utterly calm. Muted voices. She was seated in Row 1, Seat A, as always. That way, there'd be no one in front of her, and she didn't turn her head to look back.

Boarding complete. She placed *The New Yorker* on the seat beside her in a rather demonstrative way, as if she needed the magazine to remind her of where she'd come from.

'No, thank you', she replied when the flight attendant offered her a glass of champagne.

During take-off, she closed her eyes and relaxed into her seat. She had no plan – a rare occurrence, practically unheard of. No turbulence during the flight; the same could not be said of her thoughts. She thought about Jurij Pichler. What did the guy want?

She only began asking herself that during his second call. When he'd rung the first time, she hadn't been prepared. How could she have been? The phone call, this man, the whole story – it had all descended upon her so suddenly, without the slightest warning.

The guy hadn't even answered her question. There had only been silence, a long silence, and this silence suddenly struck her as quite intimate and uncomfortable. Her response was to hang up.

He hadn't called back thereafter.

She sampled the steak and vegetables that were served.

Despite herself, ever since that call, she'd been unable to get him out of her mind. She'd found no information about him on the internet. He didn't belong to any social network. He was faceless. She only knew his name and his voice. And he'd sounded frighteningly normal. Maybe even likeable?

No, she wouldn't go that far. She asked for a glass of cognac, put on the sleep mask, and reclined her seat. Jurij Pichler. What would she do when she was face to face with him? Was he looking for absolution?

She tried to remember, but she could only ever retrieve the same fragments: her father's calm voice, her mother's hands, the floral pattern on the curtains. Dušan's wooden giraffe, the ball that kept having to be pumped up: the drama of her childhood. Suddenly Dušan was gone, dead. Then her mother – gone, disappeared forever. That was the moment her childhood had ended. The last thing her father did was to hang a money pouch around her neck, stuffed full of cash, and kiss her on the forehead. 'Go where the Black folk live,' he had said. 'You won't stand out there.'

She gave a sudden start and sat upright, pushing up the sleep mask and glancing around. No, she clearly hadn't cried out loud. After Dušan's death, she had shed no more tears. She had promised to be brave. And she was in the habit of keeping her promises. She ordered coffee, to wake herself up, and returned her seat to the upright position.

They landed in Frankfurt twenty minutes ahead of

schedule. A tailwind. She had to change terminal and walk to the very last gate in the new building. By the time she got there, the plane, her connecting flight, was ready for boarding.

Row 2, Seat F. She'd left *The New Yorker* behind on the jumbo. She was in Europe now. The sun was shining, and she felt wide awake and switched on. In the seat next to her was a businessman, hogging her armrest with an air of entitlement.

She stayed seated, with her seatbelt fastened, and stared out of the window for the entire two-and-a-half-hour flight. They were approaching the country she had left twenty-two years before, and her head was empty. Then the first gaps in the clouds started to appear.

Fields, streets, the odd building. She tried to spot any differences, comparing her images of the past with the present. Down below, she could make out water meadows and pastures, and she thought of summers in the country and of her cousins. Jemal had always been the best, the fastest, the first, especially when it came to catching frogs. She'd never called him to mind before, but now here he was, right in front of her, wearing a battered hat with wire bent around the brim to form a kind of wreath. One after another, the frogs were impaled on this wire, which was then refastened to the hat to form a crown of amphibians around Jemal's head, twitching and flailing about and slapping their legs together. And when, on the following day, the white meat, sprinkled with semolina and baked in lard, was served on a plate in front of her and she couldn't bring herself to swallow a mouthful, Jemal grinned at her across the table.

'Sweet or savoury?'

She stared blankly at the stewardess, who'd addressed her in Serbian and now repeated the question in English. Eventually, she replied, 'No, thank you.'

The man in the next seat looked at her and, a moment later, withdrew his arm from the armrest.

The ground came closer, the plane touched down, and the engines roared. Desolate grassy areas on the far side of the runway, like at every airport around the world. The usual announcements, then American pop music burbling from the loudspeakers. And, shortly after, the clicking sound of seatbelts being unfastened.

On the bus to the terminal building, she remained standing directly next to the door.

No fast lane at immigration. She joined the back of the queue. A familiar script on advertisements, though the products themselves were unfamiliar. Everything was new and not as rundown as at JFK or Frankfurt Airport.

'Are you here on business or for pleasure?' The border guard behind the screen held her American passport open in both hands, like a book, and studied her.

'Pleasure.'

Stamp. He closed the passport and handed it back to her. 'Next, please!'

The frosted glass doors slid open. A throng of people were jostling behind the barrier. Children shrieked with delight and clambered onto the shoulders of their grandfathers, whose wrinkled faces looked strangely familiar. Anna passed them all by. She was sweating, her heart was racing, and she felt close to tears.

She was back in Belgrade.

6

'A piece of Damascene tart for the lady, and I'll have...' Siniša handed the menu to the waitress and, as he did so, took the opportunity to scan her long, extremely shapely legs with an appreciative glance. 'A Constantinople slice.'

'I just have one question.' Milena put on her glasses and ran her finger down the long list of cakes on offer. 'What is the "Eighth Wonder of the World"?'

'The Eighth Wonder of the World–' repeated the young woman with the white serving apron, rolling her eyes up to the ceiling with a rapturous expression on her face '– is, well, what can I say?'

'Okay,' Siniša cut her short. 'We'll take a piece anyway. Just so we can try it.'

'By all means.' The waitress gave Siniša a broad smile and left.

'And two coffees, please,' Milena called after her.

Siniša sighed and reached across the table to take her hand. 'You're getting more beautiful with every year. Why don't you marry me? Give me one reason.'

Milena withdrew her hand and put away her glasses case. She pictured the slice of cake and thought ruefully that it wouldn't be long before she was unable to button up her denim jacket – a fate that had already befallen her favourite jacket, the suede one.

Siniša propped his tanned head on his hand, his face touching his signet ring, and looked pensively at Milena. 'How's it going at the embassy with that German, that count of yours? Tell me, have you settled in all right?'

'As far as your contract is concerned, I haven't made any progress yet, I'm afraid.'

'That's not what I meant.'

'And I had to cancel a trip abroad with Kronburg at short notice because of Adam's birthday – the date just slipped through the net. He took it gracefully.'

'Pleased to hear it.' Siniša nodded approvingly. 'Don't let the guy lead you by the nose.'

'What makes you think he does that?'

'I know how these things work.' He tugged at the gold links in his cuffs. 'A little trip abroad, nice and snug, side by side, important negotiations going on late into the night, then – after the work's all done and dusted – a cosy little nightcap together in the hotel bar...'

The waitress arrived with a trayful of cakes. 'Who's having The Eighth Wonder of the World?'

'Put it in the middle, please,' said Milena.

'My dear,' said Siniša, straightening the plate, 'I think you're being a bit naïve, and as for that narcissist, Kronburg, that smart-arse windbag...'

'He's not a windbag.' Milena inspected the cakes as the waitress set down coffee cups and water glasses on the table.

'But he is a smart-arse.' Siniša gripped her hand. 'Please, listen to what I'm telling you. This is important: if that pretty boy starts getting funny with you or not treating you right, just let me know. I'll get on his case personally.'

The Eighth Wonder of the World consisted of one-third buttercream, one-third chocolate and one-third cherries delicately steeped in alcohol, all arranged in a chessboard pattern, alternating with other candied fruit and topped with a layer of fresh cream. The problem was the extremely wobbly base made from alcohol-drenched biscuit.

'Look, can you please tell me...' Milena began. With a few

stabs of her fork, she succeeded in completely destroying the Wonder of the World, and now the ruin had to be demolished layer by layer. 'What are we doing here?'

'Remember that woman from the little hotel?' Siniša asked.

'Karen Pichler, yes. I gave her your number. Did she call you?'

'Her husband has disappeared.'

Milena put down her fork.

'It's been three days now, and he seems to have vanished into thin air.'

'Have you notified the police?'

'As long as there's nothing to suggest a crime has been committed...'

'You have your suspicions, though?'

'As it happens, I was just on the point of extricating the guy from a pretty unpleasant old affair.'

'What kind of affair?'

'It goes back some twenty-five years, and my client assures me he was only indirectly involved. He was only sixteen years old at the time. His family spirited him out of the country. Real cloak-and-dagger stuff. Now he's come back and wants to make a clean breast of it.' Siniša pushed a slim envelope across the table towards her.

'What's this?'

'Everything I've been able to track down about the original case.'

Milena reached to open the envelope, but Siniša laid his hand on it.

'I want you to read it at your leisure, without prejudice if possible, and then we'll speak again.'

'This all makes no sense to me.' Milena finished her coffee and dabbed her mouth with her napkin. 'Does the wife, this Karen Pichler, have no idea where her husband might be?'

'She thinks there's a conspiracy.'

Milena took the envelope and put it in her bag. 'I'll call you.'

'When?'

'As soon as I can. And who knows, maybe the husband will have turned up by then.'

Siniša stood up and buttoned his jacket. 'Thank you.'

*

Milena enjoyed evenings at the institute, after the telephone fell silent. She could prepare for her lectures in peace and quiet and finish the tasks left over from the week. One problem – what with her teaching commitments in the criminology faculty and her consultancy at the German embassy – was that she found barely any time to work on her doctoral thesis. 'The Prosecution of War Crimes in the Former Yugoslavia Between 1990 and 1999', an important topic, was threatening to turn into a long-term project.

She greeted the youngsters who ran the art house cinema on the ground floor and climbed the stairs. The most beautiful feature of the building was the glass skylight above the stairwell. Unlike the German embassy, with its velour carpets and noise-reducing armoured windows, this building had bags of atmosphere: cracks in the masonry through which the wind whistled, parquet floors that creaked with every step. Her office was on the first floor, the penultimate room on the left. The door stood open.

'Hello?' She peered around the corner.

Cardboard boxes – standard-issue removal boxes still folded flat – were stacked against the shelves, and a man in overalls was standing next to her desk.

'Good evening,' said Milena. 'What are you doing here? Can I help you?'

'I'm looking for a pen.'

Irritated, Milena hung her bag over the chair. 'What's with these boxes?'

'Will four be enough for you? I can arrange for more if need be. But not before Monday.'

'There must be some mix-up. I don't need any boxes and I didn't order any,' Milena put one hand on her hip, 'so you can take them away right now.'

The man scratched his head with her pen. 'You sure about that?'

'Who let you in here?'

The man pulled a sheet of paper from his trouser pocket and unfolded it. 'Removal cartons, four. Room 108.' He looked around enquiringly. 'That's you, isn't it?'

'Room 108, that's right.'

'Okay, then, so everything's in order.' He ticked his list. 'How about I leave these boxes here for the time being and then see how things stand on Monday? All right?'

'Not really,' sighed Milena. 'But sure, you might as well get off now. Have a nice weekend.'

She followed the man out of her room and along the hall as far as Boris Grubač's office. The director of the institute had the tower room, the most beautiful office in the building. His door was open most of the time so he could see who passed by. It was only when he allowed himself a little tipple, close to going-home time, that he shut the door. Milena knocked.

'Yes, my darling, that's what we'll do.' Grubač rotated his swivel chair, with the receiver pressed to his ear and a toothpick between his lips. He nodded at Milena. 'Sweetheart, let's talk about this at length tonight, okay?' He pulled a face while Milena hovered in the room, at a loss for what to do except study the ornate plasterwork on the ceiling.

'Yes, my darling. Love you too.' Grubač pursed his lips to make a kissing sound and then hung up. 'Please excuse me, Ms Lukin, but sometimes my wife is terribly impractical.'

'How is she?' Milena sat down on a chair which was positioned a metre and a half away from Grubač's desk. The distance made her feel like a petitioner at court – which was precisely the effect Grubač intended.

Grubač gave a dismissive wave. 'Our son needs a new wheelchair, and you've no idea how much paperwork is involved in getting one.'

'I understand.' Milena nodded compassionately. 'Have you found something already? I mean, something affordable?'

'It's all in hand, yes, but thanks for asking.' Grubač fell silent, stared out of the window, and snapped the toothpick in half. 'What can I do for you?' He suddenly sounded quite despondent.

'It's about the removal boxes,' Milena began.

'What about them?' He leant forward and folded his hands on the desk.

'You tell me! I don't need any.'

'Didn't you get the memo? You're moving to a new office.' He consulted a piece of paper in front of him. 'Room 109.'

'I beg your pardon?'

'The move was necessary because we've got a new person joining us.'

'I don't know anything about that, either.'

'It's only a part-time position, admittedly. But adding another member of staff represents quite an upgrade for our little institute, especially in the current climate, and that's in your interest too, right?'

Milena shook her head. 'Room 109's the broom cupboard.'

'That's a bit harsh. Once you've moved in properly, it'll be very comfortable, you'll see. And in any case – how often are you in here now, on average?'

'Three times a week.'

'Hang on…' He rummaged on his desk for a piece of paper. 'So, it says here that you were in twice last week, the week before that the same, and this week–'

'Are you keeping tabs on me?'

'With her regular two and a half days a week, Ms Schröder will be spending more time here. And if I stuck her in Room 109, that'd hardly be sending out a positive message, now, would it?'

'I get the picture.' Milena replied, trying not to sound too sniffy. 'Who is this Ms Schröder anyway, if you don't mind me asking?'

'She's a fluent English speaker.' Grubač leant back and rearranged his tie over his belly. 'She was a trainee in the Ministry of Justice. And she comes highly recommended.'

'And presumably she's also young,' Milena added.

'Got it in one!' Grubač clapped his hands. 'Quit moaning, will you? At least meet the woman first.'

'I just wish I'd been consulted.'

'My decision's final.'

When Milena sat back down at her desk, she took a deep breath. She really shouldn't have risen to the bait. The fact that she had was probably down to her feeling so stretched right now. If she didn't watch out, she'd end up in the situation that her best friend Tanja had predicted. With two roles, she ran the risk of not being fully committed to either the institute or the German embassy and not doing a good job in either. That would mean that, sooner or later, she'd have to decide either to deal with Grubač and teach her students how to become good scientists – a real Sisyphean task – or to throw herself wholeheartedly into politics.

She blew her nose, pulled her bag onto her lap, took out a handful of jelly bananas, and laid them in a neat row on the table in front of her. Five bananas, that was her allocation for the evening. But she needed to eat the first one straight away. As the dark chocolate started to melt in her mouth and the cool jelly core hit her tongue, she took from her bag the envelope that Siniša had given her, containing a sheaf of about thirty sheets of paper. On top of the pile lay a twenty-five-year-old newspaper clipping.

Why Did Little Dušan Have To Die? ran the headline.

She began reading the article. In her hand, inside its cellophane wrapper, the second jelly banana began to melt without Milena even noticing.

7

'Look,' he said, 'I've got a firm hold of you, see? My arms are right here, underneath you. Nothing can happen to you.'

The little brat's arms kept flailing about, and the movements he made bore only a vague resemblance to the ones he'd been showing him for days, over and over again. Never mind. Out of the corner of his eye, he caught sight of Svenja.

She was sitting like a bronze statue on the tiled wall near the pool edge, manicuring her dainty black-varnished toenails. He noticed she was wearing the bikini top with the black polka-dots. The thin material covered just enough to leave plenty of room for the imagination. No one else in his year had such whoppers. He imagined them as being warm and firm, with gigantic nipples, just like the ones he'd seen on the websites his father liked to visit.

The little brat spluttered, thrashed about, spat out water, and gasped for breath. He quickly put his arms underneath the boy, Simon, again. 'I've got you,' he shouted. 'No need to panic.'

'You said you'd hold on to me!' The boy was bright red in the face, and his damned voice echoed throughout the entire hall. 'But you didn't hold on to me!'

'Calm down. It was just a little test. It won't happen again, okay? Come on, let's go on.'

To cap it all, the little brat started crying, and Svenja sat up and craned her neck.

He gestured to her, signalling that everything was fine. How he'd have loved to dunk the little brat beneath the surface, just briefly.

'What did I tell you?' he said sharply. 'How are you supposed to hold your hands? Like you're cutting through the water. Just try. Cut through the water. Yeah, like that. Perfect! Well done!'

Svenja sat upright again and tweaked her bikini top. Out of everyone, she'd picked him to teach her little brother how to swim. He couldn't believe his luck at first. He was the one she chose, despite the fact that all those other guys, and not just from his year, were lined up drooling outside her door. They all thought about Svenja while masturbating, but he was the one who was now spending his afternoons close to her and working up to asking her out on a date soon, by the summer at the latest. He had it all mapped out: he'd teach the little brat (Svenja called him that herself) how to swim, he'd become indispensable and win brownie points with her, and then, when summer arrived and her kid brother had got the hang of swimming, he'd go to the Danube with the two of them. He already knew exactly where to go: his favourite spot, which wasn't overlooked by the promenade. The place where he always went when he wanted to be alone with his thoughts, where he didn't have to worry about being disturbed like he was at home, with people constantly coming into his room or rattling the bathroom door.

He'd sit there on the riverbank with her, while the little brat was otherwise occupied swimming around somewhere, and he'd casually touch her hand. He didn't know how things would proceed from there, but they'd fall into place for sure. At least, that was what he imagined would happen. After so many afternoons spent together, they'd end up growing closer to one other, that much was inevitable. He wasn't quite on the home stretch yet, but he was very near to it.

'Very good,' he called out, loud enough so Svenja could

hear. 'Try to draw your arms through the whole way, yeah? Yes, just like that. That's the way to do it! Super!'

The only thing he hadn't reckoned on were all these guys hanging around here, some of them older than him, the same group every afternoon. And they all performed for Svenja – striking a pose on the starting blocks, diving in head first, putting on quite a show. For the most part, Svenja feigned complete indifference, like she hadn't even noticed the men. But, even so, he'd caught her sneaking the odd glance now and again.

'Arms and legs together,' he said. 'And keep looking straight ahead.'

The guy in the black trunks was the worst. He'd been poncing about the whole time, and what was he up to now? That cheeky bastard. He was striking a pose right in front of Svenja, pressing his hands to his knees and pushing out his fat arse. If he didn't watch out, he'd overbalance and topple face first onto her. And what a stupid face it was, too. Yeah, that's right. Watch your step, matey. And what was he gabbing on about the whole time? Meanwhile, here he was, standing around in this piss-warm kids' pool and grappling with the little brat.

Svenja was smiling at the guy, combing back her long wavy hair and tossing it showily over her left shoulder. The final straw would be if she shifted her towel and invited the guy to sit down next to her. As if that pushy bastard needed an invitation. It was hard to believe how quickly he'd moved in. And she was hanging on his every word, like she was actually interested!

'Okay, then,' he said to the little brat. 'Let's call it a day.'

Of course, the boy didn't want to know, and kept wriggling away like a tadpole.

'Tell you what,' he added. 'How'd you like to earn yourself a little money?'

The little shit splashed around and grinned. 'What if I don't want to?'

He was sorely tempted to dunk him, just for a moment. 'You'll do what I tell you, right? Otherwise, you can forget the swimming lessons, once and for all.'

'How much?'

'That depends on how smart you are.'

Half an hour later, he was on his way out of the swimming pool in the company of Svenja and the junior blackmailer. Silently, they strolled along the Danube, like they always did. Svenja was carrying her little brother's swimming trunks, and a faint smile was playing on her lips, so dreamy that it almost broke his heart. She seemed to still be thinking about Mr Black Trunks. By now, they'd almost reached the spot and he was at the end of his tether.

'I'm going to skim stones.' The boy dashed off down the track between the bushes, towards the banks of the Danube. Exactly like he'd been instructed to do.

Svenja looked up at him with a searching gaze.

With a studiedly indifferent gesture, he shrugged, while secretly exulting. Now he'd show Svenja the spot, his favourite spot. That way, she'd recognise this place later, when the time came...

Suddenly, she took his hand and pulled him after her. Was he dreaming? His hand was in hers. He followed her. She kept a tight grip on him. She ran, and he ran with her. They laughed. She looked at him. Her eyes sparkled. He'd never seen her like this, and his heart was racing like crazy.

'What are you waiting for?' she whispered.

'But the little brat...' he stammered.

'Sod the little brat!'

'What did you say?'

'Kiss me!'

He felt her breath and closed his eyes. All of a sudden, there came a shrill scream.

In shock, they let go of one another. Another scream. He'd never heard anything so piercing before. Svenja stared at him, wide-eyed and petrified.

He set off at a run, down to the river. 'Simon!' he yelled. 'Where are you?' He scrambled to kick off his shoes.

The boy didn't know how to swim yet. The bank was treacherous and the current strong. He pushed aside the reeds. Then he saw Simon.

He was standing knee-deep in the river, with a stick in his hand.

'Simon', he called out, 'what's wrong?'

With a terror-struck face and his mouth wide open, the boy pointed at a spot in the reeds.

His initial thought was that items of clothing were floating there. But then he made out the body that was bobbing in the water with its arms and legs extended, like a parachute jumper who'd fallen from the sky and landed in the reeds. The dead man's jacket had ballooned out as if it were filled with wind.

'Quick.' He took hold of the crying boy and tucked him under his arm. 'Let's get out of here.'

8

Milena took off her spectacles. Her eyes were burning. The collected newspaper articles from back then, the little boy – she slid the pieces of paper Siniša had given her to read back into the envelope. What a gruesome, senseless death. She picked up her jacket and bag, pushed her chair back, and switched off the desk lamp.

She gave the throng of people on Prince Michael Street a wide berth and, passing the Red Cockerel, turned left and walked down Gračanica Street. Dusk had fallen and the street lights had come on, though as yet their glow wasn't casting strong shadows. It had been little Dušan's fate to reach only the age of ten – almost as old as Adam was now. If he'd lived, the boy would now be – Milena did some quick mental arithmetic – a grown man in his mid-thirties. What might have become of him? Roma boys were blighted from birth and had few opportunities – quite unlike Adam Lukin, who'd grown up bilingual and was supported and pampered by all and sundry.

Milena walked on aimlessly. She didn't want to go home yet, so she crossed Paris Street at the lights and followed the narrow tarmac path that led to a wide-open space: a park with trees, lawns, and tumbledown walls – the ruins of Kale-megdan Fortress. Little Dušan had meant to buy sweets that evening. He'd gone out with his parents' permission and a handful of coins, as a reward for bringing home a good school report that day. That was what she'd read in one of the articles. The parents had let their boy go, with no inkling that he would never come back.

The souvenir sellers were about to pack up for the day and close their stalls. Milena passed the tables where old men, for the most part, were playing chess, some of them wearing old-fashioned ties. Here and there, where people had settled down for picnics, candles had been lit.

The boy had only run into the two youths by chance, so the papers back then claimed. First, they had demanded he hand over the money. Then they had started pushing and shoving him, and then hitting and kicking him, until one of them had got hold of a broken length of guttering.

The bench at the far end of the fortress was taken. Milena was just about to turn back, when the couple sitting there got up and strolled past her, arm in arm. Milena sat down. It was only when she closed her eyes that she imagined she could hear the river – two rivers in fact, the Danube and the Sava, which merged near here and flowed onward in a broad course towards Romania and then the Black Sea. The peaceful atmosphere surrounding her and the magical ambience of this place were no solace today. Quite the contrary: Milena felt the gruesomeness of the crime even more acutely here. The fact that two youths had beaten a defenceless boy to death for no reason, just out of hatred, frustration, and boredom – there was no explanation, no excuse, for such a heinous crime.

A chill wind suddenly got up. Milena wandered along the fortress wall and, after a few minutes, reached a flight of steps leading down to the harbour. Tanja's house was halfway down this path, giving straight onto the steps. Her door was open most of the time, only being locked at night or when Tanja wasn't at home. It was like living in a village where everybody knew each other, instead of in an anonymous city where crimes were committed every day. Milena did what best friends do: she knocked and then immediately opened the door. 'Hello?' she called out. 'Anybody home?'

She pushed aside two shoeboxes and hung up her jacket. The cherry branches in the big vase were starting to blossom. 'Can you believe it?' Tanja called out. 'I was just thinking of you!' She emerged from her study wearing a grey silk robe, her auburn curls done up in a topknot and a pair of spectacles perched on her nose.

Milena had never seen her wear glasses before. 'That's kismet!' she said, hugging Tanja.

'I'm just making some bookings. Hairdresser – the weekend after next. How about it? You in the mood?'

'What, to go to Munich?' Milena followed her friend to the kitchen.

'Plus a trip to the spa into the bargain. And, if you press me, a bit of culture as well. Maybe a visit to the Pinakothek?' Tanja opened the fridge. 'I've got sushi, but it's a bit old.'

'Maybe that's not such a bad idea,' Milena muttered, feeling her eyes filling with tears.

Tanja shot her friend an inquisitive glance and, without uttering another word, took a bottle of champagne out of the fridge and two glasses off the shelf. 'What's up?' she asked.

'I'm a silly cow.' Milena shook her head. 'The whole thing happened twenty-five years ago.'

Tanja peeled off the silver foil, uncorked the bottle, and filled the two glasses. Milena proceeded to tell her about the newspaper articles and the little Roma boy, Dušan Jovanović, who had been beaten to death by two youths.

Tanja raised her glass with a grim face. 'Did they at least get the bastards who did it?'

'One got banged up, but the other one got away.' Milena took a sip of her champagne. 'And now he's come back and supposedly wants to face up to his past. Jurij Pichler's his name. And Siniša is representing him – can you believe it?'

Tanja cracked an egg into the pan, making the butter hiss.

'If this guy wants to come clean after so many years, surely that's not such a bad thing,' she said. 'And, even in these circumstances, he has a right to legal representation.'

'Of course.' Milena nodded. 'But it looks like he's got cold feet again. He's disappeared without trace, and his wife's left behind wondering what the hell's going on.'

'So why did Siniša want you to familiarise yourself with the case?' Tanja scooped the fried eggs onto two open ham sandwiches.

'He obviously wanted my view on it, which I'll be happy to give him.'

Carrying plates, bottle, and glasses, they repaired to the living room, and once again Milena had cause to marvel at the sight that met her eyes. There was nowhere else in Belgrade that afforded a better night-time view of the city, the harbour, and Branko's Bridge, all lit up. If she lived here, she'd spend the whole day loafing on the couch and staring out of the window. Just like the guy who was sprawled there right now with huge headphones on, rhythmically wiggling his bare toes.

'I didn't know Stefanos was staying with you,' said Milena.

'Nor did I,' replied Tanja. 'Until yesterday, that is, when he called and then pitched up outside the door five hours later.' She sidled up to her lover from behind and yanked the earphones off his head. 'Don't you want to say hello?'

Stefanos looked up in surprise and smiled. 'Milena!' He shucked off the woollen blanket, stood up, and kissed her. 'How nice to see you!' His turquoise boxer shorts were adorned with a repeating print of toadstools; only somebody who worked as a diving instructor in Cyprus could look so good in his underpants. 'How are you?' he asked. 'I haven't seen you in ages. How long has it been? A year and a half?'

Milena smiled. 'Could well be.'

Tanja stroked his black sideburns, where the first grey hairs had begun to appear, and murmured, 'Could you make yourself scarce now? Us girls need to talk.'

'Why don't the three of us do something together one of these days?' Stefano suggested. 'Go for a bite out or something like that?' He raised his hand in farewell. 'Catch you later – promise?'

'Promise.' Milena nodded. 'How old is he now?' she asked as Stefanos disappeared with the blanket draped over his shoulders.

'Thirty-three,' Tanja sighed, 'but that's not the problem.'

'It doesn't look like there's any problem between the two of you.' Milena sat down.

'He wants to get married and won't let the stupid idea drop.'

'He loves you. What's so bad about that?'

Tanja stuffed a cushion behind Milena's back. 'I love him too, but that's not a good enough reason to have him lounging on my sofa every day. Quite the opposite, in fact. It'd be the beginning of the end, and we wouldn't be the first couple that happened to, either. Remember how it was with Philip and you? No, things are perfect just the way they are, thank you. Why go changing them? Plus...' Tanja gazed pensively out of the window.

'What?'

'Well, since Dejan, I've decided I just don't want to do the whole married-couple thing any more.'

Milena sipped from her glass. Dejan – the son of an old Belgrade medical family, who could sing and play the guitar like a dream. Tanja had met him during her practical training in a clinic and had fallen head over heels in love with him. But no sooner had they decided to get married than one thing after another started to go wrong. Suddenly, Dejan had to go to Klagenfurt, and thereafter to the US, and then Tanja read in the gutter press one day that her husband was having an affair with a well-known Russian model – a woman who now, many years later, regularly showed up at her clinic for another round of cosmetic surgery.

'Do you believe,' Milena asked, 'that people can change?'

Tanja thought for a moment. 'People just are the way they are.' She put down her glass.

'There's only one thing I believe in.'

'Which is?'

'That everybody – no matter what they've done – has the right to a second chance.'

When Milena returned home after midnight and unlocked the front door, the image of the toadstools on Stefanos' boxer shorts suddenly came back to her. The bag slipped off her shoulders, and she giggled like a teenager. Catching sight of herself in the mirror, she realised she was a bit tipsy.

Adam had fallen asleep with a book in his hand. She carefully extracted the stories of Tom Sawyer and Huckleberry Finn from his grasp and kissed him on the forehead.

She inspected the contents of the pots in the kitchen – beef stroganoff, homemade pasta, and fresh spinach – then turned off the light over the stove and went to her room. Fiona followed her. She closed the door softly behind the cat. She checked her mobile while taking off her earrings. Five missed calls. Two from Vera, and three from Siniša. And one new message in the mailbox. Received at 10:35 p.m., according to her voicemail.

'Good evening.' It was Alexander Kronburg's voice, with some muted music in the background. Surprised, Milena sat on the edge of the bed.

'Apologies for disturbing you at this late hour.' Alexander sounded very chirpy. 'But I've just had dinner with the

American ambassador. Code word "cow shit", to use your charming phrase. I'd just like to say that things aren't looking at all bad. I think I've been able to pour a little oil on troubled waters and rebuild some trust. So now it's your turn. But, first, I wanted the chance to bask in the warm glow of your approbation. Perhaps we could...' There came the soft clinking of glasses and the distant sound of laughter. 'I thought maybe you might fancy getting a drink somewhere.' All of a sudden, his voice sounded hoarse, and he cleared his throat. 'I hear there's a new bar somewhere near the theatre, and I thought that really wouldn't be too far at all from your place.' He paused. 'Assuming you're at home now, that is.' By now, his voice had reverted to its usual businesslike tone. 'Anyway, if not, we'll most likely see one another in the office tomorrow. Goodnight.' She caught the sound of a few bars of a tinkling piano before the connection was terminated.

Milena put the phone down on her bedside table and stared in astonishment at the little device. Had Alexander been a bit tipsy too, perhaps? No; if she was honest, he'd sounded perfectly clear-headed.

Spontaneously, she picked up the phone and wrote a text: *Are you still awake?*

She was just about to press 'send', when the phone lit up and Siniša's name appeared on the screen. Really? At this time of night? She sighed, accepted the call, and said, 'I suppose you know how late it is, Siniša?'

'Where the hell were you?' He was almost shouting. 'Why weren't you answering your phone?'

'Pardon me, but I was visiting Tanja,' Milena replied calmly. 'After reading all those newspaper articles you gave me, I felt the need for a bit of distraction.' She rubbed her face wearily. 'Listen, that's a really horrific story. And if you want my opinion – if I were in your shoes, I'm not sure I'd be defending this Jurij guy. But on the other hand, maybe he deserves a second chance... You still there?'

'He's dead.'

'What did you say?' whispered Milena.

'They've fished his body out of the Danube.'

'That's dreadful.'

'I had a bad feeling about this case all along.'

'What happened, then? My God, poor Mrs Pichler!'

'Damn it, Milena, I'm afraid I may have misjudged the bloke. I thought he knew full well what he was doing, with all the consequences. But maybe he wasn't as tough as we all imagined.'

'You mean...'

'Of course, I wanted to plead for a not-guilty verdict, but naturally I was careful not to raise his hopes too much. Just the opposite, actually: I also tried to prepare him for the worst-case scenario.'

'So, do you think it was suicide?'

'They found stones in his pockets, supposedly.'

'Siniša, listen to me. You wanted to help extricate him from this business, and you would have managed to. You couldn't have known the guy was so unstable. You're not a psychologist.'

'I know it's stupid of me, but I'm rather dreading this first meeting tomorrow with Mrs Pichler before we go and see the pathologist.'

Milena looked at her watch.

'So, I was wondering whether we ought to drive down there together first thing and offer her our condolences.'

'Of course, Siniša. Let's meet at nine.'

'Thanks. You're a real gem, you know that?'

Milena ended the call and put the phone back on the table, next to the leaflet advertising the Hotel Amsterdam.

An attractive typeface, with pictures of the rooms and the reception area. On the back was the price list and a small photo.

Milena put on her glasses and scrutinised the image. Jurij Pichler. He looked so harmless, this person who had been living for twenty-five years with the guilt of having taken someone's life on his conscience.

9

Karen Pichler was wearing a checked blouse – the same one she'd had on two days ago – like a jacket over her T-shirt. 'The policeman's still out the back with my mother-in-law,' she said, after Siniša and Milena had expressed their condolences. 'Can I get you anything?' She went behind the bar counter. 'I know I could really do with a coffee right now.'

Siniša, who looked very pale, declined with a wave of his hand, but Milena nodded. 'I'd love one, thanks.'

'Mrs Pichler,' said Siniša. 'It goes without saying that I'll continue to support you and do all I can for you, if that's what you want.'

Karen deftly knocked the plug of spent coffee out of the espresso machine like she'd been born into the role of barista. 'Do you take sugar?'

'Just plain and black for me, thanks,' said Milena.

'Jurij's death has hit me hard,' Siniša continued. 'We spoke so often over the past weeks, but I never noticed the slightest thing amiss.'

Karen stared fixedly through the window out into the street. The espresso cup and saucer rattled softly in her hand.

'Mrs Pichler?' prompted Siniša.

'I can't believe he'd just go and leave me here alone,' she said. 'With this hotel. With his mother and his sister, with our shared dream, and the responsibility on my shoulders alone. With the whole shooting match.'

Milena straightened up the pile of flyers. 'What do you think?' she asked. 'Could your husband possibly have taken his own life?'

Karen looked up in surprise. 'I'm glad you asked me that, Ms Lukin. And I'm telling you: no way! Jurij didn't put stones in his pockets and just walk into the water.' She shook her head. 'He'd never do that. It's complete nonsense.'

'We'll need to wait for the results of the autopsy,' Siniša interjected.

'Do you have any suspicions?' Milena asked Karen. 'I'm sorry to have to put these questions to you. After all, I'm not–'

'Ms Lukin works at the Institute for Criminology and Forensic Science,' explained Siniša.

Karen gasped, put down her coffee cup, and pressed a hand to her mouth.

Milena walked round the counter, took her gently by the shoulders, and hugged her.

And suddenly their conversation was at an end. Wiping a finger across her cheeks beneath the frame of her glasses, Karen gave a short sniff and an embarrassed smile, and then dissolved into tears once more.

Milena was handing her a tissue when a voice behind them said, 'Mrs Pichler, are you ready now?'

Milena turned around. The man with the salt-and-pepper crew cut and the alert brown eyes struck her as somehow familiar.

'Ms Lukin!' exclaimed the man in surprise. 'What brings you here?'

'Commissar Filipow!' She held out her hand. 'I almost didn't recognise you.' He'd lost weight and looked much more wiry than before but at the same time appeared rather unhealthy and pallid.

'Yes, I'm ready.' Karen blew her nose. 'Mr Stojković has kindly offered to come with me.'

Siniša stepped forward. 'The deceased was my client. The name's Stojković.'

'Yes, I've heard of you.' Filipow gave a somewhat pained smile and then told Karen, 'This won't take long. But your mother-in-law doesn't feel up to identifying her son, and your sister-in-law...'

Karen took her jacket from the coat stand. 'That's fine. Let's get this over and done with, shall we?' she said, before adding in an undertone to Milena, 'Can I call you?'

'Of course,' Milena replied. 'Anytime.' Under her breath, she asked, 'Could you let me know where the toilet is?'

Filipow escorted Karen to his car and held open the rear door for her, like he was arresting her. It was a good thing Siniša was at her side. Milena opened the door behind the counter and groped around in the dark hallway for the light switch.

For the loo, she shouldn't take the first door off the hallway, but the second, Karen had told her. She'd just taken hold of the handle, when she heard a hoarse woman's voice coming from the room opposite.

'That's enough! We just have to accept it. End of.'

There came the sound of a second voice, agitated and tearful, though she couldn't make out what it was saying. Milena was about to make herself scarce, when the door to the room was suddenly flung wide open.

A woman dressed entirely in black, wearing pink lipstick, and with her blonde hair pulled back into a bun stared at Milena in alarm.

'Sorry,' stammered Milena. 'I'm after the toilet.'

'Who are you?'

'I came with Mr Stojković...'

The woman ignored Milena's outstretched hand and, striding past her without a word, pushed open the door to the WC for her.

'Thank you,' said Milena, and she dashed in.

After she'd washed her hands and stepped out into the hallway once more, she noticed that in the room opposite a young woman was sitting at a kitchen table, resting her head wearily in her hands. Some brand-new stainless-steel kitchen cabinets stood there, still wrapped in bluish protective film.

Milena tapped tentatively on the door frame and said, 'I'm sorry about earlier. I wasn't trying to eavesdrop.'

The young woman's face was stained with tears, and her delicate-featured face looked so incredibly sad that it made Milena feel desperately miserable.

'Please accept my deepest sympathies for your loss,' she said.

The young woman gave a crooked smile.

'My name's Milena Lukin.'

The woman blew her nose quietly into a tissue. 'Did you know Jurij?'

Milena shook her head. 'All I know is that he was planning to open this hotel and that Mr Stojković was acting as his defence attorney.' She hovered in the open doorway.

'His defence attorney?' asked the young woman, taken aback. 'Why did Jurij need defending? Had he done something wrong?'

Milena thought it best to keep things vague. 'It's all a bit complicated, you know.'

'My name's Sonja, by the way.' The young woman held out her hand. 'Jurij was my brother.' She folded her arms. 'But, in truth, I didn't really know him at all.'

Milena leant against the door frame. 'How come?'

'All I was ever told was "Your brother Jurij is living in Argentina." And then, "Jurij has moved to the USA." And, sometime after that, "Jurij is in Amsterdam now."'

'I see.' At a loss for what to say, Milena cast an eye over the table, which was covered with empty jam jars, ring-bound folders, and a basket full of ironing. 'How old are you?'

'Twenty-three.'

'So you weren't born when your brother left.'

Sonja wiped her nose. 'You don't believe this story about suicide, do you?' She gave Milena a searching look. 'None of us here do. Even my mother, though she'd never admit it.'

'Is that right?' said Milena, slinging her bag over her shoulder.

'Why don't you just clear off?' The woman with the bun, Sonja's mother, suddenly materialised behind Milena. 'Leave us in peace. Can't you see how upset my daughter is by all this?'

'Please forgive me,' said Milena as she stepped back into the hallway. 'You're quite right.' She glanced back into the kitchen and said, 'Goodbye.'

But the young woman, Jurij's young sister, was gazing out of the window as though she had no interest whatsoever in the world around her.

10

He stretched out his arm and clutched at thin air – once, twice – before finally catching hold of the rope sling. Taking a firm grip of the looped cord, he puffed out his cheeks, clenched his teeth, and began to haul himself off his back.

The pain in his knees was excruciating. And he wasn't just imagining that the rope was starting to give way under his weight. In all probability, one thread parted every time he pulled himself upright on it. And if the sling were to finally snap entirely, he'd have a real problem on his hands. Then the whole contraption he'd rigged up wouldn't work any more. He'd be unable to get up, and he'd be left lying down there like a beetle on its back, waving his arms and legs about uselessly until all his strength left him. Not a pretty death, and a ridiculous one into the bargain.

He needed to sort things out, get hold of some new rope or washing line – in any event, something durable that would last until the Good Lord finally called him. But it definitely hadn't come to that yet. He still had things to do.

Once he'd got to his feet and let his dizziness subside, he knew he had to summon new strength. The old tin box under the straw-filled sacking contained all his worldly belongings: some loose change and a razor blade that had already gone rusty but still served its purpose. Beneath the false bottom of the tin were the pistol and some photos he'd taken as a young man. The camera had long since vanished, and he didn't look at the photos any more. That compartment of the tin was a dark basement where he never ventured.

He scooped up the coins and slipped them into his breast

pocket. You could never be sure of the trouser pockets, which always had some hole or other in them. He could easily fit the jam jar into one of them, though. The task he was busy with may have been an odd one, but it was simple for him to perform. And things were even easier since he'd acquired the crutch.

He dragged himself up the driveway – you couldn't call it walking – and that was the worst part over and done with. The pavement was narrow here, but passers-by gave him as wide a berth as they could and lowered their gaze; he was used to that. Now and then, someone would hand him a donation, a few coins or something to eat. But that didn't happen often, and he didn't go around asking for handouts. He wasn't a beggar. He didn't spit, but instead placed his empty bottle down beside the rubbish bin, as a distant voice instructed him to do. Up in his brain, the rusty cogs now turned slowly, but at least they were still turning.

'All right there, Mr Jovanović?' The man from the flower stall dragged on his cigarette. 'Up and about again, then?' He flicked the butt into the gutter, stuffed something in Jovan's pocket and said, 'You're welcome, Grandad. Now get lost.'

Jovan hobbled across the road at the traffic lights, passed beneath the scaffolding, and turned right. He knew every kerbstone hereabouts, every house entrance, every wad of discarded chewing gum, and every pothole in the tarmac. He'd spent his entire life here, trundling about with his handcart, transporting the laundry for Svetlana, and the household goods – all the transistor radios, coffee grinders, and spinning tops that people brought for him to repair. Now he was the last of the old inhabitants. He turned the corner by the kiosk, went over to the rainwater butt, pulled the jam jar out of his pocket, and scooped up some water.

Leaning his crutch against a parked car, he held on to

a street sign to steady himself as he placed the lilies of the valley into the jar and bent to set it down on the pavement.

The incident that had taken place here had happened a long time ago, and since then it had taken on a life of its own, like some ulcer that was an integral part of him but no longer affected him. It was as if the whole event had nothing to do with him any more. That was a lie, of course, but sometimes it paid to believe in a lie – like before, when he had believed in justice and in the future, and in the fact that he and Svetlana would finally make it together. All a mistake, all just a great big lie.

He hobbled back the way he'd come, down the street – and yet, suddenly, without thinking about it, Jovan did something he'd never done before: he stopped, turned around slowly, and narrowed his eyes. He fixed them on an indistinct shape on the opposite side of the street, a shadow that had been following him and that on closer inspection turned out to be a person. He couldn't make out whether it was a man or a woman.

He was a fool. There was no one in the whole wide world who'd bother following him. He moved on, step by step. When he stopped and turned around once more, the person had disappeared.

He needed a rope or a washing line. He shouldn't put off doing something about it for too long. He had to get things sorted.

11

In the normal course of events, Milena always took the short-cut through the rear courtyard. But today she found her path blocked, with scaffolding everywhere; the place where a wonderful peace had once reigned in the very heart of the city now reverberated with the din of pneumatic drills. Diggers were busy dumping rubble into skips, lorries were turning and reversing, and construction workers were yelling at the top of their voices. The state printing press had once been located here, and later the building had been home to artists and their studios; not long after, they'd been succeeded by a ballet school and a major picture agency. Now the large billboard by the site entrance announced the creation of luxury loft apartments and two penthouse suites, all with air-con. The firm funding the development was the City Lights investment group, and Milena took it as read that, yet again, business interests from Saudi Arabia must be behind the venture. For years, they'd been buying up not only the prime plots of land in the centre but also entire streets throughout the city, and the Serbian government was only too happy to sell this real estate to them at bargain-basement prices.

With Serbia's accession to the EU on the horizon, a gold-rush atmosphere was rife in Belgrade. It didn't take much imagination to see how politicians and bureaucrats with their hands on the levers of power took advantage of the situation to feather their nests with illicit earnings and kickbacks while the going was good, before the advent of EU regulations that would hopefully soon put an end to such criminal activity. But the damage already done to the city's building stock and infrastructure was irreparable. Milena shimmied to avoid a cement mixer and weaved her way through to Kosmaj Street.

Siniša's chambers were located in the building formerly occupied by the Socialist Youth Movement. The abandoned lobby featured an immense crumbling mosaic reminding visitors of a time when the idea of a Yugoslavian multi-ethnic state was still alive and kicking. It surely wouldn't be long before the wrecker's ball got to work on this building too, forcing Siniša to vacate his little suite of offices up on the fourth floor. But until then – there was no disguising the fact – the lawyer was busy milking a situation that pertained in Serbia quite frequently since the fall of socialism. Because property rights to the building were as yet unresolved, he was paying neither rent nor electricity bills, and furthermore had no qualms whatsoever about subletting office space and renting out individual rooms to small businesses in return for payment. Milena criticised him for these illegal practices, which made him no better than the corrupt politicians and civil servants of the ministerial bureaucracy. But Siniša's dodgy dealings brought in a nice little bit on the side, which he could comfortably use to defray some of his costs – including, for example, the wages of his secretary, Alisa.

This woman, who was in her mid-fifties, was sitting, as always, hunched over her electric typewriter and exuding a startled air. As Siniša's secretary – or his PA, as one would tend to put it nowadays – she was a seriously misjudged appointment. She had a fear and loathing of the telephone, spoke no English or other foreign languages, and even now still had an antagonistic relationship with computers. Furthermore, she was in the habit of bursting into tears at the slightest criticism or change of procedure.

'What can I do?' was Siniša's perpetual lament behind Alisa's back. 'Fire her? And what, may I ask, is she supposed to live on then?'

In greeting, Alisa straightened her sparkly plastic hairband and announced, 'Mr Stojković will be here any minute now. Can I get you a coffee in the meantime?'

Milena didn't have the heart to tell Alisa that her coffee was too weak and that, even worse, it tasted like the proverbial dishwater, so instead she replied timidly, 'That'd be nice, thanks.'

'Do go through, Ms Lukin.'

Milena took a seat at the large conference table in Siniša's office, behind piles of lever-arch files, CDs, a large bottle of aftershave and a shrink-wrapped presentation edition of Dante's *Divine Comedy*.

Alisa served a dry biscuit with the coffee.

'How's your mother?' enquired Milena.

'Thanks for asking, Ms Lukin. I mustn't grumble, but things with her aren't exactly getting easier with the passing years.'

'And your son?'

'He's just about to be discharged from the army.'

'What next? Does he have any plans?'

'Plans?' Alisa gazed glumly out of the window. 'Who can say? He likes playing computer games. And Mr Stojković promised he'd keep an ear to the ground for him. It'll all come out right in the end, don't you think?'

Just as she was leaving, Milena asked, 'By the way, did you ever meet Jurij Pichler?'

'Mr Pichler?' Alisa shook her head in alarm. 'May he rest in peace, and I know you oughtn't speak ill of the dead and all that. But all the same, I'm glad I never had to shake his hand.'

'Whenever something doesn't sit right with Alisa, she discovers she has an urgent doctor's appointment, out of the blue,' Siniša said, walking in and slamming his briefcase down on the desk. 'No coffee, thanks – and no calls, understood?' he continued. Turning to Milena, he said, 'Sorry I'm late.' His forehead was beaded with sweat as he gave Milena a peck on the cheek and handed Alisa his coat and silk scarf. 'On the way here, I've been on the phone to every Tom, Dick, and Harry, and none of the scoundrels would tell me anything about the post-mortem report.'

After Alisa had left and closed the door behind her, Milena said, 'The documents you gave me only contained press reports from the time.'

'Correct.'

'Didn't you have access to the police files when you were preparing the case?'

'My formal request to see them is with the public prosecutor.'

'And?'

'It's still pending.'

'But the authorities have to respond sometime. Haven't you pressed them?'

Siniša drew up a chair. 'As you know, my strategy in the case of Jurij Pichler was: don't bring out the big guns straight away, but instead try and resolve the matter through informal channels.'

'You were trying to pull a fast one, you mean?' Milena said.

'I was acting in my client's best interests.'

'And now he's dead.'

Siniša stood up and went to the window.

Milena went on, 'The other youth who was involved in the murder of the little Roma boy back then–'

'They're actually talking about manslaughter in this

instance,' Siniša corrected her, before adding quietly, 'Which doesn't make it any better, of course.'

'What do we know about the second perpetrator?'

'He was convicted at the time and served his sentence.'

'What's his name?'

'Luca.'

'And his surname?'

'No idea.'

'How come? The bloke's a key witness.'

'The second perp didn't figure in my strategy. Far from it, in fact. I was afraid we'd complicate things needlessly by involving him. I wanted to focus all my efforts on Pichler and disregard everything else.'

'And what about the Roma community and the family of the murdered boy – the Jovanovićs?'

'Same story. "Hold your horses until we've got the trial over and done with," I told Jurij. Everything else would have been a private matter for him to sort out then.'

'In other words, you didn't plan on calling either his accomplice – this Luca guy – or the relatives of the dead boy as witnesses?'

'I wanted to settle the matter with as little fuss as possible.'

'What's this whole thing really about when you get right down to it?' said Milena. 'It's about two youths. One of them has been convicted by a court of law and served his time, and the other turns himself in after twenty-five years and is prepared to face the music. What do think he might have got? A suspended sentence?'

Siniša raised his hands. 'Who knows – maybe I'd even have managed an acquittal.'

'Sure.' Milena nodded grimly. 'After all, Dušan Jovanović was a member of the Roma community, and the Roma don't have any clout in this society.'

'As a lawyer, my sole responsibility is to represent my client's interests. Period. So stop giving me a hard time.' Saying this, Siniša loosened the knot in his tie. 'Okay, if we assume Jurij Pichler was murdered, then what, may I ask, was the motive?'

'Dunno. Maybe the Roma wanted revenge?'

'You mean the Jovanović family? In that case, why has the public prosecutor been sitting on his hands?'

'That's the key question.'

'Very well,' said Siniša. 'Before we get carried away, I'll try and get some lowdown on the autopsy report and the police files. I'll bring some heat to bear now. Happy?'

'Sounds good to me.' Milena got up to leave.

'We'll know more by tomorrow,' Siniša called after her. 'I promise you.'

*

Milena really ought to have gone straight to the German embassy and spent her time with the telephone glued to her ear, 'putting a rocket up her Serbian friends' – to use Alexander's choice phrase – about the renewable energy sources, the accounting errors, and the emissions reports. On the other hand, she also had plenty to do at the Institute for Criminology and Forensic Science, and that was only just around the corner. People were sitting at the street cafés all around, and a farmer's wife was selling the first lilies of the valley. Milena bought a bunch. She decided it would be more sensible for her to defer the business of German-Serbian politics until the afternoon and that right now she should attend to her pet project, her doctoral thesis.

It was still before eleven when she crossed the foyer of the institute and climbed the staircase beneath the glass cupola.

In the corridor to her office, she was just taking her key from her bag when she noticed that the door to Room 109, the storage space, was open.

'Hello?' Milena peered round the door.

Behind various decommissioned desks, filing cabinets, metal boxes, and bundles of newspapers, a young woman was standing at the window smoking a cigarette.

Somewhat taken aback, Milena stepped into the room. 'Can I help you?'

The woman exhaled smoke through the window. 'Katharina Schröder's the name. I'm your new colleague.'

'Oh yes, the part-time position,' said Milena, with a surprised smile. 'I didn't know you were starting today.'

'Yes, that's right, the second of May.' The woman proffered her hand. 'It's nice to finally meet you in person.'

'You know, it's as if I had a premonition...' said Milena, handing her the little posy. 'Welcome!'

'Why, thank you!' Visibly moved, the young woman took the flowers.

Milena glanced round the room. 'I'll make sure this stuff gets moved out of here, and then I'll clear my room over the course of this week – if that's okay with you?'

'I wouldn't hear of it.' The young woman found an empty tin in a nearby crate and took it over to the washbasin. 'You're staying right where you are. I've already discussed it with Professor Grubač.'

'Are you sure, Ms Schröder?'

Milena's new co-worker put the tin containing the lilies of the valley down on the windowsill and said, 'Please call me Katharina.'

Over their first shared smoke, Milena learned that Katharina was the daughter of a German father and a Bosnian Serb mother, that she'd spent her childhood in Freiburg and her school holidays in a village near Banja Luka, and that she was 'currently' involved with a Palestinian who was studying mechanical engineering in Belgrade.

'There was an instant spark between us; you know how it goes sometimes.'

Milena stubbed out her cigarette. 'Come on, then,' she said. 'Let's just push all this into the corner for the time being. Then at least you'll have room for a desk.' She took off her jacket.

Their combined efforts succeeded in shifting the packing crates to one side and piling all the boxes and stacks of newspapers on top. Then they set to work moving the desk. It was a monster of a thing, heavier than expected.

'Perhaps,' said Katharina, 'we should take out the drawers first.'

Milena found herself wedged between the window and the desk when her mobile suddenly began ringing. She looked at the screen – a Belgrade number – and took the call.

It was Karen Pichler. She apologised for disturbing Milena and then announced, 'The hotel's going to open as of tomorrow.'

Milena brushed her hair back from her face. 'That's really wonderful news!'

'And, as it happens, I'm very near your institute right now.'

Milena turned round and looked out of the window onto the square below. Karen was sitting beneath the statue of Vojvoda Vuk; she was staring at the toes of her shoes and clearly had no idea that Milena could see her.

'If you're in your office by any chance,' Karen went on, attempting to give her voice a breezy, upbeat note, 'and fancied grabbing a cup of coffee...' She gazed heavenwards. 'You must think me terribly pushy, I know, but I really need to speak to you.'

Ten minutes later, they were crossing Prince Michael Street together. Leaving the crocodile lines of tourists, the buskers, and the whole hubbub of the pedestrian zone behind them, they carried on down King Peter Street, heading for Dorćol, the former Jewish quarter, with its crooked backyards, villas, little gardens, and small shops. Karen said she had never set foot in this part of town before.

Milena pointed out the pharmacy, which for years had been the place where the best skincare products were made, all plant-based, and noted in passing that the old jeweller's shop where her father had purchased his wedding rings had now closed. A yellowing sign in the window read: 'Many thanks for sixty-four years of your loyal custom.'

The optician's next door, where as a child Milena – and, in turn, Adam too – had had their first pairs of glasses pre-scribed, had long since ceased trading. Now some young people were running an ice-cream parlour from the prem-ises, which changed the whole character of this little corner. Outside the large plate-glass windows of the shop, a throng of hipsters in hoodies and outsize sunglasses had congre-gated, alongside housewives with shopping bags and busi-ness people in suits, all digging into environmentally friendly cardboard ice-cream cups with colourful plastic spoons. Milena had been to the parlour several times with Adam and was still trying to get used to the loud music, not to mention steadily work her way through the range on offer, which consisted of some really unusual flavours. The time was now ripe, Milena decided, to sample the marzipan ice cream, and Karen was immediately on board with her suggestion.

'Isn't it strange,' said Karen once they had sat down on a narrow wooden bench outside with their ice creams, 'that life just carries on like nothing has happened?'

'But at the same time, it's a saving grace,' replied Milena.

They ate without talking for a moment, before Milena picked up the thread again. 'It's good that you've decided to open the hotel now. When the going gets tough, the only answer is to just press on, however hard that might be. Oh, before I forget – I'll be needing your double room from Thursday to Monday inclusive.'

Karen nodded, and Milena explained that her ex-husband was coming to Belgrade to celebrate their son's birthday along with his current partner, and that she had very mixed feelings about this visit, the first for many years.

Karen continued to spoon up her ice cream in silence, while watching a stray dog doing the rounds of the customers, licking out their empty cups. Leaning back against the plate-glass window, Milena enquired, 'May I ask you a question?'

'Of course,' Karen nodded. 'It's so nice sitting here with you. Ask away.'

'Did you know about your husband's past? That he had the life of a ten-year-old boy on his conscience?'

The question did not appear to take Karen by surprise. 'He told me,' she replied. 'We'd known each other for about a year by then.'

'How did you react?'

Karen held the little spoon motionless on her lower lip. Then she turned to Milena and enquired in turn, 'What do you think – how would you have reacted to something like that?'

'I really don't know.' Milena studied the dog, which was looking up at her with its tail wagging. 'I wonder if I could live with a person who'd done something like that. I can't imagine it.'

Karen took off her glasses. 'When Jurij told me about it, it actually seemed like he was talking about someone else, a total stranger, and not himself, not the Jurij I knew.' She rubbed the bridge of her nose with her thumb and forefinger, and then she pressed them into the corners of her eyes, where tears were starting to well up. 'You see, I'm already speaking about him in the past tense.'

In sympathy, Milena laid her hand on Karen's arm.

'That was the very first time in his life,' Karen went on, her voice now quieter, 'that he'd told anyone about what he'd done. The first time he'd had to put it into words.' She replaced her glasses, straightening the large frame on her nose. 'And that was how it all began. It set something in motion inside him, which eventually led to his decision to face up to his past and hand himself in to the Serbian authorities. I really admired him for that, and he had my total respect and support.'

'What did he tell you about the crime all those years ago?' Milena enquired. 'Sorry for asking so bluntly. If you don't want to talk about it–'

Karen shook her head. 'I'm happy, Ms Lukin, to talk about it with someone who's not directly involved or part of the family.' She hugged her knees like she needed to hold fast to something, and then recounted how Jurij had described the assault to her. How he'd been drifting round the streets with his best mate Luca, tanked up on booze and a bit stoned as well, and how the young Roma boy had crossed their path, and that he'd done nothing to provoke them except hand over just a few coins when they demanded money. How the boy had come along at precisely the right time for Jurij and Luca to vent on him their frustration and rage at the world. How they bullied and jostled and punched him. How the situation began to get out of hand, and how Luca wouldn't stop laying into the boy, while Jurij stood by, as if paralysed, and did nothing to stop his friend. And then how flashing blue lights had appeared and Jurij had legged it and just kept running.

That very same night, Karen continued, Jurij's family spirited him away to an aunt who lived in the country. Barely two days after that, his father drove him to Vienna and put him on a plane to Lisbon. There, Jurij was to stay with a cousin of his, who'd been instructed to secure him a passage to Argentina as a cabin boy on a freighter. That was the plan, and indeed it all went smoothly. Not that Jurij would have raised an objection anyway – but nobody ever sought his opinion about all this.

In Buenos Aires, his great-uncle was waiting for him, and he put Jurij to work in his shoe factory. Jurij now spent almost every day on the production line, and after a year he was even given a small salary as well as being granted a residence permit by the authorities. Then, after about five years, he pooled all the money he'd saved, gathered up his belongings, told his uncle 'thanks for everything' and 'cheerio', and hit the road. He eventually made his way to Miami, where he worked illegally as a painter and decorator. That was where he got to know Karen. She was working in a gallery, and he got a job painting the walls of the house opposite, along with all the soffits, balconies, and window frames. At first, just the odd glance passed between them. Then they started waving to one another, and finally he painted a sign and held it up – 'Will you come out with me this evening?' – followed by a second one, reading simply 'Please!' and then a third – 'Otherwise, I'll die!' That made her laugh.

After the summer was over, she went back to her homeland, the Netherlands, and three months later he fetched up there outside her door. And that's where he stayed.

'And he didn't hear anything about what had become of his accomplice, this Luca guy?' asked Milena.

'You mean when he was in Argentina?'

'Or later.'

Karen shook her head. 'You know, I never quizzed Jurij about it. Maybe that was a mistake. I know that, when he returned to Belgrade, he went back to the place where it had happened – on Belgrade Street. He wanted to go there alone, and I thought that was only right. He needed to come to terms with it himself. But I do know that the question of what had got into them that night really troubled him. One time – he was really furious – he just blurted out how he wanted to get Luca to explain himself. But that was just an isolated outburst, and another time he told me he hadn't behaved any better than Luca.'

'Do you think he had any contact with the Roma clan?'

Karen shrugged. 'I've no idea. I think he made some attempts to find out what had become of the boy's family, the Jovanovićs. But I haven't a clue how far he got with that. I figured it was enough that I was there for him whenever he needed me... I'm sorry.' She blew her nose.

'You were his salvation.' Milena handed her a clean tissue. 'It was because you loved him that he plucked up the courage to confront this dark chapter in the first place. It was thanks to you that he was in a position to finally start building a life.'

'But now he's dead!'

'Whatever's happened, I promise you we'll get to the bottom of it.'

When they took leave from one another at the street corner, Milena asked, 'Was the hotel Jurij's idea?'

'Yes, it was his baby.' Karen nodded. 'Ever since I've known him, he's cut pictures out of magazines and collected them to help him envisage what his hotel might be like. And in Amsterdam he got hold of some literature that told him how to draw up a business plan, and he started talking to banks.

But the toughest nut to crack was convincing his mother. After all, the building is his parents' home.'

'She was against it, then?'

'I'm not sure that she even wanted him to come back home. Like she sensed something bad would happen. But, in the end, she gave in and signed a lease agreement with us – and on very fair terms too, I must say.'

'You know that big investors are fighting to get their hands on property and building plots in precisely your part of town, Little Sava Street?'

'Maybe so.' Karen shrugged. 'We told ourselves we'd give it ten years with the hotel and then start looking around again. But now – how am I supposed to carry on without him? And what's the point anyway?'

'Give it a go,' Milena said. 'It was your baby as well as his.'

12

Anna looked at the passing city through the side window, and the images that streamed past her at a steady pace seemed like scenes from a film. Hipsters who wouldn't have looked out of place in New York milling about outside a fast-food joint. Fountains and colourful awnings. Drugstores and supermarket chains. All of a sudden, a ruined building. You could see precisely where the rocket had struck. The war had broken out shortly after she left, and its scars were, it seems, being assiduously preserved. To what end? Anna sighed. Such behaviour was typically Serbian: defiant and backward-looking, and serving no purpose whatsoever.

'Take another turn round the block, will you?' she told the driver.

She tried to remember. As a child and an adolescent, she hadn't ventured very far afield. Hopscotch and skipping games in the driveway had been her favourite pastimes, along-side doing her homework and helping her mother fold the laundry – and keeping an eye out to check that Dušan wasn't getting up to any mischief. In the summer, they went out to the countryside to visit Uncle Davit. She'd spend her time bathing in the river, tussling with her cousins and helping her uncle collect feathers. Then, one day – it may have been at a family celebration or at the spring festival – their grand-father announced that Jemal was to marry his cousin Anna that year. Back then, she hadn't understood what such a mar-riage meant. In her eyes, Jemal was cocky and crude but oth-erwise not really so bad. But the fact that her parents vetoed the match was more than an affront to the clan.

Henceforth, there were to be no more summers in the country, and no further contact with their relatives. Her father spent all his time in the workshop, banging and hammering away, and her mother was usually to be found ironing. 'We'll get on just fine on our own,' she'd say. 'We don't need anyone else. You mark my words.'

The street sign that flitted past Anna's gaze brought her back to the present with a jolt: Belgrade Street! This was where it had happened. Unprepared, she found herself in a state of shock, and it took a few seconds for her to react. Finally, she leant forward in her seat. 'Please turn off here now,' she requested.

'What?' asked the driver, taken aback. 'To the right, you mean?'

'Wherever. Just do it!'

The driver complied and switched on his indicator.

'Now take me back to the hotel.'

She only breathed easily again when the sign for her hotel, a familiar international name, came into view on the far side of the bridge. By the time she came to pay the taxi driver, her hands had almost stopped trembling.

She ate a small snack at the bar, tipped the piano player and went to reception to pick up her room key. It was clear: she mustn't fritter away time by constantly indulging in reminiscences. Every image seemed garishly bright to her, causing a stabbing and burning sensation. But the matter at hand was crystal clear: she'd taken the first step by coming back here, and she now needed to take the second.

One factor that made things more difficult, and frankly baffled her, was Jurij Pichler. Why hadn't he got back in touch? First he goes and unsettles her by ringing her up out of the blue, only to then disappear from the scene again without a trace. Like the earth had swallowed him up. How was she supposed to find him? Engage a private detective? Even if she did manage to track him down, what then?

She hated this situation, not knowing how to proceed. She detested this city and the feeling of being hung out to dry. Perhaps she'd leave sooner than she envisaged and then just try to put the whole business out of her mind again. But there was one thing she simply had to do first. Otherwise, she'd reproach herself for the rest of her life.

In the shower, she thought about what she should wear. Best go for jeans and some sensible, unobtrusive shoes – the pair of trainers that she'd last used for jogging in Central Park. A hoodie over her cashmere sweater. Her hair plaited and tucked down into her top.

She took a taxi to Kalemegdan Fortress, like it was the most normal thing in the world to do. Just a spot of sightseeing. Getting out at Paris Street, she recognised her surroundings. She'd be able to get her bearings from here.

Finding herself caught up in a gaggle of tourists who had just alighted from a tour bus, she stopped and let them flood past. She was in no hurry. Anyhow, the place she was looking for probably wouldn't even exist any more. She'd mentally prepared for that eventuality, even assumed it would be the case. It was all such a long time ago now. Perhaps her trip, this whole undertaking, was nothing but a pretext for her to finally wallow in self-pity.

Turning a corner, she caught sight of the rough driveway and, down at the bottom, a low-roofed old shack. So, it was still standing after all! There on the left were the extension, the workshop, and the low door leading to the two rooms. It was unbelievable. Even the water butt was still there, and the old curtains, so far as she could make out from up here on the road. It was as if time had stood still and the world had bypassed this place right in the heart of Belgrade.

She tried to picture how she'd played here as a little girl, merrily skipping about and feeling happy. It all appeared so small, so dreadfully run-down, in a way she wouldn't have thought possible even in her worst nightmares. This was her place of origin, where she'd been born and had grown up until the age of sixteen. On a rubbish dump. A gypsy.

She retched, holding a tissue to her mouth, and tried to convince herself that all that stuff down there, that heap of filth, had nothing to do with her any more. And wasn't that precisely why her father had packed her off abroad and forbidden her to ever come back?

She sat down on the kerb. She could only recall fragments of the past, and the images in her mind were hazy. Leaving her father, the crossing to New York, the constant rumble of the ship's engines below deck. The immigration hall, the endless waiting, and then wandering lost around Brooklyn until she finally located the strangers who were her relatives and who took the money that her father had hung in a little purse round her neck. The damp cellar, the laundry and the way her uncle had taken every opportunity to come up to her room. She'd finally slapped his face and been thrown out, and found refuge with some students – artists, whose apartment reeked of turpentine, which even today was the smell of freedom for her. She could recall gaining a place at university, securing a scholarship and her room in the student hostel – but she had no sense of time, or of how and when this sequence of events had occurred. After just a year in America? Or had it been longer?

Likewise, she couldn't have said how long she'd been sitting here on the kerb, staring down the slope at the shed, when a figure appeared, hobbling out of the shack. Someone actually still lived down there. She couldn't believe her eyes.

The old man used a crutch to haul himself laboriously up

the drive. He was heading straight for her, though his eyes were fixed on the ground.

Like a sleepwalker, she followed him with her eyes as he proceeded down the far side of the street. His shabby suit hung limply off his frame and his small sunken face rang no bells with her. It wasn't until he reached the corner, by the flower seller's, that the old man stopped. He glanced up at the sky, and Anna suddenly felt as though the ground was about to open up beneath her feet. There was something deeply familiar about the expression on that face, a beauty and a pride she recognised instantly. Abruptly, her father turned his head and looked across the street at her, straight into her eyes.

She quickly tugged her hood over her head, got up from her spot by the driveway, and ran as fast as her legs would carry her.

13

Slap bang in the middle of the coffee table was a colourful bunch of spring flowers, whose provenance Milena was at a complete loss to explain. She bent over the bouquet and breathed in the scent. Was this really Sandra's way of saying sorry?

Milena put down her bag, hung up her jacket and went across to the outer office. 'The fresh flowers–' she began.

'Count Kronburg.'

Milena was nonplussed. 'They're from Alexander?'

The door to his room was open, but 'Count Kronburg' was, as Sandra briskly informed her, 'out on an appointment.'

'Did he give any particular reason for sending them?' Milena enquired.

The PA held up her hands. 'You'll have to ask him that yourself. Anything else?'

Milena asked Sandra if she could try and get the Serbian energy minister or the secretary of state on the phone.

'What should I say it's concerning?'

'The energy report.'

Sandra made a note.

Milena returned to her office, took the bouquet off the glass tabletop, and placed it on the desk next to her computer, tweaking some of the blooms. Then she set to work.

She tried to get her head around the calculation methods used by her Serbian negotiating partners to produce a pie chart illustrating the gap that needed to be filled regarding carbon dioxide emissions. In addition, she drew up a firm timeframe within which this shortfall would have to be made good, and she speculated on how the Serbs might try to wangle themselves some extra time within the schedule.

At some point, her landline rang. Sandra's voice told her that she had the secretary of state from the energy ministry on the line.

The man – still relatively young, and with a penchant for loud ties, if Milena remembered correctly – was very understanding and even cooperative on the phone, reassuring her he would consult with the minister 'that very day' and 'free himself up' for a working lunch on Friday, 'or next week at the very latest'.

At the end of the call, Milena immediately prepared a summary of their conversation and forwarded it to Sandra, with the request that the document be circulated to all those concerned, including Alexander and the Americans. Then she looked at her watch. It had just gone six.

She pressed the intercom button and said, 'You can go home now, Sandra; I don't need you any more. Oh, and hats off to you for getting hold of the secretary of state so promptly! Thanks very much.'

'You're welcome,' replied Sandra. 'See you tomorrow.'

Then Milena pressed the speed-dial button and, while it was ringing at the other end, took a jelly banana out of her bag. She had just squeezed the sweet out of its cellophane wrapper and popped it into her mouth when someone finally answered. It was Adam.

'Hello, love,' she said, putting her diary in her bag. 'What are you two up to – have you had dinner already?'

Her son's response was an indistinct murmur.

'Are you playing on the computer?' she asked. 'Where's Grandma?'

'Over at Mrs Bašić's.'

'Have you done your homework?'

'When are you coming home?'

'I'm on my way right now,' she said, and suddenly felt a powerful urge to give her son a hug, right there and then. 'Do you want me to bring anything for you?' she asked solicitously.

'Nah,' he replied. 'Unless it's pizza, that is.'

'Done,' answered Milena, trying not to think of Vera, who would definitely disapprove. 'If it's pizza you want, then pizza you shall have.'

'After putting on her jacket, she quickly opened her emails again and dashed off a message to Philip: *I've booked a nice room for you at the Hotel Amsterdam. It's in a lovely part of town.*

She stopped and thought for a moment. In her experience, denizens of Hamburg had a very fixed idea of what constituted 'lovely'. To be on the safe side, she changed the last sentence to read: *It's in a really lovely and interesting part of town.*

She pressed 'send' and was quickly checking her inbox for new messages when an instant reply came back: *Thanks for your message*, wrote Philip. *I hadn't heard back from you, so I went ahead and booked a room at the Hotel Moscow – not cheap, but in a very central location. All the best, Philip.*

Milena swore under her breath.

At home, this news made more of a splash than the salami pizza that Milena brought back.

'Dad's staying at the Moscow?' enthused Adam. 'Wow, that's really ritzy!'

'Adam,' Milena chided, in an attempt to calm him down, 'what have I told you about speaking with your mouth full?'

Without a word, Vera scraped the remains of the pizza onto a plate, folded up the greasy cardboard box, and demonstratively wiped the table clean.

Adam paused. 'Maybe I could spend a night at the Moscow too. I mean, it's going to be my birthday, after all!'

'Dad's only got a double room there. I don't think there'll be enough space.'

'Then Jutta can come here and sleep in my bed for a night, and I'll stay with Dad.'

'Great idea,' Vera interjected drily, clattering the dirty plates into the sink. 'Or, even better, what if your father were to rent a whole suite, then you could go ahead and invite all your friends too, eh? How about that?'

'That's enough now,' said Milena.

'You know what,' said Adam, picking a slice of salami off his pizza. 'If Dad would let me bring anyone else, then I'd invite you, Gran.'

When he was tucked up in bed, and Vera had taken him some camomile tea with a spoonful of acacia honey as a soothing nightcap, Milena slumped down in her chair, exhausted. The cat leapt onto her lap. Milena stroked her silky fur and thought about Karen. Living with her mother-in-law now, following Jurij's death, couldn't be easy for her. Or maybe the situation had brought the two women closer together? It was so stupid that she was going to have to cancel the reservation she'd only just made for Philip and Jutta.

'How come his father's staying at the Moscow?' Vera had entered the room and was busy straightening the tassels on the rug with her foot. 'Has he got money to burn, or what?'

'Just drop it, Mum,' said Milena.

'Instead of indulging in such luxuries, perhaps he'd like to cough up a bit more maintenance money to help you bring up the boy,' sniffed Vera.

'We really don't have much to complain about as it stands, Mum.'

'Only because you're holding down two jobs. Before long, you'll be run ragged!'

Milena was relieved when her mobile began to ring. 'Sorry,' she said, shoving the cat off her lap. 'It's Siniša.'

She left the room and took the call.

'I don't like to admit it,' came Siniša's voice at the other end, 'but once again you were right.'

'About what?' Milena closed the study door behind her and switched on the desk lamp.

Siniša reported that he had drawn a blank in his attempts to glean information on either the post-mortem or the police reports relating to Jurij's death.

'And did you notice,' said Milena, lighting up a cigarillo, 'that there was nothing about Jurij's death in the papers at the weekend?'

'What, not even a few measly column inches?' said Siniša, clearly disappointed. 'We shouldn't waste any more time.'

Milena drew on her cigarillo. 'How do you mean?'

'Could you try and get hold of the justice minister tomorrow? Let him know about the case and tell him it's time to lay his cards on the table.'

'I'm afraid,' Milena interrupted, 'you've got the wrong idea about my job and how much leeway I have there.' She breathed out a stream of smoke. 'My influence is very limited. For instance, if I want to speak to the secretary of state for energy, I can only manage to do so because the ambassador's PA is such a tough cookie.'

'That's perfect. So tomorrow she can ring up the justice ministry and bend their ear. Or the chief of police.'

'What planet are you on, Siniša? We're not some government authority. I need a specific reason to call someone or have the PA ring them, and I have to justify using certain official positions.'

'Then get your Count Kronburg to cover your back. He'd be able to file a completely official request.'

'On what grounds?'

'Do you need any?'

Milena sighed. 'Let me sleep on it.' She stubbed out her cigarillo. 'I need some peace and quiet to mull it over.'

After hanging up, she took off her earrings and looked out of the window at the grey concrete wall of the building opposite. Why would she go and stir up a hornets' nest by 'setting the big cogs in motion', as Siniša liked to say? Why bother going on a detour via ministers and ministries when she could simply take the direct route?

14

Zoran Filipow poked his fork around in the overcooked peas – the side dish that came with the ox tongue – and turned away from his colleagues. Because the football match against the Scots had passed off so smoothly, which had been less down to the sporting prowess of the Serbian team than to the police operation at the ground, they had all been given a half-day's special leave. The news had been greeted with loud cheers. Bully for his colleagues; let them enjoy their time off. Zoran, however, couldn't remember ever having been granted so much as a minute's special leave in the department where he worked – not even when his father had been on his deathbed or when his young daughter was born.

He dredged the dried-up slab of meat through the sauce like a rag, and only managed to swallow a piece by taking a slug of sparkling mineral water. It had finally dawned on him that there was something fishy about the case of Jurij Pichler after it transpired that, aside from a police report, absolutely nothing else on the matter had been committed to paper. His colleague Vukomanović, who was abruptly pulled off the case, was a lazy-arse bastard and incompetent to boot, but even he wouldn't have stood for such lax record-keeping.

And now Zoran was also off the case. He'd been told as much in a terse memo that very morning. Everyone knew about it, and several of his co-workers made no attempt to conceal their smirks. Zoran screwed his napkin into a ball and placed it on top of the pea sludge. There wasn't even a toothpick to be had in this dump.

If the rumours were true, then of course he ought to cross

himself three times and be glad to be shot of the Pichler case. A sensitive case like that really wasn't his thing at all, and it would actually be far better placed with his colleague Dežulović. Let him burn his fingers on it, though Zoran knew that was hardly likely to happen. Not to Dežulović.

Even so, it left a nasty taste in Zoran's mouth. It bugged him that he'd only been considered a stopgap solution. What was to be made of the whole affair? At least with Vukomanović you could be sure he'd make the most unholy hash of things in no time. All well and good – the organisation just carried people like him. But what did the powers that be really think of Zoran? That he'd do a workmanlike-enough job on the investigation, but that if the case were to get too hot to handle others would have to be called in – professionals rather than plodding bean-counters? Zoran pushed his plate aside and followed the progress of the cockroach that was busy climbing the wall, until it vanished from sight into the grubby air vent. What had been the point in him completing that postgraduate course with all its emphasis on theory, and sacrificing all those evenings and weekends to study, if they weren't prepared to give him a chance now? How was he supposed to make his mark and finally get on?

'Anyone sitting here?' Vukomanović, of all people, was standing there with his tray and the dark bags under his eyes.

'Be my guest.' Zoran nodded. Losers stick together.

'You're looking rough.' Vukomanović sat down. 'Straight up – maybe you should put in for some leave, eh?'

'How are you faring?' In response to his apathetic enquiry, Zoran learned that Vukomanović, the eternal bachelor, was looking for a buyer for his cottage out in Grocka following the death of his mother.

'If you know of anyone,' Vukomanović stuck out his elbows as he sawed into the meat, 'do send them my way.'

'Listen here.' Zoran bent forward conspiratorially. 'You know the Pichler case?'

'What about it?'

'Do you reckon there's anything to the rumours?'

'That's not our pigeon now.'

'But you attended the scene, right? Is there documentary evidence stating that the deceased had stones in his pockets?'

'There were stones at the scene, all right. But not in his pockets.' Vukomanović jabbed his knife at Zoran. 'That stays strictly between us, mind.'

'Any gunshot wounds?'

Vukomanović took a drink. 'How's it going with your building project? Got the finances together yet?'

'So, that's to say,' Zoran summarised, 'that the report that was put on my desk yesterday for me to countersign, before the case was taken away from me, didn't come from you? In other words, someone else wrote it?'

'Well, you know me. I'm not a great one for writing,' said Vukomanović between mouthfuls of food, giving Zoran a lopsided grin. 'I prefer to leave that art to the dab hands. You might like to think about doing that too.' His earlobes moved up and down as he chewed.

Zoran could cheerfully have planted a fist squarely in Vukomanović's vacuous gob right then. Instead, trying to appear nonchalant, he leant back in his chair and said, 'My father-in-law provided some start-up funding. But I need to watch that the costs don't run away from us before we even break ground.' He bent forward across the table once more. 'You know how it is with women: first they want one thing, then something else. Today it's an open hearth, tomorrow it's an induction hob, and after that it's tropical timber window frames. And my great weakness is that I can never say no to Viola. But you know what?' Zoran looked straight into Vukomanović's naïve, watery eyes. 'That's all in the past now.'

Vukomanović put his knife and fork down on his plate. 'By the by, I meant to tell you, there's someone outside who wants a word with you.'

'Who's that?'

'A civilian, a woman. She's no spring chicken.'

Zoran sighed, stood up, and picked up his tray. 'See you around.'

In the absence of a toothpick, the fragments of ox tongue between his teeth would be bothering him for the entire afternoon. It really wasn't his day.

*

If Milena tried totting up all the time she'd spent sitting on this wooden bench, what would it amount to – several weeks? Or even months? For one thing, there was the annual palaver of having to renew the residence permit that Adam required as a German citizen living in Serbia. Every year, she was sure she had everything that she needed to hand, but there always turned out to be one document that was invalid and at least one new stamp she had to obtain. When Serbia joined the EU, all this hassle would hopefully cease, and maybe one day she'd think back wistfully to this old bench in the police station on Sava Street. She crossed her legs.

In all likelihood, she'd never work out in this lifetime whether it was better not to pester the officer behind the glass partition – even though that meant you ran the risk of being forgotten on the bench – or whether it wasn't a more sensible strategy to kick up a fuss straight from the off, like the bloke beside her here with the manbag and beads of sweat on his brow. He was refusing to pay some parking fine or other and kept loudly demanding to speak to 'the officer in charge here'. But the guy behind the glass window was a sadist and simply ignored him.

Milena now crossed her legs, and with every passing minute her courage ebbed away. The truth was that she had no plan, no strategy. It was all just a gut feeling; she had nothing up her sleeve. The only incontrovertible fact in the story surrounding Jurij Pichler was that there were no hard-and-fast facts in the case. With a frosty smile and a snide remark, Filipow would send her packing with a flea in her ear. Even so, unlike Siniša, she had the feeling that Filipow was still a decent person at heart. While she was musing on whether this notion wasn't perhaps a bit too romantic, suddenly there he was in person, standing right in front of her.

'Ms Lukin?' he asked in surprise. He sounded far from pleased to see her.

Milena decided to disregard his tone of voice. 'Hello,' she said, standing up and proffering her hand.

He grasped it only fleetingly. 'Let's get down to business, then. This way, if you please,' he said in an oddly stilted way. With a brief glance over his shoulder to his colleague behind the window, he steered her in the direction of the lift. Paying no further attention to her, he watched the numbers of the floors glow dimly as the lift descended to them, greeted colleagues as they emerged from it, and then signalled that Milena should go ahead. She got the distinct impression that it would be prudent to hold her tongue for the time being.

He pressed the button for the fourth floor and, once the doors had closed, turned to her and asked, 'Did Attorney Stojković send you?'

'No, I'm here on my own account. As a friend of Mrs Pichler, so to speak.'

'Then I'm sorry to disappoint you, but I'm no longer involved with the case.'

Surprised, Milena straightened her bag on her shoulder. 'I don't get it. You were with Mrs Pichler at the pathologist's only last Friday.'

'She identified the body, and that just about wrapped up the whole case.'

'So why aren't you letting Mr Stojković have sight of the autopsy report?'

Filipow pushed down the large red emergency-stop switch, and with a jolt the lift came to an abrupt halt. 'Now just listen to me, will you?' he said, with an audible intake of breath. 'I'm going to take you to my office now, but before I do, kindly explain what I'm supposed to tell my colleagues and my superiors when they start wondering what you and I might possibly have to discuss in private. Otherwise, you'll get me into serious trouble. Don't look at me like that – just think of something! Damn it, I should have told you to get lost straight away. You and I are in deep shit, I can tell you.'

'Just calm down for a moment, will you?' Milena studied the scratched wood-veneer panelling. 'I've got it. You're planning to come and give us a talk. Simple as that. At the Institute for Criminology and Forensic Science.'

It seemed to take a few seconds for the information to sink in. 'What sort of a talk?' he enquired eventually.

'"New Concepts in Security". "Challenges in the Age of Globalisation". "Opportunities and Risks". That kind of thing. At the symposium this coming spring.'

'I'll need that in writing.'

'You'll receive a written invitation from the institute, signed by Professor Grubač – and, if the circumstances allow it, you'll even get a fee for your trouble.'

Filipow flipped the rocker switch up, and the lift started moving again.

Shortly afterwards, he flopped onto the large leather chair behind his desk and motioned at Milena to take a seat opposite. 'As I was saying, I don't have anything to do with the case any more,' he said.

Milena sat down. 'So what are we doing here, then?'

'You're asking *me* that?'

'Might I be right in thinking that the investigation in the Pichler case is pretty chaotic? There hasn't even been a press release.'

'Why are people like you and Stojković always scenting conspiracies all over the place? Serbia isn't some banana republic, you know.'

'So why isn't Mr Stojković being given any information? He's acting on behalf of the dead man's widow.'

'Perhaps it's got more to do with Mr Stojković's attitude.'

Milena sighed. 'I don't know how much you know about the background to the case. But Jurij Pichler wasn't an unknown quantity. Twenty-five years ago, he was involved in the death of a young Roma boy, Dušan Jovanović. There were two assailants, but Pichler was the one who absconded and settled abroad, while the other was tried and convicted in a court of law.'

'All water under the bridge now.'

'There must be police reports from the time, court documents. I'd be really interested to see those sometime. Is that possible?'

'Forget it, Ms Lukin. This discussion's pointless.'

'Why? Because the information is so sensitive?'

Filipow folded his hands neatly on the desk in front of him as if he were about to say something, but in fact said nothing.

'And what's happening now with the post-mortem report?' asked Milena. 'Did Jurij Pichler drown? Was there alcohol in his bloodstream? And if so, how much?'

She shifted away from him in irritation. Why didn't the guy just chuck her unceremoniously out of his office? Instead, he was just staring blankly into space. It surely wouldn't be long before dark rings started appearing beneath his eyes, marring his (actually quite handsome) face, making it look like he was a bad sleeper or suffered from chronic gastric pain. Milena noticed the bottle of whisky in its cardboard sleeve on the shelf, the dusty fan, and the shabby filing cabinets. Maybe it wasn't just her who wanted something; he did too, it seemed. Perhaps he was at least toying with the idea of weighing up his options. *Be my guest*, she thought. In that case, she'd be able to present him with a couple of possibilities.

She studied her fingernails and said, 'I don't know if you're aware of this, but I'm not only employed at the Institute for Criminology and Forensic Science right now; I've also got a job at the German embassy. We're working flat out on the legal reforms that will have to be implemented here in Serbia and, now that everything's pointing to EU accession sooner or later, there are lots of changes afoot. It's inevitable that fresh blood will be required in many different posts and at various levels of responsibility. And, of course, we're always on the lookout for suitable people.' She smiled, hating herself for putting on this charade.

Filipow picked up a pen and twirled it around pensively.

Milena stood. 'Mr Filipow,' she said, 'maybe we should draw a line under this conversation. This is all going nowhere.'

'Speaking purely hypothetically,' he began, 'if I were to find some evidence to corroborate your bold theory that some kind of cover-up has been going on in the Pichler case...'

'Yes?' replied Milena, holding her breath.

'No. No, you're quite right.' Shaking his head, Filipow laid the pen horizontally on his desk pad. 'This is all going nowhere.'

She picked up her bag without a word and made for the door. As she was on the point of opening it, she said, without looking at Filipow, 'My German ex-husband, Philip Bruns, is coming to Belgrade on Thursday. He'll be staying at the Hotel Moscow. If there's anything you need to get to me quickly and with no complications, you can leave it at reception there. He'll be there until Monday next; he's completely trustworthy and can be relied upon to pass on all information to me straight away, no questions asked.' Without turning around, she opened the door.

She walked down the corridor, thanked the police officer who opened the door for her, and took the staircase down. Only after she had left the building and reached the next corner did she stop and take her phone out of her bag. Her hands were trembling with excitement, and it took two attempts before she managed to key in the right numbers and connect to Siniša's voicemail.

'Listen,' she said, breathlessly, 'unless I'm totally mistaken, Filipow has just admitted to me that something stinks to high heaven in the Pichler case.' She lit a cigarette. 'We have to find out who this Luca guy is – Pichler's mate who was sentenced back then. Oh, and one more thing. We need to establish whether Pichler ever got in touch with the family of the murdered Roma boy.'

15

It was Monday, 4 May, shortly before 2 p.m., when, instead of turning off to the German embassy, Milena accelerated and headed out of the city. In the boot of her car, clinking around as she drove along, was a half-case of Crémant that she'd bought at the Italian wine shop on Prince Miloš Street. Champagne had been too pricey for her, plus she considered it hugely overhyped. But, on the other hand, toasting Adam's birthday with German Sekt struck her as being a bit too downmarket. No matter what she decided – which cheese she bought for supper, or whether she served fig conserve or cranberries with it – she always tried, in an act of pre-emptive submission, to view the situation through Philip's eyes. Wasn't the sofa that he'd sit on already much too threadbare, and the Madonna on the wall opposite far too gloomy? Would Philip turn up his nose, or even openly criticise the conditions in which Adam was growing up?

Milena took her foot off the pedal and changed down to third. It irritated her beyond measure that she was so wound up just because her German ex-husband was about to set foot on Serbian soil. Perhaps she should take a leaf out of Vera's book: if it turned out that Philip and his 'new lady-friend' were pleasant and affable, then at some stage a bottle of Uncle Miodrag's home-distilled spirits would be brought out – the greatest compliment that could be paid to Germans in a former-Yugoslavian partisan household. Milena switched on her indicator and followed the sweeping curve at the start of the motorway slip road. Before the route headed in the direction of Budapest, she turned off it onto a gravel road, swung around the snack bar situated there, and turned onto a dirt track. It had rained heavily in the night, and the pale-blue sky and fleecy white clouds were reflected in puddles.

She slowed down again and weaved around the puddles – less out of fear for her car's transmission, which was robust, and more because she didn't want to have to take it to the car wash again before Philip's arrival – and parked on the grass next to a BMW. It was so low-slung that Milena wondered how on earth it had made it here in one piece, with its all-round plastic spoilers. Three men were sitting in the car, smoking and listening to music. Milena put on her handbrake, picked up her handbag from the passenger's seat, and got out.

It was almost two years since she had last visited this encampment under the motorway bridge. The Roma called their village 'the Mahala'; it had been here for the past twenty-five years, and the shanty town of makeshift huts kept expanding. To begin with, it had been primarily Roma from the republics of the former Yugoslavia who had washed up here, since there had been no place for them any more after Croatia, Bosnia, and Macedonia declared their independence. Many Roma had moved on to Germany, Austria, and Switzerland, but a substantial number of them had returned here, disillusioned, and now shared the place with newcomers from Syria, Pakistan, and Afghanistan. Many of the recent refugees were also members of the Roma community, though this did not mean that they were welcomed with open arms by those already living there. Far from it, in fact. It was surely only a matter of time before the tense situation escalated and clashes broke out between the various groups. For the time being, though, everything seemed peaceful enough. Small children in underpants were launching paper boats into the puddles, while adolescents sitting on concrete blocks – massive things scattered all around the site, like they'd fallen from the sky – were glued to the screens of their smartphones.

Milena tried to recall her last time here – no easy feat. The one-storey concrete buildings with the flat roofs hadn't existed two years ago. On her last visit here, the shanty town had been exclusively built from corrugated iron, cardboard, and tarpaulins. If she remembered rightly, the Avduli family had lived in the second alleyway to the left, quite a way towards the far end.

'What you looking for then, Ma?' came a voice from behind her. 'You after car tyres or something?'

A young man wearing sunglasses pushed back onto his greasy hair was giving Milena a challenging look, while the three figures standing one pace behind him were staring at her like they'd never before set eyes on an unaccompanied woman in a denim jacket with wind-tousled hair.

'I'm looking for the Avduli family,' said Milena, adopting as a precaution the same neutral tone she used to quiz her students about the clauses of the Serbian Civil Code. 'Do you know if they're still living here?'

'The old man's been dead a long time. What do you know about the Avduli family? Do you want a handbag? We can get hold of one for you.'

'Mr Avduli's dead?' Shocked at the news, Milena took a step forward. 'What happened?'

'What do you think? Drank himself to death, that's what. Not the first time that's happened, right?'

'What about his wife and kids?'

'Last house but one, down there. The hut with the green door.' The lad lowered his sunglasses and nudged them straight on his hooked nose. 'Have a think about it. Gucci,

CHRISTIAN SCHÜNEMANN AND JELENA VOLIĆ

Prada – whatever you want, no problem. Washing machines, too. I'm Todor. That's my BMW.'

Milena pushed a strand of hair out of her face. 'I'll get back to you about that sometime, maybe.'

The alleyway between the huts was laid out with planks to help people teeter across the large, presumably ankle-deep puddles. All around, everything was sinking into a muddy quagmire, populated here and there by some pecking hens with dirty feathers. Colourful underpants and cleaning cloths were hung out to dry on washing lines. An old man was poking around with an iron bar in a metal incinerator, from which bluish smoke was rising. Muttering to himself, he chucked in the rubbish that was piled high on his handcart bit by bit. It all played out against the constant roar of traffic up on the motorway bridge.

At the end of the row, a young woman stuck her head inquisitively out of the door. Despite the streaks of peroxide blonde in her hair, Milena instantly recognised her.

Eremina Avduli was barefoot, and over her tracksuit she had thrown on a purple coat with large gold buttons. The phone in her hand suggested she'd just received a text or call from Todor.

'Ms Lukin!' she exclaimed in surprise. 'What brings you here?'

'How are things with you?' asked Milena. She held out her hand but then, after a second, pulled Eremina to her and gave her a big hug. How long was it since she'd seen the girl? Could it really be two years?

Eremina seemed a bit nonplussed. 'What a surprise,' she said. 'Come on in; take a seat. My mother's out with the kids. Can I fix you a tea? Or a coffee?'

'No, thanks.' Milena shook her head. 'First off, I owe you an apology.'

Eremina would hear none of it. 'You've got nothing to apologise for. I'll never forget what you did for me. How's your family?'

Milena sat down on the wooden bench and explained that Adam's birthday was coming up, and that everybody was getting in a flat spin about it. She watched as Eremina deftly brushed some crumbs off the table, placed a pot on the gas camping stove, and spooned coffee granules into it. Many years ago, Milena had started sponsoring this girl, paying for her schoolbooks and sending a small monthly contribution so she could have school meals. Her outlay had really been so paltry and the thanks she received in return so great that, even today, it still embarrassed Milena.

Eremina put a plate of figs on the table, and Milena said, 'The guy outside told me your father died. Is that right?'

'Yeah, his heart gave out.'

'I'm very sorry to hear that.'

Eremina divided the coffee between two large mugs and sat down. 'Mum's been really withdrawn ever since. She's got a cleaning job in the city.'

'And what about you?' asked Milena, looking at the girl. Eremina had really grown up since she'd last seen her.

'I've been looking for work, but it isn't easy,' she replied.

'How did it go with the internship?' asked Milena. 'We lost touch with one another after that.'

'I got a certificate – wait a mo.' Eremina stood up, pulled a file off the shelf above the sofa, and extracted a document in a plastic folder, which she proudly presented to Milena.

In a low tone, Milena read out the testimonial, which cited the intern's 'great input', her talent and application, and her 'outgoing personality' – none of which were news to Milena. She praised Eremina and asked, 'So, what now? Where do you go from here?'

Eremina shrugged in embarrassment. 'Without a fixed address I can't get a work permit, and without that there's no chance of a steady job.'

Milena nodded grimly. 'Understood.'

'Mum wants me to marry Davit, but I don't fancy him. And besides,' Eremina continued, tearing a fig in half, 'I've got something else in mind.'

'What's that?' asked Milena, taking the proffered piece of fig.

'I could open a little hair salon right here in the Mahala. Of course, I wouldn't earn much, but I'm sure I'd manage to scrape together a bit over time.'

'That's a great idea.'

The young woman nodded.

'So, what's stopping you?' probed Milena. 'Do you need to find premises?'

Eremina shook her head. 'The main thing I need is some kit.'

'Scissors?'

'Yeah, and a dryer.'

'Is that all?'

Eremina nodded again.

Milena took a swig of coffee, which was so strong that she momentarily had to close her eyes, and then said, 'Listen, Eremina, I need your help.'

The young woman, who until then had sat there with a solemn expression, now beamed with delight, as if Milena's request were the best news in the world. 'Sure! Tell me what I can do for you,' she responded eagerly.

'I'm looking for a family. The name's Jovanović.'

'Jovanović,' repeated Eremina, nodding.

'They had a little boy, Dušan, who was killed. He was beaten to death by two youths. It's dreadful, I know. But the whole thing's way in the past now. It all happened before you were even born.'

'There are lots of families called Jovanović,' said Eremina.

'But presumably only one with that tragic story.'

'I'll keep my ear to the ground for you,' Eremina promised.

'Thanks.' Milena took her wallet from her bag, extracted a large-denomination banknote, and laid it on the table in front of Eremina.

'No, please – put that away, will you?'

'Buy yourself some curling tongs with it, and a hairdryer, the best you can find.'

'I can't take this from you.'

'I won't take no for an answer. Then you can start earning your own money.'

'It's too much. Besides, I don't need a set of curling tongs. They're too old-fashioned for me.'

'Well, if there's anything left over, buy a mirror, or something else that might come in handy.'

'I don't know what to say, Ms Lukin.'

'And say hello to your mother for me.'

Milena was already at the door, when Eremina suddenly exclaimed, 'Hey, I know who we should ask!'

Milena turned around.

'His name's Sultan, and he's got an office in the city.'

'Sultan?'

'He knows every resident of the Mahala and every Roma. I'll find his number for you. I'll start getting some information together straight away, then I'll let you know.'

Milena smiled. 'Thanks, Eremina.'

16

'I'll be leaving first thing tomorrow,' announced Anna. 'Would you please prepare my bill?'

'With pleasure,' the hotel receptionist replied, typing on her keyboard, though the expression on her face could not have conveyed greater indifference. 'Is there anything else I can do for you, Ms Jones?'

'No, thanks,' said Anna. 'Everything's fine.'

She went up to her room. Leaving the door unlocked behind her, she sat straight down at the desk, opened up her laptop, and went to her airline's website. When she got back home, all this would just seem like a bad dream, a nightmare that had nothing to do with reality.

Within a few seconds, she'd entered all her details on the form. Departure airport: Belgrade. Arrival airport: New York, JFK. Time of departure: Earliest available flight. While the system was searching for what was available, she kept her eyes fixed on the circular aircraft icon. Her head was empty, and for days now her stomach had felt queasy. But now she'd ruminated over things long enough. Her mind was made up.

The information appeared. Tomorrow, bright and early, the first flight out of Belgrade was going to Frankfurt. An hour and a half's stopover there, and then she'd continue her onward journey to New York. It was perfect. Mechanically, she entered her name, address, bank details, and frequent-flyer number, and moved the cursor over the 'confirm' button. Then she hesitated.

If she flew back now to her old life, no one would ever know she'd been here – neither her father in his shack nor

Steven in New York, nor anyone else – and she'd never return to this city; her past would be buried forever. She stood up so abruptly that her chair toppled over.

Turning on the tap in the bath, she rolled up the sleeves of her pullover and let the cold water flow over her wrists. She was in the throes of a crisis, not to mention a state of hysteria, which she'd been in for days. She'd seen the hovel, the place where she'd spent her childhood, and the old man who'd come hobbling out of it had been her father. She'd failed to prepare herself for such an encounter because she hadn't imagined it was even possible. Or had she? She pressed a hot flannel to her face.

What had she actually been thinking of? She'd gone there like some naïve tourist to gawp at a scene of notoriety. Now hear this, everybody! This shack is the home of Jovan Jovanović and has been for the past thirty years. He's a member of the Roma community in the centre of Belgrade. And here's how his life panned out: his son was beaten to death by teenage yobs, his wife drowned herself, and his daughter lives abroad and doesn't show her face here any more. The lady in question doubtless invokes her right to suppress her past, as well as the fact that, all those years ago, her father expressly forbade her to return.

Anna massaged her temples. She mustn't do anything that she'd later regret. She had to switch off her feelings and engage her faculty for reason again. Or should that be the other way round? Yes, wouldn't she be better off doing precisely that, let herself be guided by her emotions for once in her life?

Don't do anything you'd later be ashamed of, her mother had told her before she left. She knew her mother's homilies off by heart and could recite them all like the lines of a poem. She hung the hand towel over the rail and slipped into her jogging pants. She laced up her trainers with a double knot and locked the door behind her as she left.

Then she started running, diagonally across the hotel lobby, past the waiting taxi drivers, across the forecourt to the main road, and from there down to the river. As she ran, each footfall brought new images flooding into her mind – damaged old pieces of a puzzle that she'd long since mislaid: the pot on the stove, the marker pens in the tin, the bottles next to the dustbin. Dušan's wooden giraffe with three legs, the empty space in the bed they shared, and people suddenly telling her that Dušan was now in heaven. She ran faster. The ball now belonged to her and her alone, and also the giraffe, and her mother stopped speaking. Gasping, Anna halted and put her hands on her hips.

What would have happened if her father hadn't sent her away and she'd stayed here? In all probability, she'd be married by now to someone from her clan – her cousin Jemal, say – and she'd have six children, and they'd all be shacked up together down in that dump of a place where her father still lived.

She turned around and headed back to the hotel. Dušan's death had opened a door for her to a life that she hadn't even read about in books up to that point. Because Dušan had died, strangers had collected a sum of money that her father had hung around her neck in a pouch. 'Go where the Black folk live,' he'd told her. 'You won't stand out there.' Because her little brother had died, she'd been able to leave everything behind her and start a new life.

She crossed the hotel lobby to the lift. Draw a line under the past – how do you do such a thing? Are there any guidelines for that?

She wanted to make sure just one last time that there was no trace of Jurij Pichler on the web, just like there'd been no sign of him hundreds of times before. Then she planned to board the return flight and fly back home, to her old life. She wanted to forget this episode and get on with her life, and no one – not even she herself – would be able to reproach her for that.

Once more, she sat down at the desk, opened the search engine, and typed in *Jurij Pichler Belgrade.*

She couldn't believe her eyes.

In bafflement, she clicked the URL that appeared, and a website with a cream-coloured background popped up: *Welcome to Hotel Amsterdam!*

A photo of a narrow townhouse with pilasters of red brick. A telephone number. An email address. And a thumbnail photo of the proprietors: Jurij and Karen Pichler.

Shocked, she slammed the computer shut.

17

Milena put the car into reverse, tried to judge the length of the parking space, and spoke into her phone. 'Let me think about it.'

'I'm not just talking about any old birthday wish, but something really special,' Tanja explained at the other end of the line. 'Something he's always hankered after, but that I don't know about.'

'Hang on a sec.' Milena now required both hands to get full purchase on the steering wheel, so she put the phone down on the passenger seat. Cursing, she slammed the stick into first gear. 'I can tell you right now,' she said, after picking up her mobile again. 'What he wants most of all is a Play-Station, and the most expensive one on the market to boot. But I'm dead against it, as you can imagine. So... why have I just gone and told you that? That's really stupid of me.'

'You're so old-fashioned.'

'I just think the boy ought to be stimulating his imagination by reading. And if he doesn't like reading, then at least he should be getting some exercise outdoors.'

'Then I'll buy him a basketball jersey.'

'What a great idea!'

'Oh dear, that's a bad sign. Anyhow, all right if I bring Stefanos along?'

'Be my guest, darling. We'll see each other on Saturday at the latest, then.'

Soon after, Milena walked into the Hotel Amsterdam. Behind the reception counter, all that could be seen was dyed-blonde hair in a bun and a large spray of red gladioli.

Jurij's mother was speaking quietly on the phone. Milena greeted her and glanced around the room. Despite it being the middle of the day, the green-shaded lamps above the counter were lit. A newspaper lay on one of the tables near the window, as if someone had recently been sitting there reading. In other words, the hotel had already attracted its first guests.

'What can I do for you?' asked Mrs Pichler, holding her hand over the receiver and looking enquiringly at Milena. The expression on her face was so neutral that Milena wasn't sure the woman even recognised her from before.

'I spoke to your daughter-in-law yesterday and reserved a double room,' Milena began, 'and now unfortunately I need to cancel the booking.'

Mrs Pichler put on her glasses and consulted the book she had open in front of her.

'My name's Lukin,' said Milena. 'I'm really sorry about this.'

'You didn't need to drop by in person. I'll cancel that, then.' The woman made a note. 'I can't access the computer system right now. But, like I said, no problem at all.'

'Even so, I'd like to pay for the room, so could I ask you to make out a bill for me? My stupid error in not checking back with my ex-husband before going ahead with the booking shouldn't be your loss. After all, you could have allocated the room to someone else in the meantime.'

Mrs Pichler spoke into the receiver. 'I'll call you back in a moment.' She pressed a button on the handset and looked down at the bookings diary again. 'Right. Three nights' stay. I think you'd better discuss this with my daughter-in-law.'

Milena nodded. 'Is she here?'

'No, and I've no idea when she's coming back. Do we have your number?'

'I'd have preferred to settle the matter here and now.' Milena took a business card out of her wallet and jotted her number on the back. 'And I just wanted to say I'm still very sorry I overheard your conversation with your daughter-in-law.'

'You don't have to keep apologising for everything.'

'Oh, but I do, really.' Milena put her card on the counter. 'Mr Stojković will do everything he can to find out what happened to your son.'

'Please tell him he should leave us in peace. None of this will bring Jurij back.' Mrs Pichler slammed the ledger shut. 'We just have to try and move on now and forget what happened. The same goes for my daughter-in-law.'

'But she can only do that when she knows the truth.'

'Jurij should never have come back. That's the plain truth of it. We need to stop raking over the past.'

'Did Jurij have any contact with the family of the murdered boy?'

'Not that I know of.'

'Was anyone threatening him?' asked Milena. 'Or you, for that matter?'

'What's Karen been putting in your head?' Mrs Pichler's eyes flashed in anger. 'No, nobody's been threatening us.'

Milena zipped her bag shut. 'Just one last question. Jurij's friend Luca, who was convicted back then–'

'I'm sorry; I can't help you.'

'Do you know what his surname was? Or where we can find him? Is he living here in Belgrade?'

'I can't tell you that, either.'

'I don't believe you.'

'That's not my problem. Now, please go.'

'Your son wanted to face up to his responsibilities; you really need to take that on board.' Milena picked up her bag. 'Good day to you.'

Outside, she lit a cigarette and blew her smoke irritably into the air. Jurij's mother was scared and careworn, and it wasn't Milena's place to judge her. She knew nothing of what Mrs Pichler had had to put up with and suffer in her life, or what fears and experiences she had been exposed to.

These thoughts were still whirling around her head as she drove along the King Alexander Boulevard amid the rush-hour traffic. Eventually, she realised her phone was ringing in her bag. She flicked her cigarette out of the window and took the call.

'Sultan Rostas,' said a woman's voice, and it took a few seconds for Milena to twig that it was Eremina on the other end. She sounded excited. 'His office is on Admiral Street. If anyone can help you in your search for the Jovanovićs, it'll be Sultan. Have you got something to write with? He's at number twelve. He's expecting you.'

'When?'

'Right now,' replied Eremina. 'Or is that inconvenient for you?'

'Thanks, Eremina, you've been a big help.' Milena did a U-turn at the next set of traffic lights.

Twelve Admiral Street was one of those buildings from the early Tito period that, in the general mood of euphoria affecting Yugoslavia at the time, had been designed to put a bold, modern face on the fledgling state. Admittedly, there wasn't much left of the original concept now. The attractively curved open balconies had all, in a do-it-yourself kind of way, been walled up or enclosed with a hotchpotch of windows, or even with tarpaulins. The original complementary pastel shades of the walls had been replaced by an unimaginatively uniform colour, which could not disguise the fact that the plaster was crumbling all over the place.

There was no 'Rostas' to be seen on the board of doorbells next to the entrance. But a little further along there was a second door, quite low, and a square window that had been cut into the ground-floor wall with no consideration for symmetry or the overall appearance of the building's facade. On a strip of tape stuck to a plaque above a letterbox with no flap were handwritten words, now barely legible: *Consultation by arrangement.*

Under normal circumstances, Milena wouldn't have dreamt of setting foot in such a place, but there was no question of normal circumstances now. In the meantime, she had become convinced that Jurij Pichler had contacted the Jovanović family before his death, and that this contact had led to a meeting on the banks of the Danube and very possibly to a sudden act of violence. Milena pressed the bell before realising that the door had been left ajar.

The room was in semi-darkness and was filled with both a buzzing sound and a not-unpleasant floral scent.

'Come in, do!' The man sitting behind the desk switched off his electric razor and rose from his chair. 'Ms Lukin, am I right? Pleased to meet you.' He was so tall that his head almost touched the ceiling. Sultan Rostas introduced himself and held out his hand in greeting.

It was strange, but Milena would instantly have taken him for a member of the Roma community. How so? Because of his black eyes, his dark complexion, and his slender nose? His sideburns were neatly trimmed, and his suit fitted him like it was tailor-made. He studied Milena over the top of his glasses, which had a rather unfashionable metal frame.

'Please take a seat.'

'I'm sorry,' said Milena as she put her bag down by the chair, 'but could I ask you exactly what this place is?'

'Well, you're in the Roma Welfare Agency. Right in the heart of it, as it happens.' Sultan made a sweeping hand gesture that took in the shabby seating area with its potted palm, and the rather garish wallpaper. Then he shrugged apologetically. 'We're just a handful of flaky volunteers.' He sat down. 'So, how can I help you?'

'First, I'm very grateful to you for pushing things along so quickly and making time to see me today.' Milena extracted a business card from her wallet. 'Do you remember the case of little Dušan Jovanović? A ten-year-old boy. He was beaten up and killed by two youths on Belgrade Street. The whole affair took place about twenty-five years ago now.'

'I don't recall that particular case, no, but I can think of plenty of others.' Sultan looked at the business card that Milena had handed him and continued, 'Eremina told me something about it already on the phone, but I'd be intrigued to know what your special interest in this case is.'

Milena tried to make herself comfortable on the hard chair, crossed her legs, and explained that her close friend, the lawyer Siniša Stojković, had been tasked with defending a certain Jurij Pichler – one of the two assailants back then, who had been packed off abroad by his parents straight after the incident and who had come back to Belgrade a few months ago to face up to his responsibilities by handing himself in to the Serbian authorities.

Sultan folded his arms. 'And?'

'Last week, Jurij Pichler's body was pulled out of the Danube. The police are assuming he committed suicide, but some things about it just don't add up.' Milena leant forward. 'All right, this is speculation,' she said, 'but there's some evidence to suggest Jurij Pichler may have got in contact with the family of the dead boy, the Jovanovićs. That's why I'm looking for them. I'd be very keen to speak to them.'

'So you can pin a murder on them?'

Taken aback, Milena shook her head. 'There's no question of that.'

'But, just to be on the safe side, you'll cast general suspicion on the family anyhow.'

'That's your interpretation. But, if you want to call it that, be my guest. All I'm trying to do is get to the bottom of things, even if I discover that I've been barking up completely the wrong tree.'

Sultan removed his glasses. 'Why not just leave it all to the police?'

'The police have closed the case without even properly getting started on it.'

'And you're not prepared to just let things lie?'

Milena leant back. 'Is that what you'd recommend I do?'

Sultan rubbed his eyes. 'Come with me,' he said abruptly, standing up.

'Where to?'

'I'm inviting you for a coffee.'

As they walked down the street together, Milena had trouble keeping up with Sultan's quick pace and long stride.

'I'm sorry to tell you, but I can't stand to hear this prejudiced crap any more – "The Romas are thieves and beggars, they're primitive, uncultured, archaic, and vengeful. But say what you will, there's one thing you've got to hand to them: they're really brilliant at music. Am I right or am I right? No wedding worthy of the name should be without them." But, even there, the watchword is, "Best be on your guard if you invite these people into your home. Gypsies are light-fingered and will swipe anything that isn't nailed down."'

Milena stopped in her tracks. 'I refuse to engage with you on this level.'

'Fact is, though, there's some truth in all of that stuff,' Sultan went on. 'Many Roma don't recognise the rule of law, so don't feel bound by it. Their clan takes precedence over everything for them. So, if it's a case of protecting or avenging their own – who knows? In those circumstances, they might well be capable of killing someone.'

'I never said that.'

'Ah, but you were thinking it, weren't you?' Looking straight into her eyes, Sultan held the café door open for her.

'You're guilty of making assumptions there,' she replied tartly.

She ordered an espresso, and Sultan followed suit.

'See that young woman behind the counter?' he asked. 'She's part of the modern service economy; she pays her taxes and has promotion prospects. Although she's one of us, a Roma, she's made the leap that Eremina's still hoping to make. Unlike that poor devil outside. He's one of ours, too.'

Milena followed his gaze through the window, to where a man wearing the high-vis uniform of the city maintenance department was sweeping the pavement.

'What do you mean?' she asked. 'That guy's not some poor devil; he's got a job.'

'Sure, a job that all Serbs consider beneath them. It's always been that way: we do the work that none of you lot would touch with a bargepole. I sometimes ask myself whether it'll ever change.'

'I know,' Milena nodded in assent. 'The Roma have been discriminated against and persecuted for centuries. They pick up rubbish and bottles, and it's even more difficult for them to step up to a better life than it is for others. I've got no argument with that. But, even so, you Roma aren't saints. And, to be honest, your problem lies elsewhere.'

Sultan reclined in his chair. 'Do tell. I'm all ears.'

Milena tore open a sachet of sugar and tipped it into her coffee. 'Well, the Roma aren't just street sweepers, toilet cleaners on the motorways, or cigarette smugglers at the border. They're also delegates in the Serbian parliament and professors in the Academy of Sciences. They're everywhere, in all strata of society. Except, in government and academia, they prefer not to advertise their background. No one who's made it ever looks back or – pardon my language – gives a shit about others from their own community who are still collecting rubbish and who don't have access to education or any prospects of advancement. As always, of course, any exceptions to this only go to prove the general rule.'

'Thanks for that little addendum.' Sultan drank his espresso in one gulp. 'You're not wrong about that, I grant you. The Roma don't really have a political culture or any collective consciousness of the sort that goes beyond their clan. For instance, if you hadn't helped Eremina, it's possible no one would have. I'm ashamed of that, Ms Lukin, I truly am. And I apologise. It was crass of me to suggest that you'd already prejudged the case of little Dušan Jovanović. It's probably just frustration on my part – a frustrated, flaky volunteer.'

Milena noticed the signet ring on his finger. 'What's your line of work? You're a Roma... and a Serb?'

He shook his head. 'My father had a carpet business in Croatia. When the Yugoslav Wars broke out, we were all forced to flee – except my father unfortunately chose the wrong direction, and we ended up in Kosovo. We sat out the conflict there, but afterwards, when Kosovo gained its independence, naturally it was us Roma who the ethnic Albanians came calling for first. They – how shall I put it? – politely suggested we leave our house and the country. My parents lost everything twice over, and my father can still spend entire days looking at aerial shots on Google Earth of where his shop used to be and where there's now a car park.' Sultan scraped the sugary sludge from the bottom of his cup. 'So, what's our next move?' he enquired. 'Dušan Jovanović, the little Roma boy – I'd be happy to help you, but I have to tell you, Jovanovićs are ten a penny.'

'One small matter,' said Milena, pushing her coffee cup aside. 'In one of the old newspaper articles, I read that, on the night when the murder took place, little Dušan had been running to the kiosk to buy a bag of sweets.'

'So what?'

'It was because he'd brought home a good school report. That means, in the Jovanović household, it seems like education counted for something.'

Perplexed, Sultan rubbed his chin. 'And how's that relevant to us now?'

'At the risk of this sounding like another prejudice, maybe we shouldn't be confining our search just to Roma settlements. Perhaps the Jovanovićs are registered somewhere quite legitimately as tax-paying residents.' She wrapped her scarf around her neck. 'Just something for you to bear in mind, that's all. I don't know what contacts or possible leads you have. For my part, I'm planning to go through the old newspaper articles again. Maybe there's something I missed first time round.'

Sultan picked up her bag from the floor. 'If the perpetrator back then, this bloke–' he began, handing her the bag.

'You mean Jurij Pichler?' asked Milena.

Sultan nodded. 'What I'm getting at is: if Jurij Pichler managed to find the Jovanovićs, then so will we.'

'Thanks,' said Milena, taking the bag and hitching it over her shoulder. 'It'd be a great help.'

18

With the telephone pressed to his ear, Luca sat back in his chair – his 'boss's chair', as Cecilia always called it. He even put his feet up on the desk, something he'd never normally do, as if he felt the need to prove to himself that he still had an air of calm, though that had actually deserted him on precisely the day when Jurij came back into his life. He cursed that day.

'Sorry, darling,' he said absent-mindedly, holding the receiver between his chin and shoulder so he could leaf through the dossier more easily. 'Purely from a looks point of view, she was a dead cert. But, unfortunately, the girl hardly opened her mouth throughout the entire interview. Plus, she didn't have the faintest idea what kind of operation we're running, either.'

'You're too harsh,' chided Cecilia on the line. 'And you need more staff. Preferably sooner rather than later. There are two new restaurants opening soon, and then you'll need to factor in the training period too.'

'Look, I know what I'm doing, Cecilia, I'm not some rookie.' In annoyance, he flung the portfolio onto the pile of other rejected applications, and realised in the same moment that he'd taken the wrong tone with Cecilia – which only made him even angrier. But her damned calmness, her oh-so-reasonable take on things, which she always expressed so quietly, really got on his nerves. All it succeeded in doing was showing how unprofessional he'd become. Since his meeting with Jurij a week and a half ago, he just hadn't been himself, and it was surely only a matter of time before Cecilia put two and two together, if she hadn't already done so, and started to grill him.

'I'm sorry, love,' he said. 'It's just that I'm a bit overworked right now.'

He ended the phone call, took his jacket off the back of the chair, and walked down the corridor. Coming towards him was a smell of good olive oil and roasted garlic.

In the kitchen, at least, everything was running smoothly. Samir, his latest appointment, was working quickly and efficiently – a real bright spark among his employees. As was Meike, who'd already made restaurant manager in just a few months. Unbidden, she handed him a bag containing a stack of food containers wrapped in aluminium foil.

'Ravioli and pesto,' she said, 'with aubergines, tomato salad, and some bread.'

'And for dessert?'

'Tiramisu. Will that do?'

'Pearls before swine,' muttered Luca.

'Beg pardon?'

'Yeah, everything's fine,' he replied, taking the bag.

Outside, the sun was shining, lighting up the madonnas that a street artist was sketching on the pavement in coloured chalk outside the restaurant. Luca crossed himself and dropped a banknote into the guy's hat.

His problem was that he couldn't tell Cecilia about that evening with Jurij without running the risk that one question would lead to another. Some doors simply had to remain closed. It was good for Cecilia to think that she knew everything about him already. Not because he was ashamed – quite the opposite, in fact. But it was a closed chapter in his life. The second crime had to stay secret at all costs, and he'd long since severed his ties with his old comrades. Jurij's reaction had shown him that this decision had been the right one. He'd only asked one question, in a quiet voice: 'Is that really true, Luca?' And a glance at the look of horror in Jurij's eyes had told him that a time bomb had started ticking in the guy from that moment.

Luca looked back at his restaurant through the rainbow created by spray from the public fountain. He stared at the gold lettering of the sign and the striped awnings. He'd built all this up himself, and he wasn't about to let it slip away again just because he'd let himself get carried away in a moment of madness – had taken the picture down off the wall, opened the safe, and got the damned thing out. His only thought at the time had been to scotch all the crazy stories Jurij was coming out with by showing him something momentous, something that would remove all doubt.

With the takeaway bag looped over his wrist, Luca walked down the street and, taking the shortcut, the old path, descended the steps behind the bins and emerged onto Terazije Street. No need for him to ring the doorbell – the old man wouldn't hear it anyway. He put his key in the lock, opened the door, and called out, 'It's me!'

Luca put the bag down in the kitchen. The number of drugs that the old man was now taking was quite extraordinary. The pile of bottles and packets on the sideboard kept growing larger by the day. And it stank in here, too. Luca flung open the window, took the aluminium foil off the containers, put everything on a sticky tray, and made his way down the dark hall.

The fact that he of all people should end up looking after his grandfather, after what the old man had done to him, was the biggest joke of all. That was what Cecilia said, anyhow. On the other hand, though, apart from him there was no one left to take on the job. And there was one crumb of comfort in the thought that, sooner or later, the day would come when he'd walk into the room and the old man would be sitting there in his chair not breathing any more. What would he do then? Dance for joy? Or fold the old boy's hands over his paunch, and maybe even say a little prayer?

'Sorry, Granddad, I'm a bit late.' He set the tray down. 'It was hectic at work, and I couldn't get away.'

The old man's full beard was neatly trimmed above his upper lip, while down his neck it merged seamlessly into a mat of thick chest hair. His sunken cheeks were covered with a network of broken violet-coloured veins, and in his beetle-brows there were bits of dandruff, some as big as flaked almonds. Just the same as ever. Only, this time, his eyes were closed.

Luca leant forward. His grandfather's skin wasn't normally this blue; usually it had a more yellowish hue about it. Something wasn't right. Had the moment finally come? He held his breath.

All of a sudden, the old man reared up, coughing, and a sour smell filled the room.

'You're late!' he croaked.

Luca stuck the spoon into the pasta and pushed the plastic box towards his grandfather. 'Your food,' he said. 'It's right here.'

The sofa Luca had sat down on was so low to the ground that he had to look up at the old man. As he did so, he found himself transfixed by his returned stare and his pupils as small as the heads of drawing pins. As if he'd been caught doing something wrong, Luca lowered his gaze.

'What's up?' asked the old man, between mouthfuls of food. 'Something you want to tell me?'

'Wait a minute. I'll fetch you a napkin.' Luca made to get up.

'Give me a straight answer when I ask you a question. And sit down, will you? I can see it in your eyes – something's up, isn't it?'

Luca obeyed. Placing his hands flat on his thighs, he asked, 'Do you remember Jurij Pichler?'

The old man stopped chewing. 'Pichler? The young lad from that family of fascists?'

'We met up again.'

'When?'

'Twice. Once in the restaurant and then at my place.'

'He's come back, then, has he?'

'And he's even married now.'

The old man shook his head and kept on eating. 'He's a dead loss, that one. A namby-pamby little mummy's boy, indoctrinated by that family of his. I always said as much. You'd do well to stay away from that Pichler.'

Luca closed his eyes and replied, 'Granddad, listen to me, will you? I think I've screwed up.'

The old man fixed him with a silent stare, then resumed eating.

'I don't know how it happened,' Luca went on.

'I don't want to hear about it,' the old man interrupted.

'We were sitting together, and I just started running my mouth.'

'And told him about the shameful thing you'd done, right? Wanted to make yourself look big? Well, then, looks like you've got a problem now.'

The old man reached for his stick, and Luca cowered as if by reflex.

'You're a loudmouth, and you're stupid into the bargain.' The old man looked down contemptuously at him. 'But I knew this would happen sometime. That you'd get carried away and start blabbing.'

The old man levered himself up and began to walk, step by step, out of the room.

'And I could also have predicted it'd be your bosom buddy Pichler you'd spill the beans to,' he muttered. 'Your old friends won't be at all amused, I can tell you. It'll come out and do the rounds, and then they'll search you out no matter where you try to run and hide.' By this time, the old man was already in the hallway, and his next sentence was barely audible. 'Who knows? Maybe they're already waiting outside for you.'

Luca heard the slow, regular tap of his grandfather's stick as he made his way down the hall. He knew he'd made a mistake, and he was wrestling with his thoughts and the overwhelming urge to smash everything to smithereens, here and now. Just like back then, until the only thing left was silence.

Luca got up and took the leftovers into the kitchen. If he'd learnt anything from his military training, aside from obedience and marksmanship, it was how to exercise self-control.

19

Cars and lorries crawled past one another, though the line of traffic never seemed to advance appreciably, and Milena's attempts to switch lanes didn't help. If the flight from Hamburg was on schedule, Philip would be landing any minute now.

'Hey, we'll still make it in time – you'll see,' said Milena, casting an anxious look in her rear-view mirror. 'Wanna bet? I'll bet you a scoop of marzipan ice cream!'

Adam didn't respond. Pale with tense excitement, he sat belted into the back seat gazing silently out of the side window. Milena started wishing she'd taken the rat-run behind Branko's Bridge instead of staying on the motorway leading out of the city, which was sheer madness at this time of day if you were at all in a hurry. But she'd been distracted at the time. Siniša had been on the phone, lambasting her visits to the Roma settlement and to see Sultan as 'irresponsible'. He wanted to know what she was thinking of, going to see 'the gypsies' without a man to protect her.

Milena had thought it best not to argue with him, because what Siniša was really trying to say, but couldn't bring himself to, was 'why didn't you take me with you?'

Her phone rang again.

'That'll be Dad!' yelled Adam. 'Betcha!'

A glance at the screen told Milena that her son was, unfortunately, right.

Milena took the call. 'Where are you?' she asked.

'I'll give you three guesses.' Philip's voice sounded quite

cheerful. He informed her that they'd already made it through passport control and were on their way to baggage reclaim. 'So it should only be a matter of hours,' he joked.

'Marvellous,' replied Milena.

'See you at the exit gate, then?'

'I've got a better idea,' said Milena. To buy herself some time, she suggested they meet instead at the café in the departure lounge, on the first floor. 'The cappuccino there is fantastic,' she lied.

After Milena had hung up, Adam asked quietly, 'So they're there already?'

'And they can hardly wait to see you.'

It was pure luck that, in the last few kilometres to the airport, the congestion unexpectedly eased, and they made quicker progress than she'd feared. The fact that a space became free on the parking deck right in front of the over-pass leading to the terminal was nothing short of miraculous. Milena scarcely had time to switch off the engine before Adam had flung open the car door.

'Wait!' she called, while trying to scoop up as quickly as she could a mass of sweet wrappers and other rubbish from the centre console. 'Watch out for the traffic!'

She hurried after him, across the zebra crossing, and into the main terminal, weaving a zig-zag course around people and baggage trolleys – but with no hope of ever catching him. It was only on the upper floor at the top of the escalator, where Adam stopped and began looking frantically around, that she finally caught up with him. Her height gave her a distinct advantage for spotting Philip.

'There they are!' She pointed at two figures at the café counter.

Adam raced ahead, and Milena noticed how Philip, sensing his son's energy, turned around and caught sight of him. And how he only just managed to put his cup down and open his arms wide in time.

He caught hold of his son and, clutching the boy, spun around once. The sheer delight of these two finally meeting one another again was so absolute, and caught Milena so unawares, that it almost overwhelmed her. When was the last time they'd seen each other? She normally put her son on a flight to Hamburg, or Paris, or wherever Philip happened to be at the time, during the Easter or autumn vacation and picked him up again from the airport a week later. She tried her best to suppress her jealousy, but the feeling that she was now steadily becoming increasingly surplus to requirements brought her close to tears.

Putting on a brave smile, she turned to the young woman who was standing off to one side by some bags while looking at Philip and Adam with such unadulterated joy that it could only be one person.

'Hello, you must be Jutta,' said Milena. 'Welcome to Belgrade.'

Jutta ignored Milena's outstretched hand and instead gave her a huge bear hug like she'd been waiting forever for this moment. After taking an instant to recover from the shock, Milena responded with a less full-on hug and kiss of her own and tried to ignore the blonde hair that got caught between her lips in the process. After all, the woman couldn't help being a good fifteen years younger than Milena, not to mention blonde and sporty and fit. And in any case, in Milena's eyes, any woman on Philip's arm was always bound to be a difficult person to get on with.

Philip's embrace was far more perfunctory and less heartfelt, bespeaking an honesty that Milena found at once gratifying and shocking.

'Did you have a good flight?' she asked.

'Yes, apart from the doughy rolls we were given,' said Philip. He'd begun to develop a little paunch above his belt, though the small bald patch on the crown of his head had started to show even when they'd been together. Nonetheless, he was still handsome in an odd way. Adam had definitely inherited his father's mouth, with its sensuously curved lips.

'And rather than hand things to us,' added Philip, 'they virtually chucked them at us. Typical Eastern European service.'

His words stung Milena, but before she could reply Adam pointed at the larger of the two bags and called out excitedly, 'Are my presents in there?'

On the drive into the city centre, father and son sat huddled together on the back seat, while Jutta sat up front next to Milena. Milena feared this might well be the pattern for the next few days.

'It's so nice to meet you at last,' said Jutta as she fastened her seat belt. She continued, 'Oh my God, I'm so excited – my first time in Belgrade!'

Milena smiled and began by explaining the story of Nikola Tesla, the person after whom the city's airport was named: a Serb by birth, who had discovered alternating electrical current. And while she was in lecturing mode, she went on to tell Jutta that, in Serbian, Belgrade meant 'the white city', and that it had been occupied by the Ottoman Turks for several centuries, and then by the Habsburgs, and that the Eastern and Western influences could still be seen today not only in the architecture but also in the food on offer, especially the tarts and pastries. She pointed in passing at her favourite building, the Palace of Serbia, an architectural landmark dating from the early 1960s, the Tito period – though admittedly a sight that made more of an impression was the Pobednik, the towering victory column set right at the tip of Kalemegdan Fortress, and of course the panoramic view of the Old Town, with Princess Ljubica's Residence, the magnificent domes of the Patriarchate, and the graceful greenish-gold tower of St Michael's Cathedral.

'Belgrade is the most beautiful city on Earth,' declared Adam, and Milena decided to put off mentioning the bombing raids by German forces in 1941 and 1999 – which had left scars that were still visible today all over the city – to a later date.

'So, here we are, then,' she announced, bringing the car to a halt in front of the main entrance of the Hotel Moscow. As the bellboy fetched the bags from the boot, and Adam started leaping about with delight, Philip placed an arm lovingly around Jutta's shoulders, and Milena suddenly felt like a taxi driver, an uninvolved observer of someone else's life that she had nothing whatsoever to do with.

'See you later, lovey,' she said, stroking Adam's hair. 'I'll come back and pick you up around eight.' But the boy ducked away from her hand, seemingly fascinated by the sight of the bellboy slinging both a rucksack and a duffel bag over his shoulders and yet still managing to pick up the battered little suitcase, an old-fashioned rigid number, that Milena recognised with a shock as one that she'd owned when they were married.

Only once she'd threaded her way back into the Belgrade traffic did she allow herself to burst into tears. So that was that: the happy times, her marriage with the love of her life, Philip – all gone. The past and all the shit she'd gone through suddenly overwhelmed her with such force that she had to pull over to the side of the road and stop.

After she'd blown her nose several times and lit a cigarette, she decided she needed to stretch her legs and get some fresh air. She got out of the car. It was just so stupid, wallowing in self-pity like this, as if the next few days were all about her.

She was a grown-up and had learned to take the rough with the smooth where the family situation was concerned. Adam was the one she needed to worry about and protect. As the child of a divorce, he was fatefully torn between two worlds, two languages, and two egocentric parents.

She was dying for a coffee, but the chances of finding one hereabouts looked slim. Only now did she notice she'd fetched up in Crown Street; Belgrade Street was just round the corner from here. The place where the young Roma boy had met his end – that grim location suited her present mood. She pulled her mobile out of her bag and scrolled through the call history, selecting Siniša's number. She got hold of him straight away.

'Has that Sultan Rostas been in touch with you yet?' he asked.

'No,' replied Milena. 'I'm in Belgrade Street right now, and I'm wondering where exactly the murder was committed.'

'In front of number fifty-six,' Siniša told her. 'The kiosk's still there.'

'Thanks.'

'What are you up to? Are you okay? You sound so odd.'

'I'm just trying to build up a picture of the crime scene.'

'By the way, I'm sorry if I spoke out of turn earlier,' said Siniša. 'I'm just worried about you.'

'Adam's with his father right now,' Milena answered.

'Do you want me to swing by Belgrade Street?'

'No need,' said Milena. 'Let's talk later.' She ended the call.

Number fifty-six was in the next-but-one block, and, being on foot rather than in a car, it suddenly struck her how steep the road was in this section. Eventually, a colourful banner advertising ice cream came into view on the right-hand side of the street.

Milena cast a look around. Perhaps little Dušan had come

the same way she had today. Here, on this corner, must be the place where the two youths – Jurij Pichler and his friend Luca – accosted him. From there, they'd jostled and kicked and punched him as he tried to make his way to the kiosk. And that was where he was finally killed.

A small set of steps led up to the kiosk door, which was covered with bright stickers. *Open 24 Hours*, proclaimed a sign hanging from the door handle. Assuming the large picture window next to the door had been in place back then, whoever was inside might well have been able to follow the unfolding tragedy outside as it happened. The murder took place at around 10 p.m. and no one, including several passers-by, had intervened. Just one person, who'd remained anonymous, had called the police, but by that time it was too late.

'Can I help you?' In the open doorway stood a man in jeans and a T-shirt, lighting a cigarette.

Milena shielded her eyes with her hand so as to get a better look at him. The man was sporting a fashionable full beard. 'Have you been working here long?' she asked.

He puffed out a cloud of smoke. 'What's it to you?'

By the kerb, right next to a *No Parking* sign, stood a small jam jar containing a bunch of half-withered lilies of the valley.

The flower of the Roma, thought Milena. 'Who put those there?' she enquired.

'I reckon the bloke who keeps leaving them there's got a screw loose. He puts the flowers down, says nothing, and then walks on. I sometimes give him a glass of schnapps and, if I'm honest with you, I think that's the only reason he keeps reappearing.'

'Do you know his name?'

'Haven't a clue.'

Milena placed her foot on the first step. 'Do you know

what happened twenty-five years ago at that spot where the flowers are?'

The man flicked away his cigarette butt. It bounced across the pavement, kicking up a few sparks, and rolled to a stop on the kerb, not far from the lilies of the valley. 'No, but I get the feeling you're about to tell me.'

'A young Roma boy was beaten to death there, right outside your kiosk.'

'A gypsy?'

'By two youths.'

'Are you a journalist?'

Milena shook her head. 'No, I'm here in a private capacity. How often does the guy with the flowers come?'

'What, the tramp? You think he has something to do with it?'

'Maybe he's a relative of the dead boy. Look, if he turns up here again, or a woman, can you let me know?'

The man took her business card, glanced at it quickly, and promptly handed it back.

'Sorry,' he said. 'I don't want to get involved.' He abruptly turned his back on her, went back inside the kiosk, and closed the door behind him.

Milena turned away in resignation. The idea that someone around here, after twenty-five years, might possibly be leaving flowers as a tribute to the little boy was insane. But then she suddenly had a thought.

Taking a biro from her jacket pocket, she wrote *please call me* on the back of the business card and stuck it between the flowers in the jam jar.

20

He tested the length of the washing line. He planned to double up the cord in order to fashion a really strong sling. Fancy chancing upon such a great find just a block away from his usual route! Why hadn't he tried looking in this court-yard before? He folded up the line and was just stuffing it into his trouser pocket when he was caught in a glaring beam of light.

'Hey, you, get out of here!' screamed a shrill voice. 'Dirty gyppo! Get out, you hear me? Or I'll call the police!'

He reeled away, groping for his crutch. Dazzled by the torchlight, he was ducking in an attempt to evade the beam when, all of a sudden, something struck him, almost knocking him off his feet.

He drew breath sharply – someone had hurled a bucket-ful of water over him, ice-cold. Gasping for air, he stumbled backwards and banged against his crutch.

'Piss off, and don't show your face here again. Bloody vermin!' A window slammed shut.

The water was trickling down his neck and his back, and slowly seeping into the waistband of his trousers. He hobbled off and stumbled, shivering, out of the entranceway, where he bumped into a man walking past. He nearly lost his balance but had the presence of mind to steady himself with his crutch and a little sideways hop. But then he noticed that the washing line had fallen out of his pocket. His precious find – gone!

He retraced his steps for a few metres and tried to bend over to reach the ground with his outstretched hand, but couldn't manage it. He was an old man with stiff limbs. He could have wept like a child.

'Do you think he's shat himself?' Passers-by gave him a wide berth. 'Don't give him anything. They only go and waste it all on drink.'

Then, suddenly, he had the line again; someone pressed the tangled ball into his hand. 'There you go, Gramps. Things aren't so bad, eh?'

Trembling, he stuffed his prize back into his pocket. His wet jacket was clinging to his back and his soaking trousers were starting to slip down. It was getting late; he should have been back home a long time ago.

He had no conception of how long the return route took him – an eternity. Finally, he found himself limping down the driveway, turning the key in the lock and, with his last ounce of strength, pushing open the door. He was sweating and freezing and smelled so dreadful that even he couldn't stand the stench. What would his Svetlana have said if she could have seen him in this state? He closed his eyes in exhaustion.

'Svetlana,' he whispered, as if she were standing there in person at the oven. He stretched his hand out to her. 'My darling.'

A shaft of light slipped across the table, the oven, the straw sack, and the hook on the ceiling where the old rope sling was hanging.

It was most common in the evenings, when people were looking for a parking space, for someone to come down the driveway in a car. Then, after spending the night carousing, they'd return as dawn was breaking. He'd be woken by their raucous drunken singing and the sound of them pissing against his door.

He began unravelling the washing line. *How best to attach*

the line to the hook up there? he wondered. *Should I stand on a chair?* No, he really wasn't up to that.

He put the tangled line aside and ran his hand over the table, with its worn surface and the dents and scratch marks in its wood. He hadn't properly thought this through. And maybe that was a sign. If the old rope arrangement snapped, then that would be that. Could he stand to wait that long, though? And why now, of all times, had Svetlana chosen to reappear to him after such a long absence?

He was quite calm. The thought of ending it all on the bridge wasn't new, but for the first time in his life he had no fear of the river. On the contrary: the river would be his salvation, like it had been for Svetlana all those years ago.

His heart was beating just as it always had done – no stronger and no weaker. He picked up his crutch. One last walk. Along the same route that Svetlana had taken. He still had strength enough for that.

Putting his hand on the doorknob, he took one last look back. At some stage, someone would come in here and wonder who in God's name had ever lived in this hole. But then there'd be no one to reply, 'This was where Jovan and Svetlana Jovanović lived with their children Anna and Dušan. They were a family, and, even though it might not look like it now, there was a time when they were happy here, in this room.'

He hesitated, suddenly remembering the metal box – under his mattress, with the old photos. Shouldn't he erase all these traces of the past? As he was mulling this over, he caught sight of a shadow looming up behind the glass panel of the front door. The shadow was huge but, the nearer it came, the more it resolved into the shape of a person. Jovan stood stock still and held his breath.

Then came a noise, a rustling sound he couldn't place. He

strained to listen in the darkness and waited. But nothing happened. By now, the shadow had disappeared again, as swiftly as it had come.

He opened the door and took a step outside. As he did so, his foot kicked against something.

A plastic bag. Had he completely lost his mind?

With his heart pounding, he stared into the darkness. 'Is anyone there?' he called. 'Is that you, Svetlana?'

*

Anna ran, weaving her way around all kinds of rubbish and debris until she reached the top of the slope.

Having made it to the road up top, she moved off slowly, breathing heavily with her hands on her hips like she'd just competed in a race. She choked back tears but didn't look back.

The bar was stuffy and noisy, and it reeked of beer. Anna squeezed her way through a crowd of people to the counter. The very fact that nobody here knew a thing about her history or the ongoing drama she was caught up in had an instant calming effect on her.

She moved aside to let one of the bar staff pass with a tray of drinks for players at the billiards table. Her wanderings round the streets of Belgrade had been a quest for something familiar, for her family, for her father, and when she encountered that familiarity she'd been shocked, overwhelmed by memories and images that she hadn't reckoned with, and her only thought had been to take to her heels and get away from it all. Without a word of greeting, she'd put the bag down outside his door and run off. Running away was all she'd ever done – since that night twenty-five years ago when she'd seen Dušan, on the other side of the street, and those teenagers who wouldn't leave him alone and who started kicking him. She'd been frozen to the spot in fear until someone told her to clear off, get away as fast as she could. She'd called for help, begged people and pleaded with them, fallen weeping at the feet of passers-by, but no one had understood her or responded, and when she finally crept silently into bed past her sleeping parents, she'd hoped against hope that it had all been a bad dream, that she hadn't seen what she'd seen, that she'd witnessed nothing untoward, and that when she woke up in the morning Dušan would be there and everything would be back to normal.

'Mind if I join you?' A guy in a suit and a checked business shirt plonked down his beer stein beside her glass. 'I'm guessing you're not from around here, right?' he enquired, giving her a broad grin. 'At least, I haven't seen you in here before.'

She could have replied that she'd been born and bred in Belgrade and that her father lived 200 metres from here, right in the city centre, but instead she silently sipped her wine, with the corners of her mouth twitching.

Amid the hubbub of noise and laughter, he bent down to her and yelled in her ear, 'When I saw you come in a moment ago, do you know what I thought?' He lifted his glass and gave her a suggestive look. Before she knew it, she'd clinked glasses with him.

'I thought,' he continued, '*that woman's on the run*. So I'm wondering if you might need a strong shoulder to lean on.'

She got up from her stool and paid.

'No need to be so uptight!' he called after her as she left.

It was already approaching 8 p.m. and groups of youths were roaming the streets. One guy in a bomber jacket had his arm draped around his mate, while another hollered out 'Cheers!' and raised his beer bottle to her when she passed. As Anna turned a corner, she could already see from some way off an ornate sign illuminated by two spotlights: Hotel Amsterdam, a narrow house located on a slight bend in the road, freshly stuccoed and brightly painted. She stopped, half-hidden from view by parked cars, and looked at the green-shaded lights that gave the interior a homely glow. Her heart was in her mouth.

When she came face to face with him, what would she say? 'Hello, I'm Anna Jones, formerly Anna Jovanović. The sister of little Dušan'?

On no account should she be tongue-tied. It was imperative that she didn't come across as confused or nervous, but neither should she do too much explaining. After all, he was the one who'd called her and then failed to get in touch again.

She crossed the street, clenching her fists in her trouser pockets. Still ten metres to go, then five, and then she was flinging the glass entrance door open in fury.

She recognised the woman behind the counter. She'd seen her before – not once, but hundreds of times, in that photo on the hotel's website: Jurij Pichler's wife, who now greeted her cheerily.

'Hello – did you have a good journey here?'

'Yes, thank you,' replied Anna.

Mrs Pichler handed her a registration form and asked her to sign it, gave her the room key, and reassured her she'd do all she could to ensure that Anna had a pleasant stay at the Amsterdam. It dawned on Anna that this woman didn't have the faintest idea who she was or what she had to do with Jurij Pichler.

'Don't you have any luggage, Ms Jones?'

'Luggage?' Anna shook her head. 'No, it's being forwarded.'

The room was small, tiny even, but pretty, with floral wallpaper, red curtains, and cushions trimmed with lace. Anna went to the window, which had a view of a house opposite and a pile of rubble, and then sat down on the edge of the bed.

Here she was, then, under the same roof as Jurij Pichler. So, what now? Just wait until he deigned to show his face? Presumably he wanted to stay undercover for now and size her up in his own good time. What more had she expected? He was a coward. A murderer and a coward.

The ticking of the clock on the bedside table pounded in her ears. She imagined how terror-stricken he'd surely be when he caught sight of the name on her internet reservation. She was the spirit he'd summoned up, who'd now haunt him for evermore. And what about when she finally got hold of him and stood face to face with him?

She wasn't planning on doing anything drastic or taking any steps she'd later regret. She wouldn't overstep any marks. But, even so, it'd be good to have something to use against him now. To see him tremble with fear, if only for a few seconds. To show him just what it was like to feel terrified and utterly exposed.

Somewhere in the building, a door slammed. An engine started up, and a car drove off. Where had this hatred come from? That was what she wanted to ask him.

Maybe she should go and sit downstairs by the fireplace with a drink, play the cool New York woman, and bide her time to see what transpired.

In that instant, there was a knock at her door. Anna didn't move a muscle.

Another knock.

She stood up. The person on the other side of the door had to be Jurij Pichler – she was in no doubt. In all likelihood, his heart would be pounding just like hers. Before he thought better of it, or she lost her nerve, she turned the knob and tugged open the door.

An elderly woman with an old-fashioned bun stood there in the dimly-lit corridor and announced, 'Sorry to disturb you.' Anna couldn't see her face properly, just her outstretched arm and the object she was thrusting at her. 'I thought you might need this.'

Mechanically, Anna took the power adapter. She hadn't asked for it.

'Is there anything else I can do for you?' asked the woman. Her voice didn't convey any genuine willingness to help; instead, it had a challenging tone to it, as if she actually wanted to say something quite different. Like 'what are you doing here?' or 'what's your game?'

'Are you Jurij Pichler's mother?' Anna heard herself asking.

'The very same.' The woman came closer. 'And you? Who are you?'

Anna didn't budge an inch. Holding the woman's gaze, she replied, 'Tell your son I'm waiting for him.'

This woman's eyes – they could well be the same as Jurij Pichler's. It seemed to Anna as though the woman were growing in stature, becoming huge, while she grew ever smaller, shrinking to the little girl who lived in the shack. She had to call upon all her inner strength to resist the feeling that she was inferior, a supplicant, a gypsy.

'I think you and I need to have a talk,' said Mrs Pichler, pushing her way past Anna into the room.

21

Milena took the package that Philip handed to her – a square lilac-covered cardboard box with ornate gold lettering on the front spelling out the name of the patisserie on Queen Zorka Street – not necessarily the best in the city, but certainly the most expensive.

'Oh, my, you really didn't need to!' she said.

The tart that she lifted from the box was decorated with exotic fruits and covered with a shiny glaze. Alongside this extravagant gift, Vera's crown cake and snow tart appeared somewhat rustic, positively homely, and Milena could predict the comment Vera would pass on this unsolicited contribution to the cake selection: 'So, my desserts aren't good enough now?'

Philip held out his hand in formal greeting to his ex-mother-in-law, instead of giving her a hug – as Jutta did – and cast a baleful eye over the old three-piece suite, the old shelving unit, and the old rug with the stupid tassels. In that instant, it was plain to see on his face that all these things were bringing back less-than-happy memories of the visit he'd been obliged to make to Belgrade when he was with Milena.

Jutta gushed about the 'charming little flat', while Adam impatiently tore the wrapping paper off his present and, with a triumphant yell, held up the long-awaited PlayStation. Vera chose to adopt an expression of astonishment – suitable for all occasions – and planted herself imperiously in her chair, leaving it to Milena to cut the cakes, pass around the whipped cream, and politely ask the visitors from Hamburg about their first impressions of Belgrade.

'Hmm,' said Philip, reaching for a cake fork. 'That's a bit of a tricky subject.'

'Tricky?' enquired Milena, trying hard to suppress any kind of undertone in her voice.

'I mean, it's all very nice and interesting, but when you take a closer look at the houses, everything seems so dreadfully grey. Just think how much better it'd look with a lick or two of paint.'

'Mind you, there are some great cafés,' Jutta chipped in diplomatically. 'And people here even have a smattering of English.'

Milena nodded, put on a brave smile, and thought to herself, *what on Earth had Jutta expected? That the Serbs would be running around with daggers clenched in their teeth?* Oh well, she had asked them for their opinion. Maybe she ought to have organised today quite differently, say, by inviting Eremina from the Roma settlement. After all, Adam was completely hyper and Vera was all out of sorts. It made Milena realise how little these different worlds had in common, and she thought of the man living on Belgrade Street who was quietly tending a shrine by regularly leaving flowers at the spot where Dušan Jovanović had met his death.

Things perked up somewhat the moment Tanja appeared. She made a point of saying hello to Vera before anyone else, thereby giving the old lady the sense that she was the real star of the show. She kidded around with Jutta like they'd known one another for years, and even managed to feign pleasure at seeing Philip again. Looking at Vera's snow tart, she jabbed Stefanos – whom she introduced as 'my partner' – in the ribs and said, 'See, I wasn't overselling it, was I?'

Milena put a large slice on his plate. He took a first bite, let out an appreciative sigh, and rolled his eyes in ecstasy, and it was evident he'd made a friend for life in Vera.

CHRISTIAN SCHÜNEMANN AND JELENA VOLIĆ

'And how are things with you?' asked Tanja, sitting down next to Milena. 'Everything okay?'

Milena pushed aside the cat, which had made itself comfortable on the warm pair of socks that Vera had knitted for Adam, and looked at her watch. 'I don't know where Siniša's got to. He was meant to be here by four.'

'Oh, did you ever find out what happened to his client?' asked Tanja. 'I haven't seen anything about it in the papers.'

'It's a complex case,' Milena replied quietly. She explained to Tanja that neither she nor Siniša had so far managed to break through the wall of silence surrounding it. Far from it, actually: no information whatsoever had been forthcoming from either the public prosecutor's office or the police.

'But the Roma have a powerful motive, right?' whispered Tanja.

'I know it seems obvious that the Roma might have taken belated revenge,' said Milena, pressing her finger onto Tanja's plate to pick up pieces of praline, 'but, at the same time, there's something about that theory that bothers me.'

'Hey, what's this?' Adam asked in puzzlement, turning a diving mask and an invitation card over in his hands. 'A diving course? In Cyprus?'

'In the summer holidays.' Tanja stroked his head. 'Stefanos will teach you. And we'll all go there together.' She laid a hand appeasingly on Milena's arm. 'Go on, let me indulge him. I'm his godmother, after all.'

Adam let Stefanos help him try on the mask and bombarded him with questions. How deep would he dive? And would he get to use a proper scuba tank? And would he see coral down there? Or seahorses?

A diving course at Stefanos's sub-aqua school in Cyprus, complete with flight, holiday villa, and all the frills: all Milena could do for now was shake her head and observe with a certain sense of satisfaction how Stefanos answered all of Adam's questions calmly and knowledgeably, and how Philip and his PlayStation had been eclipsed for the time being.

By the time Siniša finally appeared – considerably later than billed – and discreetly placed a slim envelope on Adam's table of presents, Milena was feeling quite upbeat again.

'How was Belgrade Street?' Siniša asked, after he had greeted everyone in turn and Milena had poured him a cup of coffee. 'And did that Sultan Rostas from the Roma Welfare Agency get back to you?'

Milena handed him the sugar. 'I think we're barking up the wrong tree there.'

'How do you mean?' Siniša asked, picking up his cup and following her across the hallway.

Milena shut the study door behind him and took the flat box of cigarillos down off her bookshelf. 'I've been thinking about it,' she said, as Siniša gave her a light. 'Maybe Jurij Pichler's murder has nothing to do with the Roma after all.'

Siniša sat down on Milena's office chair. 'What makes you say that?'

Milena exhaled pensively. 'If the Roma had wanted to avenge little Dušan's death and kill Jurij Pichler, then surely they'd have beaten him to death, or possibly slit his throat. They wouldn't have gone to all the trouble of filling his pockets with stones and making it look like suicide.'

'So, what you're saying,' said Siniša, 'is that the Roma would have been up-front about their crime, rather than trying to conceal it.'

Milena nodded. 'Or is that just stupid prejudice on my part?'

There was a perfunctory knock, and the door burst open. Philip stood there, fuming. 'Are you out of your tiny minds?'

'Pardon me,' said Milena. 'We're in the middle of a conversation here.'

'I ask you – shooting practice! It's totally insane!'

Milena could see the anger in his eyes, but, before she could do or ask anything, Siniša stood up, buttoned his jacket, and announced solemnly, 'My present to Adam for his birthday.' He extended his hand to Philip. 'The name's Stojković. I'm pleased to finally make your acquaintance, Mr Bruns.'

Philip recoiled from the greeting, holding up his hands. 'We're trying to teach the boy that violence solves nothing, and here you are with nothing better to do than teach him how to handle a gun?'

'I can see where you're coming from,' said Siniša, putting his hand on Philip's shoulder. 'But honestly, you needn't worry.'

'Interesting that this is the way I discover how Adam's being brought up here. Shooting practice – he's a kid of eleven, for God's sake!'

'Okay, I get it,' interrupted Milena. 'Adam can do archery instead.'

'I didn't realise you were so against it,' said Siniša. 'Please accept my profound apologies.'

'That settles the matter, then,' added Milena.

'No, it doesn't,' a new voice chimed in. Vera was standing in the doorway, with her arms crossed.

'Mum, please,' implored Milena, but Vera wasn't about to be stopped.

'Adam *should* learn how to defend his country. It's essential.'

Philip looked incredulously from one to the other. 'Are you saying that Adam should learn how to wage war here in Serbia?'

'No,' said Milena.

'Do I need to remind you of the German invasion?' Vera asked. 'Or the NATO bombing? The Germans were involved in that, too.'

'That's just absurd!' Philip made to leave, but by now Jutta had joined the group in the doorway, blocking his exit.

'Isn't Adam a German citizen?' she asked in surprise. 'So, surely he can't fight for Serbia anyway.'

'He shouldn't be fighting for anyone!' shouted Philip.

'The boy has German nationality, but he's a Serb too,' Vera declared. 'Let's pray that he never has to decide which side he should go to war for. Let's sincerely hope and pray–'

'Enough of this!' Milena cut her off. 'The shooting practice isn't happening. The topic's off the table, so let's just drink a glass of fizz.'

As the corks were popping and Stefanos was busy filling the best crystal champagne glasses, which Tanja had retrieved from the dresser in the living room, Milena said under her breath to Siniša, 'Now I intend to find out exactly what Jurij Pichler did in the final days and hours before he turned up dead on the banks of the Danube.'

22

Karen Pichler's flat was right at the top of the building, in the attic, and the steep staircase revealed quite how out of shape Milena was and where she would end up if she kept putting off her swimming sessions and treating herself to generous slices of Adam's birthday cake on a regular basis before going to bed. By the time she'd made it to the top landing, she was puffed.

The most striking thing about the room into which Karen bade her enter was its high ceiling, with black-painted beams and a sharply tapered gable end. Other than that, the whole place was white – the walls, kitchen units, and shelves – and the only thing visible from the two windows was a bleached-out sky.

'It'll be quieter up here than downstairs in the hotel.' Karen lifted a pile of newspapers off a chair. 'Please, do sit down.'

Breakfast plates and an empty glass of red wine – presumably from the night before – stood on the table. On one side of the room, packing cases bearing the name of a Dutch removals firm were stacked beneath the sloping roof, while on the opposite wall shelving had been built around a narrow doorway. The shelves were completely empty except for a couple of illustrated books.

Karen put the espresso maker on the stove. 'I must apologise for my mother-in-law,' she said. 'She can be a bit brusque with people sometimes. You shouldn't take it personally.'

'Of course, no problem.' Milena hung her bag over the arm of the chair; as she did so, she caught sight of a small framed photograph showing two people on a beach, with a foaming sea and blue skies. In the picture, Karen was standing on one leg like a flamingo, and Jurij was holding her tight. A crack, with four small side branches, ran diagonally across the glass in the frame.

'Our engagement photo,' Karen explained. 'I found it in the wheelie bin, just by chance.'

'How did it end up there?'

Karen said nothing but cast a meaningful look towards the door to the floors below.

'You mean your mother-in-law threw the picture out?'

'Not that she made any special effort to hide it from me. It was right on top.'

Milena took a closer look at the photo. If it was their engagement photo, then it must have been taken around the same time as when Jurij told Karen about his past. Jurij was beaming like someone who was certain they'd found their ultimate happiness. Perhaps this was the first time he'd held in his arms someone he didn't have to keep any secrets from.

'Just so you know how things stand between the two of us here – it was yesterday, I think.' Karen put out two coffee cups. 'She was having a go at me again, accusing me of having done nothing throughout my entire marriage but stir up Jurij's feelings of guilt.'

'What makes her think that?'

'Good question. I reckon all that matters to her is that it's always someone else's fault. Whatever, you name it: the fact that Jurij's dead, or that the plumber stood us up, or that we've only got one guest. She nags and taunts and just won't let things lie. Eventually, when I can't take it any more, I start lashing out, or crying, or both. It really is a nightmare – for everyone involved, Sonja too. She's retreating into herself more and more.'

'What about the guests?'

'Like I said, there's only one, an American woman, and she only showed up yesterday.'

Milena drank her coffee in silence, put her cup down gingerly and asked, 'What's happened to his personal belongings? Have the police taken them all? Maybe there's something, however trivial, that might help us reconstruct his final days.'

'You're welcome to have a look,' said Karen, opening a drawer, taking out a bag, and spreading its contents over the tabletop: a mobile phone, coins, postcards, and a tattered paint-colour swatch. 'That's all I have left of Jurij – can you imagine that? The phone's the only thing the police returned to me straight away, but you can forget that; it's knackered. It was lying around in the water for too long.'

'What about the rest? Wallet, diary, laptop?'

'It was all seized and taken away.'

Milena looked at the postcards: pictures of Florida and Amsterdam, none of them written on. Apart from them, the only thing was a broken folding ruler. How absurd and sad, thought Milena, that this was all that remained of a person's life. She needed to ask Commissar Filipow if it wasn't about time the police handed back Jurij's personal effects. Even if it was fair to assume that all promising lines of enquiry had been exhausted, it would still be an opportunity for her to get in contact with him again. On the other hand, if he'd been at all minded to play ball and divulge information, he'd presumably have done so long since.

'I could have sworn...' Karen rummaged around in the drawer. 'There was some kind of a flyer here, too. I found it in one of Jurij's trouser pockets. I think it's just a promotion for something or other, but even so...'

'Have you gone through his coats and jackets as well?'

Milena enquired. 'Maybe there'll be something there. Receipts, bus and train tickets, business cards – anything at all.'

'That's just the problem. At the same time as I'm trying to pick up every thread and asking myself whether the smallest little thing might be significant, my mother-in-law's busy throwing everything away. Like she can't erase the memory of her son quickly enough.' Karen blew her nose. 'Believe me, there are moments when I could just smash her head against the wall.'

'Why don't you, then?' Old Mrs Pichler was standing in the doorway, looking pallid and almost transparent, like a spectre. They hadn't heard her approaching.

'Have you been in my drawer?' asked Karen.

'You're really obsessed, aren't you?' replied her mother-in-law.

'Answer me! I'm looking for a flyer from Little Italy. It was right here in this drawer.'

'I haven't got the slightest interest in your drawer!' In an instant, Mrs Pichler's face, which had been roughly the same colour as the greyish-beige housecoat she was wearing, flushed scarlet with rage.

Milena stood up. 'Why don't you sit down?' she asked in concern. 'Would you like a glass of water?'

The old woman ignored Milena. 'I just came up to tell you that I have an appointment now, so there's no one on reception.'

'What you think of as rubbish are my mementoes, you hear me?'

Mrs Pichler turned her back without a word and left the room.

'Just get that through your thick skull once and for all, will you?' Karen shouted after her. 'And keep your nose out of my fucking stuff!' Tears welled up in her eyes. 'If I know her, she'll probably go and get hold of a new flyer for me, or better still a whole sheaf of them, just to spite me.'

'Little Italy,' said Milena. 'Isn't that the restaurant on Academy Square? Do you think he might have had a special reason for keeping the flyer? To get some ideas from, maybe?'

'What, for our hotel?' Karen wiped her nose. 'No, their pitch was far too pushy. Plus, that sort of restaurant really wasn't his thing.'

'Or had he jotted something down on it? A telephone number, perhaps?'

'I'm sure I'd have noticed that.'

'I don't know if it'll do any good,' said Milena, casting a glance at her watch, 'but have you got a photo of Jurij that you can let me have?'

Sunk in misery, Karen buried her head in her hands. 'It's really terrible,' she began, 'but in hindsight I should have paid far more attention. And when I think about it now, I realise I don't have even the beginnings of an idea what was going through his mind at the time.'

*

Naturally, Milena could think of better ways to spend a Saturday than trolling round the city centre with her ex-husband's new partner. But she did it all the same, so that Adam would have his father all to himself for the day. Milena had suggested that the two of them should take the riverboat trip they'd been talking about for months, while she'd go off and do something else with Jutta.

She'd actually had in mind something like visiting the National Museum, or showing Jutta round the university, and maybe seeing the National Library. But Jutta had announced that she wanted to hit the main shopping drag on Prince Michael Street. She'd called it 'our girl time'.

The conditions were perfect, with the temperature almost at a summer level, and a street musician on every corner serenading the customers sitting at tables outside cafés, who, with their sunglasses, all looked like they'd leapt straight off the pages of a fashion magazine. Jutta bent down to drop some coins into the instrument case of a saxophonist and signal her appreciation of his playing, and all the while Milena couldn't rid herself of the image of Karen and her mother-in-law making life hell for one another.

As Jutta glued her nose to the window of Belgrade's oldest and most exclusive lingerie emporium, Milena tried her best to dispel these gloomy thoughts – though, in truth, she wasn't exactly dying to hear which négligées, thongs, and scanties were Jutta's favourites, or that everything here cost a fraction of what you had to shell out back in Hamburg. Milena patiently translated every word of the shop assistant's professional advice. Finally, Jutta made her selection, and Milena found herself unable to suppress the images that automatically flooded into her mind's eye of Jutta parading in front of Philip in these skimpy little gossamer numbers.

Picking up her bags, Jutta cheerfully linked arms with Milena and said, 'You know what sometimes really bugs me about Philip?'

Although Milena could have reeled off a whole catalogue of things there and then, she shook her head. She'd moved on from ruminating over Philip and everything to do with him and their life together, and her thoughts had for some time now been firmly trained once more on her investigation, which to date had only uncovered one solitary piece of information – namely that, in the days leading up to his death, Jurij Pichler must have been in a restaurant called Little Italy.

Milena sighed to herself. Meanwhile, Jutta was cheerfully prattling on. 'Of course, you'd know all about that. But I'll tell you one thing for free: I'm going to break him of that particular habit, you can bet your bottom dollar!'

Having tuned out, Milena simply nodded automatic agreement and added, 'Yeah, don't let yourself be dictated to by Philip.'

Jutta giggled and then asked, 'Tell me, are Serbian men like that too?'

Over on the far side of the square, several green-white-and-red flags were fluttering in the breeze, and Milena explained that the building now sporting the *Little Italy* sign in gold cursive script had, until two years ago, been home to Belgrade's largest and oldest bookshop. Yet neither the protest meetings by longstanding customers and students nor the petition with the mass of signatures that was handed over to the mayor in the presence of local television cameras managed to save that institution from closing.

'Just like everywhere,' was Jutta's reply, as they stepped inside the fast-food restaurant and Milena cast a baleful eye around the place.

Of course, the tall old bookshelves were now gone, along with the ornate plasterwork on the ceiling, the chandeliers, and the old parquet flooring. Instead, the building now boasted polystyrene ceiling tiles, terracotta floor tiles, spot-lights, and lots of chrome. A young woman in uniform with a tightly knotted neckerchief was standing next to the salad bar and giving a dressing-down to a man wearing a chef's checked trousers and white jacket.

Jutta declared she didn't fancy eating Italian right now and headed off in the direction of the toilet. Milena took the opportunity to get out the photo of Jurij Pichler that Karen had handed to her in a small envelope.

The woman in the uniform finished her conversation and looked enquiringly at Milena.

'I'm sorry to bother you,' said Milena, stepping closer and showing her the photo. 'But have you seen this man before?'

The woman looked Milena up and down before peering somewhat reluctantly at the photograph. After a couple of seconds, her lips parted in surprise, as though she wanted to say something. But then she shook her head. 'I'm sorry, no.'

Undeterred, Milena kept holding the picture under her nose. 'Take another look, why don't you?'

The young woman motioned with her head to the man in the cook's jacket that he should make himself scarce. Her name badge identified her as Meike. 'Are you from the police?' she asked.

'No, this is a purely private inquiry,' replied Milena. 'I've reason to believe this man must have been in here sometime over the past few weeks. His name's Jurij Pichler.'

'Really, I've never seen the guy.'

'How about your colleagues?' enquired Milena. 'Mind if I ask them?'

'In all honesty, we've got our hands full here.' The young woman smiled regretfully. 'Besides, how many people do you think come in and out of here every day?' She picked up a menu. 'Anyhow, would you like to see our weekend special?'

'Maybe another time. Thanks.' Milena took a flyer from the counter and went outside.

Printed diagonally across the flyer, in imitation of a rubber stamp, were the words *25% Off All Soft Drinks – Only Until 31 May*. It seemed Karen was right: the advertising was far too full-on for the Hotel Amsterdam to have used it as a model. At the top of the leaflet was the restaurant's trademark gold lettering, while at the bottom there was a tear-off voucher.

'Oh, that's another thing we've got in common,' said Jutta,

who by this time had rejoined Milena. 'I'm a big coupon collector too. You can save quite a bit over time.'

They strolled through the pedestrian zone, slaloming around stressed-out fathers with their families, fashionably dressed women laden with shopping bags, and reckless pensioners on mobility scooters. Milena pondered whether the manager at Little Italy, that Meike woman, had been telling the truth.

Her thoughts were interrupted by Jutta. 'I know it's a bit much to ask of you,' she said, 'but tomorrow's Sunday, and they're so much cheaper here than back home.'

'What are?' asked Milena.

'The trainers I've been telling you about.'

'No problem; go ahead. I'll be fine here for the time being.'

'Are you sure?'

'Absolutely.' Milena got out her cigarettes.

'I'll be as quick as I can,' Jutta promised, then promptly disappeared into the crowd milling around the glass doors of a department store.

Milena lit a cigarette. Maybe Jurij Pichler had got himself mixed up in drug dealing or in some other shady goings-on, she thought. As she stood there, she noticed out of the corner of her eye that a man had appeared beside her and also lit up a smoke. He was wearing checked trousers and struck Milena as familiar.

'You work at Little Italy, right?' she asked.

'Could I see that photo again?' he asked. The guy looked totally drained.

She pulled the picture out of her bag and handed it to him.

He exhaled smoke over the photo, gave it back to her, and said, 'He had a pow-wow with our boss.'

'Are you sure?'

'Yeah, they had a plate of cold antipasti.'

'When was this?'

'Sunday 24 April.'

'How can you say so precisely?'

'Because it was the first day of my traineeship.'

'Okay.' Milena put the photo away again. 'And today was your last, am I right? Did I pick the signals up correctly earlier?'

'You're from the police, aren't you?'

'No, I'm not. You can rest easy. But if you're spinning me some yarn here just because you want to get back at your boss–'

'Make that "ex-boss".'

'– then you've picked the wrong person to piss about.'

'I understand.' The man grinned, exposing a row of manky teeth. 'So, what's the guy in the picture done wrong? Did he kill someone?' He took a long drag of his cigarette. 'Don't mind me, I was just kidding. But just to make it clear, 'cos I'm out of a job now, any more information...'

'What did the two of them talk about?' said Milena, getting out her wallet.

'Like I said, I wasn't standing close to them, but it looked to me like some kind of job interview. Maybe for a new restaurant manager. Marović is planning to open a couple more places soon. Though I think it's his wife who really owns the business. She deals in wine and real estate, I've heard. Have you ever seen her?' He stuck the money Milena had given him into his pocket.

'Marović?' repeated Milena. 'And what's the first name?'

'Cecilia. And believe me, she looks like a Cecilia too.'

'I meant him. What's he called?' Milena looked past him, down the street. 'Could it be... Luca?' she prompted.

The man pointed his index finger at her like a pistol and replied, 'Bullseye, got it in one. Luca Marović.'

After he'd scrounged another cigarette and taken his leave,

Milena watched him walk away with her heart beating fit to burst. *Luca Marović*, she thought.

'What did that guy want with you?' asked Jutta, who in the meantime had reappeared at her shoulder. 'Did you give him a handout or what?'

'Jurij Pichler and Luca Marović,' Milena muttered to herself.

'Hey, you're as white as a sheet!'

Milena's first impulse was to march straight back into Little Italy. Why shouldn't she? Catch Luca Marović on the hop. He was a key witness, after all.

'I'm sorry for asking so directly,' said Jutta, 'but what's going on here?'

'It's all a bit complicated,' Milena replied, relieving Jutta of one of her bags. 'Let me walk you back to the hotel.'

'You know what Philip once told me?' said Jutta once they'd crossed the street. 'Mind you, he really only said it as a joke.'

'What?'

'That sometimes he thinks you might be a spook. And today's making me think he may be on to something. I mean, first that business with the woman in the restaurant, and now this bloke. And what's with that photo you keep showing people?'

'Interesting theory,' said Milena, 'but I can set your mind at rest on that score.'

'Does the letter have anything to do with it?' asked Jutta.

'What letter?'

'This envelope we were given. We were a bit puzzled. We wondered why the guy brought it to us in the hotel rather than going straight to you at home or in your office.'

Milena stood rooted to the spot, thunderstruck. 'Where is this letter?'

'Didn't Philip give it to you?'

'No,' said Milena, 'he didn't.'

'What, not at Adam's birthday coffee and cake? Hey – what's up?'

Milena was already on her mobile. 'Philip, it's me,' she began when his voicemail kicked in, making no attempt to hide her anger. 'Please call me back the minute you get this.'

23

It beggared belief quite how many people flooded into Belgrade on the intercity buses on a Saturday. He wasn't thinking about the hunchbacked pensioners from the surrounding villages, who were perennially lugging something around with them. Sacks, bags, you name it – the main thing was it had to be large and unwieldy. No, those figures were just part of the cityscape, like the pigeons in the gutters or the potholes in the tarmac. He meant the young women, who looked like they'd made a special effort to tart themselves up before making their big entrance to the capital. They teetered across the station forecourt with bare midriffs, wearing tight little hot pants and clutching fake designer handbags, clearly imagining they were strutting their stuff on the Champs-Élysées. And then there were the lads, with their balloon-silk tracksuits and their bumfluff moustaches, so muscle-bound from working out that they could barely walk.

In search of a parking space, he circled around the station, describing the scene to Cecilia on his phone, yet thinking to himself all the while, *what have I got to sneer about? I used to be just like them, going around with that same look on my face that said 'get out of my way or I'll smack you in the mouth faster than you can think'.* Plus Cecilia had quite rightly remarked that it was exactly these sorts of people who'd end up in Little Italy later as, so to speak, the high point of their Saturday out in Belgrade – and that they'd ensure the restaurant made another tidy profit that night.

'You know,' said Cecilia – her voice on the speakerphone sounding so close he could scarcely believe that she was at that moment sitting in a taxi in Dubai heading for the airport – 'once I'm back and we've got the new restaurant launches out of the way, let's go away somewhere. Just the two of us. What do you say? To Rome, maybe.'

'That sounds fantastic,' he said.

'But you have to promise me one thing.'

'What?'

'That you'll keep yourself out of trouble till then. Don't let anyone talk you into doing anything stupid.'

'Stupid?' He pressed the clutch, put the car into neutral, and turned off the engine. 'What do you mean?'

'Listen, everything's cool. No one's got anything on you. You did your time long ago, and since then you've kept your nose clean. Just remember that.'

'Receiving you loud and clear, my dear.'

'I'm serious. And don't let anyone tell you different, you promise?'

'Promise.'

'And if anyone turns up wanting to take a stroll down memory lane with you, just tell them where to get off. It's not your problem.'

As he made his way over the pedestrian crossing a few minutes later, he got to thinking how strange it was that at the same time as he was making this little excursion into the past he should be getting harangued by Cecilia from thousands of kilometres away. The woman must have a sixth sense.

The station clock ticked over to twelve. He briefly thought about taking another stroll round the block and turning up a bit late, say ten minutes, so as to show how little this whole business meant to him. But, on the other hand, did he need to indulge in such play-acting? It was like Cecilia said: he had nothing to blame himself for, and he should act accordingly.

His mind made up, he pushed open the door to the station bar and strode in.

The glass counter had a selection of dry-looking cakes, and every second table was decorated with a vase containing plastic flowers. Lining the bar were the usual suspects: down-and-outs exchanging the profits of their begging for spirits. A handful of travellers with luggage had tucked themselves away in a far corner of the room, while a table in the middle was occupied by a solitary woman, who was sitting with her back to the door. As a kid, Luca recalled, he'd had to go and collect his drunk father from dives like this. If Luca ever refused, he'd get a hiding from his grandfather, but if he obeyed he'd be treated to a diatribe of very public slurred abuse from his father all the way home.

'Well, what are you waiting for?' The woman at the table had turned around to look at him.

Jurij's mother had always appeared old to Luca and, above all, stern. It looked like she hadn't changed a bit. That bun and her dark eyebrows – painted lines – were just like before.

He motioned to the waiter, ordered, and took a seat.

'Nice suit,' she said. 'Italian?'

'What are we doing here?' he asked. 'Why so cloak and dagger? Any special reason?' Luca nodded nervously as the waiter set down a beer in front of him.

'Would you rather I paid you a visit at home? And had a nice cup of coffee with your wife?' Mrs Pichler watched as he took a sip of his beer and set the glass straight on the mat.

'Typical Marović,' she remarked snidely. 'Never let anyone get under your skin.'

'I don't know what you're after,' he said, 'but let's get one thing straight right now. What I told Jurij when he came to my restaurant the other day – all that was just so much crazy bullshit.' He looked into his glass, shook his head, and feigned amusement. 'Always the same old story, see,' he said. 'One glass too many, and my imagination runs away with me.'

'Your imagination, eh?' Mrs Pichler repeated, holding Luca firmly in her gaze.

'And the things I come up with then are way out there,' he went on. 'But I'm afraid Jurij took them for real.'

'Oh, he did, did he?' she replied.

'Or maybe not.' Luca smiled nervously. 'Anyhow, it's all a big misunderstanding,' he explained, trying not to avert his eyes. 'So why don't you just forget what you've heard? In fact, forget the whole evening ever took place. Tell Jurij that and – no, let me finish – no matter what Jurij may have said to you, or what he thinks happened, I advise you all to keep quiet about it. Not a word to anyone. Please tell him that.'

'Callous and arrogant – just what I'd expect from a Marović.' Mrs Pichler's lips had narrowed to a line, and Luca could feel himself breaking into a sweat and the blood draining from his veins. All of a sudden, he understood what the problem was. Jurij was dead. She'd let him rattle on, and now everything was too late, the whole game was up.

'Did you kill him?' she asked.

'Jurij's dead?' he whispered hoarsely. 'He's really dead?'

'Speak up!' she barked at him.

Luca cleared his throat. 'I could never have harmed a hair on Jurij's head, you know that.'

'All I know is this: you're a Marović, and the Marovićs are capable of anything. You're to blame for Jurij's death, every bit as much as your grandfather.'

'Listen, that's enough. It's completely absurd. My grandfather's old and near death's door.'

'All it would have taken was a word from him back then, and we could have brought Jurij home from Argentina. Our lives would have been completely different. But he wouldn't even listen to us.'

'It was your decision to send Jurij abroad in the first place.'

'I didn't have a choice. Jurij wouldn't have survived doing time.'

'Jurij wasn't as delicate as you might think.'

'Easy for you to say. You always had your grandfather looking out for you, along with all his damned cronies. Just look at you: seven years in the clink, and now you're sitting prettier than you could ever have imagined in your wildest dreams. But Jurij spent his whole life on the run. And now–'

'You don't know the half of it,' Luca said quietly.

Mrs Pichler pressed her clenched fist to her mouth. In the silence, the only sound was the piped music coming from the loudspeakers, the upbeat tempo of a pop song.

'How did it happen?' asked Luca, keeping his voice low.

'What does that matter?' She seemed to take a long, deep breath. 'It happened.'

'Listen, if I can do anything for you, just say,' said Luca. 'I really mean that.'

Her eyes, red from exhaustion, narrowed to dark points. 'How could you help me?'

'You tell me.'

She wiped her mouth with the back of her hand. 'Very well,' she said. 'You can't bring Jurij back, but there is something you can do. I want a million.'

'What?'

'In return, you get the hotel.'

'A million?'

'The land it's on alone is probably worth double that. But I'm sure I don't need to tell you that.'

'I don't know what to say,' muttered Luca.

'Give me the money, and you'll never see me again. I'll

disappear and not breathe a word to anyone. Regardless of what's happened or what you've got to do with it.' She stood and picked up her coat. 'Think about my offer,' she said, 'but don't take too long about it.'

Luca was staring straight across the table, at her coffee cup with a trace of red lipstick on the rim. He felt her hand on his shoulder.

'In case you're interested,' she said, 'that gypsy boy's sister is back in town, and I get the impression she's very keen to meet you.'

'Are you trying to threaten me?'

'Just don't force me to do things I really don't want to.' Without a backward glance, Mrs Pichler left the bar.

Luca sat there, dumbstruck. In an unguarded moment of weakness – the briefest instant – he let out a small sound, not even a sob, but loud enough to make the men at the counter turn and look at him.

He rubbed a hand over his face. Then he stood up, took out his wallet, and walked over to the group of men. Some of their faces – broken-veined masks ravaged by alcohol abuse – struck him as vaguely familiar. They could well have been the faces of old comrades who'd fallen by the wayside.

'My friend is dead,' he said, putting a note down on the counter. 'His name's Jurij. Drink a toast to him for me.'

He drove back slowly, aimlessly, turning off at places where the traffic became too heavy. He'd never been a crybaby. If he'd ever cried, it had only been from rage. And he wasn't even feeling that now.

It had been an illusion, a romantic folly, to think that he could relive the old days and pick up the threads of old friendships again after such a long time. He'd tried and failed. He should have known he would. On that night when the gypsy boy had crossed their path, their ways had parted forever.

Jurij had taken one route, and Luca another. He'd gone into construction and then done time, while Jurij had gone to stay with his Nazi uncle in Argentina and then worked in the shoe factory. End of story.

He slowed down when he got to Belgrade Street, drove past the place first, turned around at the next opportunity, then drove back, parked up to the right of the carriageway, and turned off the engine.

Over there. That was where it must have happened. Had they been drunk? He couldn't remember. He undid his seat belt and got out. He didn't have the faintest idea why he was putting himself through this.

He'd always felt strong with Jurij at his side, but Jurij had started making plans for the future. Australia, women, adventures, all kinds of stupid stuff. And the worst part of it was that he, Luca, didn't figure in any of them. He couldn't bear the thought that Jurij would move away one day. He was more afraid of that than he was of the beatings at home. But he was powerless, and couldn't bring himself to say 'Jurij, please stay here', or 'take me with you'. After all, he wasn't a loser, a weakling, a pussy.

And then this gypsy boy had crossed their path.

When he saw the flowers by the roadside, he knew it had been a mistake to come here. Had the lilies of the valley been put there by this sister who'd supposedly come back? Had the gypsies made some kind of shrine here? There was something wedged between the wilted flower stalks: a business card. He bent down and extracted it.

There was a handwritten note on the back. *Please call me.* He turned the card over.

'You looking for something, mate?' A young man with a pair of sunglasses perched on his slicked-back hair was heading towards him, like a dog scenting that something wasn't quite right here. Luca could tell a gypsy at a thousand paces. It was like they gave off a smell that no amount of aftershave or pomade could mask.

'No, I'm fine, pal,' answered Luca. 'Jog on. Get lost.'

'What's your problem?' the guy asked.

Luca slipped the business card into his trouser pocket and crossed to the other side of the road.

'Hey, brother, just hold it right there!'

He got into the car, locked the doors, and started the engine. But, by this time, the guy had loomed up in front of his radiator and was standing there, looking straight into his eyes.

Luca put the car into gear and revved the engine twice in warning. Then he stepped on the gas.

24

Milena and Jutta had already gone through all the newspapers
and magazines on the mahogany table, likewise the writing
case that lay so decoratively on the antique bureau. But all
they'd found were advertising brochures, writing paper, and
any number of empty envelopes with the embossed letter-
head of the Hotel Moscow. Jutta called out from the walk-in
wardrobe that there was nothing in the pockets of Philip's
jackets or trousers either, and wondered aloud whether the
chambermaid might have thrown the letter away.

'Did the envelope have an address on it?' asked Milena.

'Just "Lukin", in thick felt-tip pen.' Philip replied, snap-
ping his suitcase shut in annoyance. 'You know what I don't
get?' he said. 'If this letter's so important, why didn't you have
it delivered to you at home or at one of your many offices?
How many have you got now? Two, is it? Is that not enough?
What's the point of this whole charade?'

Milena was familiar with this aggressive manner of his,
and she didn't feel like explaining that this clandestine letter
was explosive information being passed to her by Commissar
Filipow, just as she had suggested he should do, and that the
information would in all probability help her prove that Jurij
Pichler's death was due to an act of criminal violence.

Instead, in a pointedly friendly tone, she replied, 'It'd be
going a bit far to explain it all to you right now.'

'What's that supposed to mean?'

'It's too complicated.'

'It's got to do with the photo, right?' asked Jutta, with a
knowing nod.

'Okay.' Philip slammed the drawer of the bedside table. 'So, if you're using us here for your intrigues and something's gone wrong, then you've only got yourself to blame.'

'Absolutely!' replied Milena, folding her arms across her chest. 'Some things never change, do they?'

'Beg your pardon?'

'Never mind!' responded Milena, in a tone that came across every bit as tartly as she intended.

'Feel free to speak your mind,' said Philip. 'Don't hold back on my account.'

'All I'm saying is – how is this possible? An envelope is left for me, and all you have to do is pass it on, nothing more. But even that's asking too much of you, apparently. Whenever somebody wants you to do something for them one time, or needs to rely on you for the smallest of favours, they might as well forget it. It always backfires.'

'And you're in a class of your own when it comes to holding other people responsible for your screw-ups.'

'Stop fighting, will you?' pleaded Jutta.

'We're not fighting,' said Milena.

'That's rich coming from you, Milena!'

'Just leave it, will you, Philip?' said Jutta.

'No.' Philip lay back on the bed and crossed his arms behind his head. 'I won't leave it. I'm sick and tired of always carrying the can when something goes pear-shaped in Milena's strange life.'

'You want to know what's "strange" about my life?' said Milena, putting on a wry smile. 'It's that absolutely nothing goes wrong in it until you put in an appearance.'

'I'll be down in the lobby,' said Jutta, taking her coat off the hook.

A moment later, the door clicked shut, and Milena let out a sigh. 'Okay,' she said. 'I'm sorry.'

'Hallelujah!' Philip laughed. 'So, problem solved?'

Worn out, Milena slumped onto the small chair. This meant she'd have to get in touch with Filipow again. And, in all likelihood, he'd act like he didn't know what she was talking about. It was all very aggravating.

Now that Jutta had gone, it was as if they lacked an audience, so they fell silent, and Milena suddenly realised quite how exhausted she was – and how little she had to say to Philip any more. She'd spent so much time with this man. And it hadn't all been bad, by any means. There'd been some exciting and happy years, but it was all over far too quickly. And now here they were, sitting in a luxury hotel in Belgrade, with nothing to say to one another. If it was possible to find any connection whatsoever left between them, it was their son.

'So what was up with you and Adam?' Milena broke the silence by asking.

'I told you already when I called you back.'

'Did you really have a row?'

'Spare me the cross-examination, please.' Philip lifted his arm and let it drop theatrically onto the bed. 'Adam was tired and wanted to go home. That was all. Don't go blowing it out of proportion.' He stared at the ceiling, like he always used to, and continued, 'But I'll tell you one thing: you and Vera are really spoiling that boy something rotten.'

'Of course we are. So what?'

'Well, it's just that I can't think of any eleven-year-old in Hamburg who'd stand by the roadside and hail a taxi for himself when he wanted to go home. Honestly, I couldn't believe my eyes. It was like that's what he always does as a matter of course.'

'Don't exaggerate. He was tired – you said so yourself.'

'How come he can't take a bus? You're giving the boy

completely false expectations. I mean it, Milena. The example you're setting him here's way off beam, if you ask me.'

'Interesting. Do tell me more.'

'And you don't seem to realise how your mother's indoctrinating him'.

'I don't have to listen to this, Philip.'

'Do you really not hear the sort of things he comes out with sometimes? His hero-worship of Tito, for instance. That's straight out of Vera's mouth. "Our hero, Tito. We must be grateful for all he did for us." It's really appalling, this black-and-white way of thinking. And Adam takes it all as gospel.'

'Look, the boy's not stupid. It's just a phase he's going through. Last time it was the Middle Ages; now it's Tito. And I haven't a clue what the next thing he'll fixate on will be – Willy Brandt and the Vietnam War, for all I know. And I fail to understand what's wrong with him learning about different points of view. Anyhow, I really object to you and your thought-policing. It's so German of you!'

'If that's really what you think, then we have a problem.'

'No, Philip, *you* have a problem.'

'Then we'll seriously have to consider whether this is the right environment for him to be growing up in.'

'Right, I've heard enough!' Milena stood up and grabbed her bag. 'I hope you have a nice life.'

She made to go, but by now Philip had stood up and was blocking her path. 'That's typical of you. Run away when things get difficult. Avoid talking things through at all costs, 'cos that might get a bit uncomfortable for you.'

'Running away?' Milena rejoined furiously. 'Who is it that ran away? And who vetoed all discussion and opted to bring the whole house of cards down instead, just because things got a bit difficult? It definitely wasn't me, that's for sure!'

'For some reason, I remember things differently,' Philip said, giving her an insolent grin. 'And I'm afraid, sweetheart, that where failed marriages are concerned it takes two to tango.'

'I'm not your sweetheart, and I'll happily take responsibility for everything, but certainly not for your affairs.'

'Are you telling me you were faithful the whole time?'

'Of course I was. Why wouldn't I have been?'

'So what about that young guy from your postgrad study group? Don't pretend you don't know who I mean. That bloke with the ponytail you spent evening after evening with, while I was sitting at home twiddling my thumbs.' He was gripping her arm tightly. 'You're staying here until I get an answer from you.'

'Let go of me!'

Suddenly, his face was right in front of hers; his lips were close to hers and she could feel his breath. He wasn't squeezing her arm any longer; his grip had loosened, and his eyes flashed with a look, an intimate look she'd forgotten had ever existed.

Confusion overcame Milena, and her heart began beating nineteen to the dozen.

*

As she opened the door of her flat and stepped over the threshold, she was greeted by a round of thunderous applause.

'You're late!' came Vera's voice from the kitchen, accompanied by the cacophony of a Saturday night TV game show. 'Where have you been all this time?'

Milena hung up her jacket and put on her slippers. The flat was filled with the smell of fried onions and bacon. Fiona, the cat, was sitting like a beautiful sculpture next to the umbrella stand and giving her a reproachful look – or, at least, so it seemed to Milena.

While she was washing her hands, she noticed in the mirror the dark circles under her eyes and the lines around her mouth – something that Tanja, when describing her clients in the beauty clinic, always referred to as 'that divor-cée look'. Milena bent down and splashed cold water on her face.

'The boy's asleep.' Vera had put her feet up and used the button on the remote to turn down the volume. 'Did you hear that he came home early from that stupid boat trip?'

'Yeah.' Milena said, flattening the rug where it had got rucked up. 'The two of them fell out, I hear.'

'So, Philip mentioned that, did he?' Vera kept a watchful, critical eye on Milena as she tried to straighten the tassel on the rug with her foot.

'Is everything okay with you?' asked Vera. 'Did the two of you finally talk things through?'

'I'll tell you about it tomorrow,' said Milena, giving her mother a kiss.

'It's about time. By the way – if you're still hungry,' she called after Milena, 'we left you some dinner. It's on the stove.'

It was true; Adam's bedside lamp was already switched off, and he'd buried his head under his pillow.

'Darling?' Milena said softly, listening to his breathing in the darkness. Then she carefully straightened the bedspread over his feet.

A saucepan of homemade tagliatelle and a skillet contain-ing some braised mushrooms stood on top of the oven, along with a small dish of chopped parsley on the side. But Milena had no appetite. She grabbed a handful of grapes and the rest of the cold coffee and, with Fiona in pursuit, walked down the hallway to her room.

By now, Philip had long since receded to what he actually was: her ex-husband, with a spare tyre, a bald patch, and certain unpalatable views, and Milena could only hope that her departure from his hotel room hadn't looked too much like a hasty getaway. A brief email was probably called for. She tilted open the window and reached for her cigarillos on the shelf.

She would wish him and Jutta a pleasant trip and at the same time make it clear that she unfortunately wouldn't be available for any more jaunts. The pressure of work in the office, too much unfinished business – no, better fabricate a business trip. She switched on the desk lamp and opened her inbox.

Philip had evidently also felt the need to get in touch again. *You left so quickly*, he wrote. Apparently, that drew a line under the matter as far as he was concerned, for he went on, *Incidentally, there was something I meant to ask you. We'd like to take you out to eat somewhere tomorrow, before we head off on Monday. Would 8 p.m. suit? And do you have any recommendations? Philip. PS – Please forgive me; sometimes I behave like a complete ass.*

'Oh well,' Milena muttered to herself. 'It's like you said: it takes two to tango.'

She smoked and stared out of the window at the concrete wall. The lost letter... The fact that Commissar Filipow had conspiratorially left a letter for her at reception proved that there really had been a cover-up over the death of Jurij Pichler. Presumably something had come to light that was so sensitive it had to be swept under the carpet. There was no other possible explanation. She took off her earrings.

Despite the fact that she'd left a message on Siniša's voicemail, so far he hadn't got back to her. And yet it was truly sensational news that she'd found out who the second assailant was: Jurij Pichler's childhood and teenage friend Luca Marović, proprietor of the Little Italy restaurant on Academy Square. The guy was a key witness, who might just be able to provide the vital clue required to piece together Jurij Pichler's final days – and also to ascertain what Pichler had been up to, and maybe even how he had met his death.

She turned off the light and pulled back the bedcover, but her mind wouldn't stop churning. By and by, her thoughts turned to Philip and that oddly charged situation in his hotel room, and to Jutta, whose taste in underwear she now knew. As she drifted to sleep, she found herself walking into Little Italy once more, and then talking to her informant on the street. Then, all of a sudden, Berlin came into her mind, and the question of what Alexander was doing there right now.

Milena rolled onto her other side. According to Alexander's last communication, the negotiations at the Foreign Office should have come to an end this evening. The talks had been extended for a day, but she found it hard to judge whether that was a good sign or not. What little information Alexander had divulged sounded somewhat guarded. No major breakthrough, then, and a lot of hard work still lay ahead, yet Milena found this prospect by no means disheartening. Quite the opposite. She turned over again.

Presumably Alexander was now out on the town, sampling the nightlife of Berlin in the company of the other conference members, with a whole host of female delegates making eyes at him at the bar. *So what if they are? Good luck to the lot of you*, she thought. She could do without all that kind of stuff.

By now, she was wide awake. She sat up and furiously plumped the pillows behind her back.

She might as well just come right out and admit it: it would have been nice if Alexander had got in touch after the end of the conference. She'd have liked to hear his voice. Yes, she was even missing him. How many days had it been now since she'd last seen him and spoken to him? She counted. Precisely three. But it seemed to her like an eternity.

She stood up and closed the window. She was all at sixes and sevens right now; in this state, and in the middle of the night to boot, it'd be unwise to start shooting off messages to people, especially German ambassadors. Just as she was thinking this, her mobile buzzed with a newly received text. Picking up the phone, she couldn't believe her eyes.

Are you still awake? Alexander had written. *Can we talk?*

At that moment, she felt close to him, maybe closer than she'd ever felt before. Without thinking about it, she pressed the call button.

'Mum?' Her bedroom door eased open a crack, and Adam's face appeared. 'I can't sleep.'

Milena cancelled the call and put down the phone. 'Come here, you,' she said.

She pulled back the cover and shifted aside a bit. 'What's up then, love?'

As Adam nestled into the crook of her arm and began to tell her about the boat trip, Milena turned off her mobile and realised how small and insignificant her thoughts, fears, and anxieties were in comparison to the catastrophes and upheavals that were playing out in the mind of her young son right now. She could just picture it: the Second World War, the German fascists, Tito the partisan leader. Maybe Philip's criticism hadn't been so wide of the mark after all. The topics filling Adam's head at the moment, encouraged by his grandmother, were momentous and, understandably, they'd overwhelmed the boy.

Adam finally got to the heart of the matter. 'Gran says Tito's a hero, but Dad says he's a criminal.' Holding out his open palms in a gesture of helplessness, he asked, 'So one of them must be lying, right?'

'No one's lying,' said Milena, pressing him closer to her. 'It's not such a simple matter, see. It's like this: Tito may be a hero, but he also did some bad things.'

'What kinds of things?'

'Well, he persecuted people who didn't agree with him.'

'But he won the war. He showed the Germans what's what. That's the truth, just ask Gran, but it seems Dad just can't stomach it.'

'Your grandma forgives Tito everything because he liberated us from the German fascists. She's forever grateful to him for that, and that's the reason she only sees his positive side. Dad thinks differently. He sees the negative side, too.'

'And what about you?' asked Adam.

Milena thought for a moment. 'Tito's a hero, all right. I don't have a problem with that. But heroes shouldn't think they can get away with murder. Dad's right as far as that goes.'

They sat in silence for a while, with Milena wondering how she could better explain to him the Serbs' and Germans' different perspectives on history, as well as the wartime and post-war generations, when she noticed that his breathing had become deeper and more regular. She bent down and noticed a piece of paper poking out from beneath his pyjama jacket.

'For you,' he whispered, half-asleep. 'I found it in Dad's hotel room...'

From under his brushed cotton top she extracted a small crumpled pale-blue envelope. Written on the front in bold letters was her surname. No indication of the sender. *Typical Adam*, she thought. Cautious boy that he was, he'd squirreled the envelope away without telling anyone.

Taking care not to wake her sleeping son, she slit open

the thin envelope with her fingernail and pulled out a white sheet of paper.

The information from Commissar Filipow consisted of three numbers, a point, and an exclamation mark: *6.36!*

Other than that, no explanation – nothing. Milena was incredulous. *Is this meant to be some kind of joke, or what?*

25

'Thanks.' Milena closed the menu and handed it back to the waitress. 'I'll just have peppermint tea today.'

'What's up with you?' asked Siniša, laying his hand solicitously on her arm. 'Are you unwell? Or just on a diet?'

'The latter, if anything. As of today.' Milena rummaged in her handbag.

'What's the point of that?' Siniša leant back in his chair. 'You know I can't stand stick insects!'

'No need to worry on that score!' laughed Milena, pulling the note out of the pale blue envelope and pushing it across the table to him. 'Here's Filipow's cryptic message,' she said. 'I'd actually been hoping he'd send us some hard facts, like a copy of the coroner's report. Or that he'd pass us some secret memo explaining why investigations in the Jurij Pichler case were suspended. Instead, all we get is this set of figures.'

Siniša took Milena's reading glasses and peered through them at the sheet. 'Is that a comma or a point between the six and the three?' he asked.

'A point. Six-point-three-six. I've already started wondering if it might be the calibre of the weapon used to kill Pichler.'

Siniša furrowed his brow. 'Could very well be.'

Milena picked up a fork and sampled a piece of his cake. 'But why the exclamation mark?' She speared a raspberry. 'Is he trying to tell us "you're right; this was a crime of violence – calibre 6.36"?' She pressed the small tines of the cake fork to her lips pensively. 'But, if so, why not just write a complete sentence? "Jurij Pichler was shot with a 6.36-calibre weapon." Is the information really so sensitive?'

Siniša folded the paper and put it back in the envelope. 'I know someone in ballistics. I'll check it out with him.'

'So, all we know so far,' said a deflated Milena, 'is that Jurij Pichler ate a plate of cold antipasti with Luca Marović on Sunday, 24 April, two days before he vanished without a trace.'

Siniša stood up and gave her a peck on the cheek. 'I'll call you.'

'In any event, tomorrow morning let's pay a visit to Luca Marović at Little Italy,' said Milena. 'Unannounced, what's more.'

'Agreed. And until then, no going it alone. You promise?'

Saying this, Siniša left, leaving Milena to hoover up the leftovers on his plate. She reflected that if, as had been proved, Jurij Pichler had made contact with Luca Marović and met up with his childhood friend, he might also have tried to get in touch with the Roma family, the Jovanovićs. And what if a meeting had taken place between Jurij Pichler and the Roma family – which as yet remained unproven – and things had got out of hand? But of course that was all pure speculation. It was equally possible that the two friends Jurij Pichler and Luca Marović had fallen out. Resignedly, Milena picked up her bag and stood up to go. None of this made any sense.

Thirty minutes later, she walked into the Institute for Criminology and Forensic Science. It was Sunday, and the place was quiet. She unlocked her office, opened the window, and, with no more ado, sat down at the desk. Into the search engine she typed two words: *Luca Marović*.

The first hit was the Little Italy website. Luca Marović: manager of the franchise business, located on Academy Square. Full-time employees: 28. Planned openings: Victory Square and Macedonia Street. *Send Us Your CV, Sample Menus, Specials, Events.*

The next hit was an interview that Luca Marović had given to a business magazine two years earlier. Milena skim-read the piece. A glowing success story, of course. But amidst the self-promotion were a few personal details: Luca Marović was married, had no children, and was the son of a professional tennis player.

Milena popped a jelly banana into her mouth and was clicking through the photos accompanying the article, when she heard footsteps in the corridor. She recognised the rhythm. A loose piece of parquet flooring let out a squeak. She counted to two, and then the door of her office opened.

'What are you doing here?' asked Boris Grubač. He was sucking on a sweet. 'And on a Sunday, too. In this lovely weather!'

'I might ask you the same question,' Milena responded.

'Believe it or not, when you sneaked past my office, I was just reading your memo.'

'Great,' replied Milena, leaning back in her chair. 'And?'

'With respect, what you've cobbled together sounds a bit half-baked: "New Concepts in Security", "Challenges in the Age of Globalisation", "Opportunities and Risks".'

'First off, I just wanted to sound out whether we've budgeted for it.'

'Can I give you a bit of advice?' He closed the door and pushed aside a pile of books on her desk to create a space to perch half his buttocks on. 'If you really want to seal the deal on this sort of conference, don't put forward the name of some middle-ranking detective like Zoran Filipow for my consideration, just because he made eyes at you one time. That's the truth of it, isn't it?'

Milena shook her head. It went without saying that Grubač's insinuation was complete nonsense, but, at the same time, she somehow felt she'd been rumbled.

'Aha, I thought so!' Taking her silence as an admission of guilt, Grubač triumphantly slapped his thigh with the flat of his hand. 'Ms Lukin, forget this Filipow guy. You've got far more impressive contacts! Try schmoozing the right people, like the German foreign minister or, even better, the defence minister – it doesn't matter; the main thing is to play the big league, then we can really push out the boat. Then we wouldn't have to hide ourselves away in the little auditorium down here. Instead, we could hire the Congress Centre. Are you even listening to me?' Following her gaze, he looked at the screen and exclaimed, 'Hey! Who's that? Isn't that Marović's grandson?'

'Yeah, his name's Luca. He runs a restaurant on Academy Square. Do you know him?'

'Not personally, but I knew his grandfather.'

'Do you mean his father, the tennis player?'

'Tennis player! I ask you! No, I'm talking about Vladimir Marović. And you can see the resemblance, too. Just look at his nose. Do you want to invite him too? Interesting idea. But the grandson – that's so typical of you.' Grubač squeezed his thumb and index finger together. 'You're thinking small again!'

Milena clicked on the picture of Luca Marović, enlarged it until it filled almost the entire screen, and asked incredulously, 'You mean to tell me this guy is the grandson of Vladimir Marović, former head of the Yugoslavian secret service?'

'And recipient of the Order of the Yugoslav Star, First Class.'

'The man's a criminal, more like.'

'Vladimir Marović, my dear Ms Lukin, was responsible for ensuring that you had a carefree and peaceful childhood growing up in our beautiful Yugoslavia.'

'He had thousands persecuted and deported just because they disagreed with him politically.'

'He guided this country's destiny from behind the scenes with courage and vision.'

'He has so much blood on his hands I wouldn't even give him my little finger to shake.'

'No one's forcing you to,' said Grubač, shaking his head as he looked at the photo of Luca Marović. 'A restaurant owner, you say? So why would you want him at your security conference, when you didn't even know about his family connection to General Marović?'

'It doesn't matter,' muttered Milena, as she feverishly tried to work out if this new information – that Luca Marović was General Marović's grandson – had any bearing on her case.

'He's done time,' she said. 'Did you know that?'

Grubač gave her a thoughtful look. 'That's right,' he said. 'Now you mention it, there was something. But quite a while ago, right? Twenty, thirty years?'

Milena's phone rang. She quickly pressed the mute button and asked, 'Do you know what he was charged with back then?'

Grubač gave a dismissive wave of his hand. 'Oh, I dunno, he blotted his copybook somehow – some kind of hooliganism, if I remember rightly.' He straightened his tie over his paunch. 'I was pretty young myself at the time, fresh out of the party school and working as a very junior official in the intelligence department. But I'll tell you something that'll interest you.' Grubač leant across the desk, exuding a mixed aroma of alcohol, peppermint, and aftershave. 'This guy, Marović's grandson,' he said, tapping the screen with his fingernail, 'who was really wet behind the ears back then, was up in court for some stupid nonsense or other, and my boss wanted to ensure that he only received a short suspended sentence. An act of pre-emptive obedience on his part, so to speak. You understand? This was the grandson of General Marović, after all. And do you know what happened then? The same General Marović you've been calling a criminal hit the roof! He was adamant that his grandson should receive the maximum sentence and genuinely pay for what he'd done.' Still perched on the edge of the desk, Grubač put his hands on his hips and shot Milena a challenging look.

'And?' she asked. 'Did he pay?'

'I assume so.' Grubač helped himself to a jelly banana. 'But you see what I'm driving at? General Marović behaved in an utterly correct and proper manner. He came down hard on others, but he was hard on his own kin too. So, Ms Lukin, before you go high-handedly condemning all and sundry, you should show a bit more respect.' Grubač went over to the door and reached for the handle. 'And as for your symposium, you really need to go back to the drawing board.'

Once Milena had heard his footsteps recede down the corridor, she picked up her mobile to call Siniša.

The screen lit up, and she was reminded of the earlier call she'd sent to voicemail. The unknown caller had left a message.

'Hello,' came a high-pitched, girlish voice. 'It's Eremina. I've got some good news for you. Would you believe it – we've found him!'

26

Jovan Jovanović had had a bad feeling about it right from the start. The bag outside his front door wasn't his; it was someone else's property – and, to be honest, he didn't want anything to do with it.

All the same, he crept around it like an inquisitive dog. He still hoped, and yet at the same time feared, that someone might simply come and take it away again. Maybe the people who parked their cars here, or the teenage yobs who racketed around after dark, revving their engines.

But the next morning the bag was still there, with its gaudy colours and bulging contents. He got the feeling it might be giving off secret invisible signals.

Eventually, he grabbed it by its handles and took it inside. The thing was heavy. So, what now? What should he do with it? Stow it under the wash basin, or put it down by the bin? No, he decided, the bag belonged on a chair, like a guest you'd welcomed into your home.

He lifted it up and immediately noticed a wonderful smell filling the room. There were some oranges right on top. Where on Earth could oranges still be had at this time of year? He took one of the fruits, dug his fingers into the thick peel, and took a bite, making juice run down the sides of his mouth. He finished it and then ate another; that left him with three more.

He worked his way through the bag, bit by bit. A flannel shirt. Some long johns. Warm socks. Pulling on the socks, he felt the warmth return to his legs for the first time in ages. He'd have danced about in delight if he were able to. What a treat!

His heart was pounding wildly as he speculated who was being so charitable to old Jovan – and, above all, why? He was a filthy old beggar, and lugubrious with it. Svetlana had always said as much, and she was right. Whenever something good happened to him, he'd be afraid it would slip from his grasp or that something bad would happen to him in recompense. It had always been that way. When Svetlana spent her evenings ironing to bring in a bit more money, he didn't see the extra cash she was earning but instead worried about her dropping the iron on her foot out of sheer exhaustion. And hadn't he been proved right about it all in the end? Indeed, things had turned out worse – far worse – than he'd ever imagined in his worst nightmares.

And now, here was this bag. Just how stupid was he? Did he in all seriousness think someone would do him a good turn like that without expecting something in return? Nothing on Earth, or even in paradise, was for free.

He picked up the bag, intending to put it aside, when he suddenly hesitated. Though there were some screwed-up sheets of wrapping paper left inside, they couldn't account for how heavy it still felt. As if he were still eager to find more, he began rummaging again – and finally emerged with a small package.

He needed to sit down when he saw what it was: sweet waffles wrapped in gold paper. Suddenly, they all came flooding back to him, hazy images he wasn't even aware still existed in his head. He saw the children standing around the table here, their eyes wide with anticipation.

He took a knife and, like Svetlana had always done, carefully cut the seals, making sure he didn't tear the gold paper as he unwrapped the packet. Svetlana had always strictly rationed the waffles – one every Sunday – and had divided each little piece into still smaller pieces, thereby multiplying the number of special treat days.

Anna was capable of endlessly nibbling away on her piece of waffle, whereas Dušan always wolfed his straight down. And now he, their father, this derelict specimen of humanity, had been given a whole packet all to himself? He felt it was somehow improper – and he didn't believe in coincidences.

He washed himself, put on the new underwear, and wore the flannel shirt over it. Then he slipped the rewrapped pack of waffles into his trouser pocket, picked up his crutch, and left the house.

All those years ago, when he'd hung the money pouch around Anna's neck and sent her away, he'd given her clear instructions. 'Go where the Black folk live,' he'd told her, 'and don't ever look back.' Anna had been a clever, obedient girl; otherwise, he'd never have let her go. She went to America, and he never thought he'd set eyes on her again.

He crossed the junction and hobbled down Belgrade Street. At the traffic sign that was level with the kiosk, he took the gold waffle packet out of his pocket, stooped down, and laid it near the jam jar.

Using his crutch, he pushed the waffles as close as he could to the wilted lilies of the valley. Back then, when it happened, he hadn't known how he could go on living and had prayed that Svetlana might come to him, dispel his fear, and take him with her. And now, just when he was ready to follow her, this bag suddenly turned up. Had Anna returned? How was she doing? Was she healthy? Had she had a happy life?

Dogs appeared and started sniffing around. Jovan looked on as they tore open the paper wrapping and ate the sweet confection inside; when they'd finished, pigeons flew down to peck at the crumbs. The waffles were gone, and none of it made any sense. Or, if it did, he couldn't see it. He turned for home.

The car had been following him for a while, though he

hadn't noticed it. He wanted to get home, bide his time, and listen to the voices in his mind to hear what Svetlana whispered to him. She'd watch out for him and show him the right path.

'Hey, Gramps.' The voice came from the car. Its window was wound down, and the man was leaning across the passenger seat. 'What were you up to there? Feeding the pigeons? Stand still when I'm talking to you. Tell me.'

Without replying, Jovan walked on, supporting himself on his crutch. He heard the car door open, but he didn't turn around. On the contrary, he tried to quicken his pace.

Suddenly, from behind, a hand grabbed his shoulder. 'Are you Dušan Jovanović's father?' the man asked. 'Answer me! Are you Jovan Jovanović?'

He didn't recognise the man's face. He raised his crutch in what he hoped would be a threatening manner, but the man simply snatched it from him, grabbed his arm, and snapped, 'Where do you live?'

His arm felt like it had been trapped in a vice. Jovan turned around imploringly, looking for passers-by to come to his aid, but they averted their eyes and hurried past.

'Come with me,' the man hissed. 'We're going to have a quiet little chat, you and me.'

Now that Jovan no longer had his crutch, he was powerless. He only had one weapon left – a last resort. He took a deep breath.

His saliva hit the man square in the face. It ran down his cheek and clung to his neatly trimmed sideburns, where it formed a slowly lengthening thread that dripped to the ground.

Jovan found himself staring into a face contorted with fury, and in the very next moment the ground gave way beneath his feet.

27

It was coming up to 4 p.m. when Milena flicked on her indicator and took the large, sweeping bend. This was the second time within five days that she'd found herself driving down the slip road for the motorway to Budapest. But instead of hitting the accelerating lane and putting her foot down, she slowed down, turned onto the gravel road, braked, and came to an abrupt halt in front of the snack bar. Her path was blocked by at least twenty motorbikes.

She had to sound her horn several times, wind down her window, wave vigorously, and call out 'Excuse me, could you please...?' before the leather-clad bikers who were taking a break here finally deigned to put down their French fries and – with no particular urgency – manoeuvre their heavy motorbikes off the carriageway. Milena drummed her fingers nervously on the steering wheel.

'Where are you trying to get to, then, darling?' asked one of the bikers, a guy with a long straggly ponytail. 'This is a dead end.'

She took off along the dirt road at twenty miles an hour, kicking up a cloud of dust behind her as she went. She ignored her ringing phone, as she needed both hands firmly on the wheel to negotiate the bumpy, potholed track.

By the time she parked up on the patch of grass and pulled on the handbrake, her mobile had stopped ringing. *One missed call* appeared on the screen. Alexander had left a voice message saying that he was at the airport, where he'd just landed, and that he'd really like to 'go out for a bite to eat' with her that evening.

Furious, Milena grabbed her bag from the passenger seat. This evening, of all evenings, she was committed to going out with Philip and Jutta.

'Oh – look who's here again!' called out one of the young men who were loafing around on the concrete blocks, looking at their smartphones.

'All right?' replied Milena, slamming her car door.

'That all depends.' The young man in the white tracksuit bottoms grinned. 'Todor's totally hacked off.'

'Todor?' Milena said, as she put her car keys away. 'I've come to see Eremina.'

'Yeah, I know that.'

'So what's happened?'

'I'll tell you what's happened. Yesterday he almost got himself run over, and today the old man went and pissed all over his car seat.'

'Sorry, I don't know what you're talking about.'

The young man jumped down from his perch and swaggered towards her. 'In case you've forgotten, Todor's the guy with the BMW, and it might be a good idea if you paid him something for his pains. He really stuck his neck out for you.'

'Yeah, right,' Milena replied with a nod. 'Like I've got a magic money tree at home.'

'It's called compensation for damages,' the young man called after her.

Milena teetered her way across the planks over the waste ground and tried to ignore the dog that kept barking incessantly at her from one of the compounds, setting off all the other dogs in the Mahala. Children were playing half-naked in the puddles, and somewhere a television set was blaring at full volume. As far as she could tell from the din, there was a live football match on.

What Milena had taken to be a line of colourful bunting

turned out upon closer inspection to be dusters and dish-cloths hung out to dry on a washing line strung diagonally across the alleyway. Underneath this was a parked car with wide tyres and twin exhaust pipes – Todor's BMW, Milena assumed. The door to the Avduli place, the home of Eremina's family, stood open.

'Hello?' Milena knocked, fending off some small children who were trying to tug her bag off her shoulder.

Eremina appeared from behind a striped curtain, carrying a bowl and some hand towels. She put them down and greeted Milena. The house smelled of coffee and perfume, or possibly hairspray.

'I've given him some clean togs,' Eremina announced, rolling down the sleeves of her thin blouse. 'A pair of my dad's old trousers. Todor's helping him get into them right now. The old guy was pretty rattled by the whole business, and I have to tell you I've got a bit of a guilty conscience about it all.'

'What's happened?' asked Milena. 'How did you find him?'

Eremina put her hands on her hips. 'What did I tell you?' she said sternly. 'Go outside and play!' She shoved the knot of children who had gathered inquisitively at the door outside, and then closed the door behind them. 'Todor didn't exactly treat him with kid gloves,' she confessed. She put a lid on the large pot on the stove and proceeded to tell Milena the whole story about how Todor had offered his help after she'd told him that Milena was looking for the family of the young murdered boy. She knew from Sultan Rostas of the Roma Welfare Agency that the murder had been committed on Belgrade Street and that flowers were still regularly being laid at the spot where it happened. Todor had immediately declared himself willing to drive there and keep a lookout for anyone who showed up.

'Great,' Milena said approvingly. 'That's real commitment.'

'Isn't it just?' Eremina then went on to explain that, late the previous evening, there'd been an encounter with some unknown guy at the roadside shrine, but that Todor, by his own admission, had failed to apprehend him. Today, though, at around lunchtime, he had – in his own words – 'got a result'.

'So you really have got hold of the father of Dušan Jovanović?' Milena asked.

'Looks like it,' replied Eremina. Saying this, she pushed the curtain aside.

Milena followed her down two steps and around a corner, and found herself in a windowless room, a little cell of a place. On the wall were a mirror, two lamps, and posters of Sophia Loren, Princess Diana, and Leonardo DiCaprio. A hairdryer, comb, and scissors lay on a small dressing table, along with two neatly folded hand towels. The centrepiece of Eremina's little hairdressing salon was an office chair with one of its arms missing. On this sat an old man with sparse hair and a sunburned, heavily lined face covered with snow-white stubble. His striped shirt was buttoned right up to his neck, and the collar was too loose for him. He sat there as if petrified, staring vacantly into space.

'Mission accomplished, as you see.' Todor stood leaning against the wall behind the door, half in darkness; his sunglasses were perched on his gelled hair and he was just putting his smartphone away. 'He put up a bit of a fight, but he's behaving himself now. All you've got to do is take him away.'

'He's not some criminal, you know,' said Milena, noticing that the old man was trembling. He clearly hadn't drunk any of the cup of tea in front of him. Milena deposited her bag on a low stool. 'Please forgive me,' she said, turning to the old man. 'I hope you're more or less okay?' She crouched down in front of him. 'We didn't mean to frighten you.'

The old man continued to stare blankly ahead. Milena turned around and asked the others, 'Can you leave us alone for a moment, please?'

Eremina shot Todor a look indicating that he should hold his peace and follow her. He complied, confining himself to shrugging at Eremina and looking at her more questioningly than indignantly.

The old man blinked, which was at least a sign of life, and Milena began. 'My name's Lukin. I've been searching for the relatives of Dušan Jovanović, the young boy who was killed many years ago on Belgrade Street.'

He turned his head and looked at her without saying a word.

'Are you related to Dušan?' Milena asked quietly. She laid her hand on his arm. 'Mr Jovanović?'

'Please,' he whispered, groping for Milena's hand. 'Take me home.'

Shortly afterwards, Milena was helping the old man get into the passenger seat of her car and securing his seat belt. Eremina passed her the bag containing the clothes that he'd had to change out of, while Todor stowed his crutch in the boot. It was only then that Milena noticed a nasty graze on Todor's cheek. Startled, she asked him what had happened.

Todor waved away her concern. 'It's nothing. I'm just glad to have been of assistance.'

'I explained,' Eremina said softly, touching his arm, 'that you were keeping an eye on someone yesterday on Belgrade Street.'

Todor shrugged. 'My first thought was that he was about to nick the flowers.'

'What happened then?' enquired Milena.

'I approached him and spoke to him. I wasn't sure...' He searched for words.

'How old was this man?' Milena asked.

'There was something fearful about the way the guy looked at me. I went after him, but there was no chance.' Todor rubbed his chin. 'How old? No idea. About the same age as you, maybe. No, probably a bit younger.'

Milena nodded. 'And what did he look like?'

'He took off like a shot when he saw me – I didn't really get a good look at him. I'd say he was a real Mr Average. But he wasn't a bad driver, I'll give him that. He shot off pretty smartish. In a Lancia, too.'

'Did you get the number plate?'

'Getting a bit like the cop shop here, isn't it?' Todor said with a wry grin. 'Sorry, numbers and letters really aren't my thing.'

The journey back to the city centre passed in silence. In the passenger seat, old Mr Jovanović had closed his eyes. He looked so small, sitting there. But maybe it'd be a mistake to underestimate him.

'I'm afraid it all went a bit badly,' Milena began, but he continued to say nothing. He kept his eyes firmly closed and just seemed to be counting the minutes until he was free once more and back on familiar ground. She wondered if he knew that one of the perpetrators from back then had returned to Belgrade, after twenty-five years, and had been killed in mysterious circumstances.

The sun's rays were only just clearing the tops of the tall houses on Prince Miloš Street by the time they got to the centre. Milena drove around Victory Square, passed the Grand Hotel, turned into King Alexander Boulevard, and decided to refrain from asking Jovan Jovanović any more questions for the time being. She'd drive him back home now, make a note of where he lived, and then take it from there.

She parked on Belgrade Street, not far from the kiosk, and hadn't even had time to turn off the engine before he flung open his door.

'Steady on, there,' said Milena. She walked around the car, helped him unbuckle his seat belt and get out, and passed him his crutch from the boot. He set off with no more ado.

She followed him, carrying the bag with his clothes in, and, as she watched him lumbering along ahead of her, it struck her that she might well have seen him somewhere before in the city. Men like Jovan Jovanović – a bit raggedy, constantly on the move, vulnerable, with something of the hunted fugitive about them – were as much a part of this city as the chewing gum stuck to the pavements, the potholes in the roads, and the verdigris-tinged domes on the presidential palace.

Jovan Jovanović made his way laboriously down the street, looking to neither the right nor the left. They were already below Kalemegdan Fortress by this time, passing a line of tour buses, and Milena began to wonder where this trek would end. Here, near the entrance to the catacombs, was the site of Club 24, a venue her students were always talking about; DJs from Berlin and New York were regularly flown in to perform here, but also at other places in the city, like the former Cuban embassy and the old warehouses along the Danube. Milena turned around. Old Jovanović had vanished into thin air.

How was that possible? The next door she came to was nailed shut, with the window next to it firmly barred.

On the far side of the street, by the sumac trees, all that was visible were weeds and fly-tipped refuse. A tram rushed past. On the corner, an old washing machine stood by the roadside like a pillar, marking an entranceway that would most likely otherwise have escaped Milena's attention.

The driveway led down the bank and seemed to peter out into nothing. A whole new level of gloom reigned down here, and it was clammily damp as well. 'Mr Jovanović?' she called out.

Behind some parked cars, a low-roofed shack came into view. Milena took a large step to avoid a muddy puddle, squeezed past an abandoned armchair, and in the hazy twilight caught sight of a second low building. A dim light came from inside, and the door was open.

'Hello?' Milena hovered on the threshold.

A candle was burning on the table, and a pan with a lid stood on a lit gas ring. Old Jovanović pulled up a stool and made a gesture to her that clearly meant 'come in'.

From the low roof of the hut, a line was dangling; it ended just above a pile of cardboard boxes and old straw mats. Apart from junk, there was really nothing in the shack except for a shelf next to the cooker with crockery on it, a couple of oranges, an assortment of plates and cups, a bin, and some empty bottles.

Leaning on his crutch, Jovan Jovanović put a flower-patterned cup down on the table. 'You're a good person, right?' he said in a hoarse voice.

'What makes you say that?' Milena said, taking a couple of jelly bananas from her bag. She was glad that he'd instigated a conversation. 'Did you live here with your family?'

He stared at her fingers.

'Mr Jovanović?'

In the flickering candlelight, she could see that all the colour had drained from his face, making the lines on it appear deep and black, as if they'd been crudely engraved into his pale skin with a knife. Jovan Jovanović was sunk in thought.

'Do you remember?' asked Milena. 'When Dušan died

– it's all so long ago now. Twenty-five years. One of the two perpetrators came back. Do you understand what I'm saying, Mr Jovanović?'

Milena waited until he returned her gaze, and then went on. 'The man's name was Jurij Pichler. Now, it's really important I know this, Mr Jovanović – did Jurij Pichler try and get in touch with you? Did he make contact with you? Or with anyone else from your family?'

'Pichler?' he asked, staring into space – and slowly shook his head.

'Mr Jovanović?' Again, she waited until he looked at her. 'Does the name Luca Marović mean anything to you?'

He shook his head once more. 'Anna came back,' he said.

'Anna?' Milena repeated. 'Your daughter?'

He nodded.

'Where is she? Can I speak to her?'

'I don't know where she is. I haven't seen her, but I know she's here.'

'How do you know?'

He tugged at the collar of his shirt, pointed at his socks, and gestured at the oranges. 'Presents,' he said.

'From your daughter?'

'I sent Anna away, back then, to America. She was supposed to start a new life there and forget her old one. She wasn't meant to come back.'

'But you say you don't know where she is or how to get in touch with her?'

He shook his head and suddenly narrowed his eyes suspiciously. 'Why do you want to know that?' he asked. 'Has she been up to no good?' He extended his arm and put his hand next to Milena's cup. 'Look, Anna's a good girl,' he said imploringly. 'Believe me. She's clever and respectable. Like her mother.'

Milena started to fish in her bag. 'It's imperative that I talk to your daughter,' she said. 'There are some questions I really need to ask her. Look, I'll give you my card. My phone number's on it. If you see Anna, please ask her to contact me, okay?'

Without a word, the old man stood up and limped over to the straw mats.

'If you've no objection, I'd like to come and see you again in the next few days,' said Milena, getting up from the table. 'Maybe even as soon as tomorrow. Would you be okay with that? You just rest up now, and we'll talk again tomorrow. Perhaps I might bring a friend along, too?'

What was the old man doing? He appeared to be trying to lift the mats. Milena had no idea what he was up to but pitched in to help him all the same. The mats and boxes were clammy to the touch. She'd definitely bring him a proper blanket.

Then she realised what he was about. In the floor, which was just bare earth, was a hole covered with a board. With their combined efforts, they pushed the board aside, revealing a tin box of exactly the same dimensions as the hole.

Rebuffing her attempts to help him, he picked up the box and carried it over to the table. He lifted the lid and, with trembling fingers, began to search around in it.

He placed a photo on the table, a somewhat crumpled colour print. It showed a young woman with her hair tightly scraped back from her face; she had a long nose, dark eyebrows, and a wide mouth, which her smile made seem even larger. Around her neck hung a chain with bright links that looked like they were made of barley sugar.

'Is that your Anna?' asked Milena.

'Svetlana. My wife.' He thrust his chin forward. 'She went just a few months after Dušan. She couldn't take it any more. She jumped from the bridge.'

Milena carefully took hold of the next photo he handed her. A small boy in a striped pullover, with his hands shoved defiantly in the pockets of his jeans. The boy looked healthy, with fine features and alert brown eyes. The girl standing beside him was a good head taller than her brother. She had long hair, a small bust under a jumper, and full lips. The black brows above her eyes merged into one, making the look on her face appear even more serious. The siblings: Anna and Dušan Jovanović.

The old man nodded wistfully.

The third photograph was of a house. Stuccoed and painted yellow, it had a single storey with a veranda supported by pillars. A sandy track led up to it. It was a manor house, quite large.

'Did you live there?' asked Milena in disbelief.

Jovan Jovanović was trying to lever up a second lid, which formed a false bottom to the box. Eventually, in frustration, he tipped the whole thing upside-down. Razor blades, hairpins, and bulldog clips spilled out, and two small gold-coloured cylinders rolled across the table.

Milena picked one of them up and held it in her hand. A bullet, smooth and cold to the touch. 'Have you got a gun?' she asked.

'A Beretta,' he replied.

'Where is it?'

Jovan Jovanović looked at her, dumbstruck. 'It's gone,' he said.

28

Anna peeled the price label off the soles and put the sandals right at the bottom of the carrier bag, and on top of them the smoked hams in their vacuum packs, the goat's cheese, and a packet of biscuits. She left the shirt in its plastic wrapping and slipped it vertically down the side, like a board, which also made the whole bag a bit more stable. Had she forgotten anything? Oh, yes, the money.

Five notes. Or would six be better? Why not just make it a nice round figure? Ten. Then again, too much cash in one lump sum – who knew what her father might go and spend it on? Maybe he'd go on a splurge and buy a television that would flicker in the dark or other expensive goods – which he was perfectly entitled to do, of course – but in doing so draw the attention of crooks, whom he'd be powerless to fight off down in that shack of his.

Undecided, she slipped the notes back into her purse, rolled up the underclothes and shoved them in anywhere they'd fit, and put the bag in the wardrobe. It was truly remarkable how, after all this time, she'd suddenly discovered a sense of responsibility for her father. She'd sort out the money question and other things tomorrow. She put on her trainers, opened the drawer, and pulled out the gun.

The evening sun bathed the clouds in a delicate shade of pink, and a cool breeze wafted up from the river. Anna strode briskly down the street, making for the Danube, with her hands in the pockets of her hoodie. She could feel the cold metal of the gun barrel. She had no idea if the thing was in working order. She'd found the pistol under the bed at her father's place, safe and sound after all those years in the box where it had always been kept. She'd made a conscious effort not to look right or left but to keep her attention focused on the tin box, and she had slipped unnoticed out of the house just a few minutes later. In the meantime, her fear had given way to a feeling of elation. She was in a state of euphoria, as if there were some narcotic in the clear air that she was sucking in in deep breaths, and she began to imagine that her father had kept the gun all the while especially for her, for this day and this act, as if he were now by her side, a silent accomplice, giving her strength and casting an approving eye over every step she took. This, along with the pistol, gave her a wonderful feeling of security.

The riverside promenade lay before her like a dead-straight ribbon, with no bends, no curves, no impediments. She started to jog, running without any haste in a steady rhythm. Her anger at the fact Jurij Pichler had just vanished into thin air had dissipated. She didn't give a damn if he'd drowned, or been shot, or done himself in. He'd called her, and she'd come, and now she was going to bring the story to an end, and everything would make sense. Before she returned to resume her old life, she wanted to look at least one of the perpetrators from back then squarely in the eye.

Level with the jetty, a path led up the embankment. She'd closely scrutinised the locality on the internet and had the lie of the land in her head. She didn't encounter a single walker or jogger, and the drone and chug of ships' engines on the Danube grew ever fainter as she ascended. All she could hear now were the sounds of her own breathing, her footsteps, and the cracking of twigs beneath her shoes.

Luca Marović's house was a white-rendered box of a place. Anna peered through the garden gate and up the driveway. Aside from the light that had come on at the gate when she activated the motion sensor, and a wall lamp next to the door of the house, the whole place lay shrouded in darkness.

She pressed the bell, shifting nervously from one foot to the other.

The second time, she kept her finger on the buzzer for longer. She'd played through this encounter innumerable times in her head, but somehow she'd never anticipated that no one would be at home.

The wall along the road was studded with broken glass. At the corner, a fence began. It was the height of a man and surmounted by a double coil of barbed wire. Anna walked along it; the further from the road she got, and the darker it became, the more difficult and uncertain her task appeared. What was she going to do now? Go back to her hotel? Come back again tomorrow or wait outside the gate until Luca Marović came home? And what if he was out of town?

The ground now beneath her feet was all churned up, as if wild boars had been rooting there. A chain-link gate hung askew on its hinges and the abutting fence had sagged slightly, leaving a clear gap in between – just a narrow opening. The heavy padlocked chain on the gate was entirely ineffective; Anna had no problem squeezing herself between the fence and the gate. What she was doing here was quite illegal, but nothing compared to what Luca Marović had done.

She pushed aside some shrubbery, taking care not to cut herself or snag her jacket on its thorns. Presently, the bushes became more sparse, and she found herself standing among shrubs and trees on the edge of a lawn.

The house, barely twenty metres away, was in complete darkness. With its pretty round arches above all the windows and doors, the rear elevation looked far more inviting than the austere frontage. Wicker chairs were arranged on the patio, and Anna thought of the old picture of the house with the roofed veranda. When she'd opened the tin box at her father's, the photo had been lying on top. As a child, she'd looked at the tattered print countless times with her mother. It had been her mother's great dream to one day live in a house like that. Of course, it was a total fantasy that could never have become a reality. But Dušan and Anna – their mother prophesied it, and told them time and time again – would one day get to live the dream.

All of a sudden, light flooded into the garden. Inside the house, the uplighters had been switched on. Two men were entering the living room. One of them, presumably the owner, Luca Marović, took off his jacket and opened the patio door.

Anna quickly concealed herself behind a tree. She heard their voices but couldn't make out what they were saying. How normal Luca Marović appeared! A regular-looking guy, the kind of bloke who'd surely give you useful tips about buying a second-hand car. He looked like he'd never done a thing wrong in his entire life. But he seemed nervous and was gesticulating, while the other man sat patiently listening to him. Now the two of them stepped out onto the patio and shone a torch into the garden. Had they spotted her in the darkness? Anna held her breath in alarm and crouched down slowly between the bushes.

'... cameras at the corner,' she heard a voice say. 'As for the fence, mind, the gyppos would only need a pair of wire-cutters to get through that...'

'Don't worry, we can arrange everything, Mr Marović.'

'... as quickly as you can, before those vermin get the idea...'

As if in slow motion, she crept around the tree while the two men passed right by her, less than ten metres away, and vanished into the darkness – presumably to inspect the gap in the fence, the weak link in Luca's security system.

She thought about following them, calling out Luca Marović's name and challenging him; after all, she was armed. She could watch him shake with fear, get him to dance for her to her heart's content, or quite calmly request a one-to-one conversation. Then again, there were two of them. Anna hesitated, got slowly to her feet again, and looked over at the house.

On this side, the property ended with the garage. There was no exit that way, and she couldn't make out from where she was standing what the other side of the building looked like. She needed to hurry up and come to a decision. The men could return at any moment.

Her best bet would be to play things by the book and go and ring the bell at the front gate once more. In order to do that, though, she had to get around to the front of the house again, and as quickly as possible.

She flitted across the lawn and onto the patio. A quick step across the threshold, and she was in Luca Marović's living room.

His jacket was draped over a chair. Firewood was laid ready in the grate, and the marble floor was covered with rugs. Modernist drawings hung on the walls, along with an oil painting in a gilded frame.

These were just fleeting impressions that she took in in her haste, yet the effect was so singular that Anna stopped dead in her tracks.

What she was feeling wasn't hatred or envy. It was something else, an emotion she'd never experienced before with regard to her brother's death and the people who'd murdered him. She struggled to place it.

Perhaps it could best be described as pity for a man who evidently no longer felt safe even on his own property, in his own home. He was terrified of the gypsies and had no idea that one of them was at this very moment lurking in his house. Wasn't that enough? Wouldn't it be a sweet victory simply to leave this guy to be preyed upon forever by his own fears?

As she crossed the dining room, running her fingertips over the furniture, she heard a key turn in the entrance-hall door.

'Hello?' called a woman's voice. 'I'm back!'

Startled, Anna hid behind the dining-room door. She heard the sound of luggage being deposited on the floor.

'Are you there, Luca?'

Suddenly, all was quiet. Anna stood in her dark corner, holding her breath and not daring to move a muscle. On the other side of the open door, less than a metre away from her, the unknown person asked, 'Is anybody here?'

29

The distance between the lanterns – little candles in glass bowls – corresponded roughly to Milena's length of stride. She was late, by over half an hour, and Philip would have every reason to be annoyed. Even so, the fact remained that not everything could be resolved in the twinkling of an eye. Some things took time, especially when you had to explain to an eleven-year-old why – at this late hour, and after such an exhausting week, which would continue tomorrow with a very early start – he couldn't come to the restaurant with you.

Adam's strongest counterargument – 'But it's Dad's last day here!' – had failed to win her over. She'd stuck to her guns, refused to get drawn into debate, and guessed she'd just have to learn to live with her son's condemnation of her as 'the most cold-hearted and selfish mother *ever*'.

There was a slow-moving queue at the entrance. Milena took the opportunity to rearrange the collar of her silk blouse and straighten her denim jacket. She wondered whether she'd have time to give Siniša a call and bring him up to speed. He still didn't know about her meeting with Jovan Jovanović. And if it was true what the old man had said, and his daughter really had come back to Belgrade – well, didn't that change everything? Wouldn't that entail a complete rethink on their part? At that moment, her mobile started to ring in her bag. Thought transference, perhaps?

Without her glasses, though, and in this light, she couldn't read the screen. She pressed the green button all the same and said, 'Hello?'

'Milena?'

'Yes?'

On the other end of the line, a familiar male voice enquired, 'Where are you?'

'Alexander!' she exclaimed, her heart skipping a beat. 'How are you?'

'I'm pleased to have finally caught up with you.'

'I was delighted to hear your news,' said Milena. 'But I was rushed off my feet when you called, and now–'

The receptionist behind the lectern, a pretty young woman, beckoned her forward.

'Lukin,' Milena told her, with one hand over the receiver. 'I reserved a table for 7 p.m. My friends will be here already.'

The young woman pointed across the dining room. 'Please, go ahead. They're at the back, on the left.'

'Ah, I can hear you're otherwise engaged,' said Alexander.

'Dinner with my ex,' replied Milena under her breath. 'I'm at the Meat Factory – remember when the farming minister tried to drink us under the table here?'

At the other end of the line, Alexander gave a sigh. 'I've missed you,' he said. 'Not just at the Foreign Ministry negotiations, either. We could have done so much together in Berlin, gone to the opera or a jazz club, and maybe taken in a quick tour of the National Gallery in between. Or we could have just gone with the flow and drifted about.'

'Sounds very tempting – but would we have had time for all that?'

'We'd have made time.'

'Really?'

'Absolutely!'

Milena was heartened by his words as she peered across the dining room, trying to spot Philip and Jutta. Almost all the tables were occupied, and the high-ceilinged room was filled with the hum of chatter and laughter. Waitresses and waiters dressed in long aprons, with studiedly upright postures and inscrutable expressions on their faces, bustled to and fro between the tables like they were on a catwalk.

'So, were the negotiations a success, at least?' Milena asked.

'Let's put it this way,' replied Alexander. 'All is not yet lost. But these technocrats who don't really know what they're about – what's that phrase of yours for them?'

'Desk jockeys?'

'Yeah – well, somehow I just used to have more patience at these conferences.'

Milena laughed. There was so much more she wanted to ask him – for instance, if there was any prospect of individual Balkan states that were already part of the EU renouncing their power of veto over Serbia's negotiations on accession, and whether the president of the West Balkan Conference might play a mediating role in this – but then she caught sight of Philip and Jutta right at the back of the room, in front of the obliquely lit brick wall. They were sitting close together, and Philip had one hand on the back of Jutta's neck and the other on her thigh. It didn't exactly look like the pair of them had much need of Milena's company this evening.

'Any chance we could meet up later?' Alexander asked. 'For a nightcap, at least?'

'I'm not sure,' muttered Milena. She observed how Philip, with half-closed eyes, whispered something in Jutta's ear. She could imagine the kind of stuff he'd be saying; in all likelihood, he'd be forever finding some bimbo or other who'd sit and listen with rapt attention to the crap he came out with.

'You still there?' asked Alexander.

'Listen, I've got to go,' said Milena, startled at how dismissive her tone sounded. No doubt it was the old feeling of jealousy – which vied with tearfulness whenever she thought of Philip – rearing its ugly head again. That, and an indefinable sorrow, and at the same time a realisation that she was at the wrong occasion this evening – that she'd be forced into the degrading position of being a spectator of Philip and Jutta's happiness instead of doing something to ensure her own.

When she finally got to the table and excused herself for her late arrival, Philip, who had his arm slung around Jutta, squinted at his smartphone and chided her. 'Almost an hour. We were beginning to think you weren't coming.'

As they all set about deciding whether they'd have steak tartare or salad, monkfish or rump steak, Milena's thoughts kept wandering to Alexander and to old Jovanović, who'd been robbed of his entire life by the loss of his family and who, if he got to eat anything at all this evening, would only be having the most frugal of fare. Had his daughter really come home, or was that just a father's vain wishfulness talking?

Jutta opted for a side salad with honey dressing – 'but easy on the honey, please' – and, when the waiter had departed with their order, Philip recounted in that rather smug manner of his that Milena so detested how he and Jutta had had a real adventure that afternoon: they'd travelled on Belgrade public transport.

He waited to see whether Milena would say anything, but she just smiled politely and instead fell to wondering where Anna Jovanović, assuming she was still in Belgrade, might be now.

While Philip proceeded to embroider an account of a straightforward bus journey to the far side of the River Sava as an expedition to visit the 'slums of Belgrade', and Jutta punctuated the anecdote with little chuckles of agreement, Milena tried to put herself in Anna Jovanović's shoes. Why had she hidden from her father? Did she have some mission to fulfil? Had she secretly let herself into his shack and taken his pistol? There was every reason to suspect she had. And, if that were so, didn't it mean she was executing a plan? Or had she simply found herself overwhelmed by the situation? As far as Milena could make out, there was no coherent, logical picture.

'And of course, it's still the case that no one around here speaks English.' Philip reached for his wine glass. 'And then,' he continued, 'this old dear comes tottering up to us, carrying a handbag and with her hair permed, and she asks us in perfect German with hardly a trace of an accent whether we've lost our way, and do we need any help?'

Milena placed her napkin at the side of her plate. 'Excuse me, please,' she said, picking up her bag and pushing back her chair. 'I've just got to make a quick phone call.' As she made her way back across the dining room, she dialled Siniša's number.

He picked up immediately – like he'd been waiting for her call. 'Where are you?' he asked. 'Have you finished already? I'm standing right outside the restaurant.'

'What?' said Milena in astonishment, as she squeezed past people in the foyer. 'You're outside the Meat Factory? Why didn't you come in and find me?'

Siniša explained that Vera had told him where he could track Milena down, and had said that she was having dinner with Philip. 'I thought it'd be easier if I just waited here,' he said, and after a short pause he added, 'There's something I have to tell you.'

'About what?' asked Milena, finally emerging onto the street, where there was still a queue of people waiting to get into the restaurant.

'Not on the phone,' said Siniša.

'That sensitive, huh?' she replied, crossing the forecourt and looking around. 'What's happened?'

Milena saw headlights flashing in the line of parked cars. She recognised Siniša's car, crossed the street, and opened the passenger door. 'So,' she said breathlessly, 'what's up?'

'Sit down.' Siniša gave an approving flourish of his hand and remarked, 'Hey, you're looking good!'

'Thanks.' She pulled the door shut. 'What's the urgency?'

He propped his elbow on the armrest between them and explained that it had to do with the message from Commissar Filipow and that ominous *6.36* with the exclamation mark. He'd asked around at the Institute for Ballistics and learned from someone he knew there that the figures might indeed refer to a calibre and, if that were so, not just any calibre.

Siniša turned to face Milena so he could get a better look at her. 'Get ready for this,' he said. 'It's the same calibre of bullet as the ones that killed the Serbian prime minister back in 2003.'

Milena stared at the dashboard in total bewilderment. At length, she asked, 'Are you trying to tell me that Jurij Pichler was shot with the same weapon that was used to assassinate our PM?'

'Apparently, the murder weapon was never recovered at the time, and no further shootings using that calibre have taken place since. Until a fortnight ago, that is – on the day Jurij Pichler was gunned down.'

'Says who? Filipow?'

'I suppose so, yes. But the information was so sensitive that it seems he didn't even feel safe committing it to paper anonymously in a fully formulated sentence. Especially because he most likely figured that it'd ring a bell with us the minute we heard that number. That calibre is legendary in military circles. Ultimately, my friend in ballistics only confirmed something that's an open secret anyway: that 6.36-calibre cartridge cases were found at the scene where the PM was assassinated. The fact that the same calibre weapon was used to kill Jurij Pichler was like a calling card. And, of course, as soon as that came to light, the police closed down the investigation.

'Wait a minute.' Milena squeezed the bridge of her nose with two fingers. 'Just run that by me again: the prime minister and Jurij Pichler were shot with the same gun? That means we must be dealing with the same perpetrators, right? And what kind of calling card? Do you mean the secret service might be behind it?'

'I think you're getting dangerously close to the truth there.'

'But what could Jurij Pichler have to do with the secret service?'

'That's the million-dollar question, and I must confess I never thought along those lines before now. But it's perfectly possible that he might have worked as an agent abroad, and that he maybe wanted out of the whole business.'

'And was eliminated as a result?'

'If he was party to state secrets, then we can't rule out that possibility.'

'But why shoot him with the same weapon that was used to kill the prime minister back then?'

Siniša grimaced. 'You really are sharp, aren't you?' he said. 'That is genuinely mystifying, I grant you.'

'I might just be able to make some sense of it if Jurij Pichler had been a political figure, with a specific agenda, and contacts, and big ambitions. But all he wanted to do was open a hotel. None of it adds up.'

'You realise,' said Siniša, choosing his words carefully, 'we've reached a point where it might be wise for us to leave this case well alone?'

Without responding, Milena produced a shiny gold cylinder from her trouser pocket. 'Take a look at this,' she said.

'Where did you get that?'

'It's from old Jovanović's Beretta.' She told him how she'd met the old man that afternoon, while Siniša held the bullet between his fingers and examined it closely.

'Three millimetres,' he announced.

'At most.'

'In other words, not the murder weapon.'

'No way.' She put the bullet back in her pocket. 'Old Jovanović's pistol that fires these rounds has gone missing,' she said, 'but there's something else that's odd too.' She recounted how Jovanović had sworn blind that his daughter, Anna Jovanović, was in the city. According to him, she'd come back from America, where he'd sent her many years ago after Dušan's murder and his wife's suicide.

'What makes him think she's come back?' asked Siniša, and in reply Milena told him that he'd found a large shopping bag outside his door one day, full of presents, and he'd taken that to mean she'd returned. 'I know it all sounds a bit nebulous, but I somehow get the feeling we should take what the guy's saying seriously,' she said. 'And the idea that Anna Jovanović may now be in possession of that old Beretta and could be about to stumble into the same mess as Jurij Pichler–'

'Okay.' Siniša pressed his hands together pensively. 'How about this? Tomorrow we'll go and see Filipow, or, even better – let's arrange to meet him at some secret location, and then we'll confront him with all our theories and suppositions. But until then...'

Distracted, Milena dived into her bag for her mobile.

'What's up?'

'Why didn't I think of it before?' she muttered to herself.

Siniša looked on as Milena scrolled through her list of recent calls and began, 'Could you at least tell me–'

'Karen Pichler told me the only guest in her hotel was an American woman.' She rang and waited for a reply, but no one picked up at the other end. 'Let's get going, right now!' she said, putting her phone away.

'Where to?'

'Hotel Amsterdam. Don't you get it? The American woman who took a room there might well be Anna Jovanović.'

Without another word, Siniša turned the ignition key and started the engine. Suddenly, he looked across at Milena. 'What about Philip, though?'

'What about him?'

'Isn't he sitting in there waiting for you to come back?'

Milena cursed under her breath and got out her phone again. 'What are you waiting for?' she said. 'Drive!'

A text would have to do. This was an emergency. Philip would be royally pissed off, but she could live with that.

*

When, shortly after 9 p.m., they turned into Little Sava Street, the narrow house on the bend lay in darkness. The spotlights on the facade were switched off, the *Hotel Amsterdam* sign wasn't illuminated, and none of the rooms were lit. Siniša parked in the entrance and turned off the engine.

The glass entrance door was locked and bolted. Milena shielded her eyes and peered inside the dark room. The reception-desk-cum-bar, the club chair by the fireplace – on the face of it, everything seemed normal. But on the table nearest the window, there was a screwed-up tea towel and, further back in the room, a chair had been knocked over.

'Should I try them again?' Siniša keyed the number into his phone, and shortly afterwards the sound of ringing could be heard inside, quite faintly – probably the handset at reception. But there was no sign of movement.

Milena pondered for a moment. At their first meeting, Karen had gone down a side alleyway and disappeared behind the building.

The path ended at a large pile of builders' rubble. Alongside it there was a vacant lot, with room for plenty of cars to park. Next to the wheelie bins against the hotel wall, stones had been stacked and covered with a tarpaulin, and four steps without a balustrade led up to a white door surrounded by decorative moulding.

Milena could find no bell, and the brass doorknob wouldn't turn.

'Look over there,' said Siniša.

From the darkness behind the rubble came the glow of a lit cigarette. A figure was sitting motionless on the edge of a discarded bathtub.

'Excuse me,' Siniša called, 'are you from the hotel?'

'That's Sonja Pichler,' said Milena quietly. 'Jurij's younger sister.' They picked their way around the pile of rubble.

'Good evening, Ms Pichler,' said Siniša. 'We tried phoning, but there was no reply.'

The young woman didn't respond. Thin cables leading up to her ears revealed she had earphones in, and next to her on the ground was a bottle of beer.

Milena took a step closer and leant forward. 'Is your sister-in-law at home?'

Startled, Sonja looked up, reluctantly tugged out her earphones, and replied, 'What are you doing here again?'

'We were just wondering if we could speak to your sister-in-law,' said Siniša.

'Karen's not here, and the hotel's closed.'

Sonja made to put her earphones back in, but Milena asked in consternation, 'Karen's gone, and the hotel's closed? What – you mean for good? What's happened, then?'

'Don't act like you're concerned.' Sonja threw her cigarette butt on the ground; it kicked up a few sparks and then went out. 'You're forever coming round here, pestering us with questions, and every time you do the shit hits the fan once you've gone.'

'Your family's been arguing, then?' enquired Siniša.

'That's what I said, didn't I?' Sonja replied snippily.

'Whatever,' said Milena. 'We're looking for someone, an American woman who may have been staying at your hotel. Karen mentioned her one time. Or have all your guests checked out now?'

'You know what?' Sonja replied, leaning truculently against the edge of the bath. 'I think I'll ask the questions here, if it's all the same to you. First off, I want to know what my brother did wrong. What was so terrible that no one will even breathe a word about it in my earshot? I'm not a kid any more.' She pointed the beer bottle at Siniša. 'You were Jurij's lawyer, weren't you? Maybe you can give me a straight answer for once.'

'I'm sorry. I'm sure you'll understand.' Siniša smiled hesitantly. 'But if your mother's clammed up and doesn't want to talk about it, then she'll have her reasons. I have to respect that and not go behind her back.'

'Then I hereby refuse to testify.'

'Didn't Jurij ever drop a hint to you about what he'd done?' asked Milena.

'A hint? Is that meant to be a joke or something?' Sonja gave a hollow laugh. 'As far as he was concerned, I might as well have not existed. My mysterious brother, always somewhere far away... and then, when he suddenly turns up here again...' She took a swig from her bottle and let out a soft burp. '... we have absolutely nothing to say to one another. Sad but true. Which isn't to say that we might not have got along given time. Who knows? I mean, we could have gone fishing together or something. I've no idea what people do with their big brothers. I just didn't think that he'd be here one day and gone...' She turned her face away.

'The police halted the investigation,' said Milena, 'but there are still lots of inconsistencies.' She handed Sonja a pack of tissues. 'This American woman – is she still staying here?'

Sonja took a tissue, blew her nose, and sniffed. 'I think so. Though I don't remember seeing her today yet.'

'What's her name?' asked Siniša.

'Jones.' Sonja balled up the tissue in her hand. 'Anna, I think. Speaks fluent Serbian, mind.' She gazed up at the dark wall of the hotel. 'Oh, that'd just be the final straw!' she groaned.

'What?'

'If the woman's done a moonlight flit on us.'

'What makes you think she'd do that?'

'My mother had a chat with her, and afterwards she said to me, "I hope that gyppo woman doesn't end up pulling a fast one on the bill." I was a bit puzzled, to tell you the truth, 'cos this Ms Jones doesn't exactly look like a gypsy.'

Milena and Siniša exchanged glances, and Milena asked, 'Is your mother in?'

Sonja shook her head. 'She's gone off to drown her sorrows somewhere. She always does that after she's had a row with Karen. She calls it "taking a turn round the block".' Sonja looked up at the house again. 'Who is this Ms Jones, then? Did she know Jurij?'

'It's complicated,' Siniša told her.

'Could you ring us when Ms Jones puts in an appearance again?' Milena asked.

'Did she have an affair with Jurij?' enquired Sonja.

'No. She once had a little brother,' Milena explained. 'Assuming, that is, that this woman really is Anna Jovanović.'

'So what? Gypsies always have loads of siblings. What's that got to do with Jurij?'

'Hey, look up there!' Siniša suddenly exclaimed, catching hold of Milena's arm. A light had come on in one of the windows on the second floor.

'That's her,' said Sonja. 'Room 3. I'll take you up there if you tell me what Jurij had to do with this woman's little brother.'

'If Ms Jones is the Anna Jovanović we've been looking for,' said Milena, 'then she can tell you the whole story herself.' She adjusted her bag strap on her shoulder. 'So, could you give us access to the room, then, please?'

A few moments later, they were up on the second floor of the hotel, outside Room 3. Siniša knocked. A strip of light was visible beneath the door.

'Ms Jones?' he called. 'Could you please open the door?'

'Maybe she's just getting ready for bed,' said Sonja, shifting nervously from foot to foot. 'Just tell me, will you? What's this about the boy?'

All of a sudden, the door was yanked open. Milena took a step back in astonishment.

'What are you doing here?' asked Sonja, equally taken aback.

Over her nightdress, Mrs Pichler was wearing a cardigan, and her loose straw-coloured hair tumbled down below her shoulders. The glasses that were perched on her nose made her eyes look huge. 'What do you people want?' the old woman exclaimed exasperatedly. 'Why can't you just leave us in peace?'

'And what about you?' replied Siniša. 'What are you doing here, at this time of night, in a guest's room?' He pushed open the door. 'Hello? Are you in there, Ms Jones?'

'I've been tidying her room,' said Mrs Pichler, stepping into the hallway and attempting to pull the door shut behind her. 'That's my job.'

'Has Ms Jones checked out?' Siniša simply pushed his way past her.

'Get out of this room this instant!' the old woman protested.

'Mum,' Sonja interrupted quietly, 'what has Jurij got to do with this Ms Jones, and what's all this about her little brother?'

Mrs Pichler now let Milena walk past her unimpeded, leant wearily against the wall, and said in a flat voice, 'It wasn't Jurij's fault. Luca was to blame, and that's why he got sent down.'

'To blame for what?' asked Sonja. 'What do you mean by that? Is the boy dead?'

In the open wardrobe, Milena found a suitcase and, next to it, a bag.

'You have no right–' Mrs Pichler started to object, as Sonja took hold of her shoulder.

'Answer me, Mum! What was Luca sent down for?'

'An accident.' Mrs Pichler replied. Her breathing was laboured. 'It was an accident. Get out of my house right now! Or I'll call the police!'

'Be my guest,' said Siniša.

Milena saw that the bag was full of provisions and presents. Turning, she said to Siniša, 'It's her, all right. Anna Jones is Anna Jovanović.' She turned to face Mrs Pichler. 'Have you spoken to her?'

'And why would I do that?' rejoined the old woman.

'Mum, you spent almost half an hour with her,' said Sonja. 'You were talking to one another.'

'Did Ms Jones have any contact with your son?' asked Milena. 'Did she and Jurij ever meet?'

Siniša was leafing through an official document, a dark blue US passport. 'When Anna Jones entered Serbia, on 28 April,' he announced, 'Jurij was already dead.' He replaced the passport in the drawer.

'What sort of accident are you talking about?' asked Sonja. Her face had drained of colour, and she kept her gaze fixed on her mother. 'Do you mean Jurij was responsible for someone's death? How could something like that have happened? Was it just negligence? Or are you telling me he was a killer, a murderer?'

'Stop it!' her mother screamed at her. 'Stop saying these stupid things!'

'Just tell your daughter what happened,' Milena urged.

'You keep out of it,' snapped Mrs Pichler. 'Go to your room – now!' she shouted at Sonja.

Sonja remained rooted to the spot.

Mrs Pichler shut her eyes and, struggling to control her emotions, painfully recounted, 'Back then, Jurij was still a boy himself, just like Luca. And this gypsy brat – well, he must have really got under their skin somehow. And when you annoy a lad at that age, you shouldn't be surprised if you get beaten up. That's just the way of the world. And the fact that the boy upped and died was a pure accident.'

'The boy died?' Sonja asked in disbelief.

'Did you have this same conversation with Ms Jovanović?' asked Milena.

Mrs Pichler shook her head. 'She was just after some information.'

'What information?'

'Luca's address.'

'And did you give it to her?'

'I had no reason not to.'

'Where does he live?' asked Milena.

Mrs Pichler shook her head stubbornly. 'Just let Ms Jovanović deal with the matter in her own way. We shouldn't get involved.'

'We've reason to believe Ms Jovanović is armed,' Siniša told her.

'Oh, I know for a fact she is,' said Mrs Pichler, crossing her arms defiantly. 'The pistol was in that drawer, right there, where you've been snooping about all this time, next to her passport.'

'Mrs Pichler,' said Milena, 'if anything happens to Luca Marović–'

'We can't do a thing about it.' Mrs Pichler took her daughter firmly by the shoulders and propelled her towards the door. 'Come along, child. The show's over.'

'I think I know where he lives!' Sonja suddenly announced.

'You've been drinking,' insisted Mrs Pichler, pushing her daughter out of the room.

'Jurij wrote *Cherry Blossom Quarter* in his diary – *Bella Vista*,' Sonja called out over her shoulder. 'Hurry!'

30

The van's brake lights came on briefly before it turned the corner and disappeared into the night. Once it had gone, the street lay as quiet as the grave. No movement, no sound, not a breath of wind – everything dead still.

Despite being dressed in only a thin shirt, Luca felt warm, as if his anxiety were providing a constant source of heat – despite the fact that he'd called the security firm with the precise purpose of getting some peace of mind. The end result of his consultation had been the Premium Package: an alarm system, surveillance cameras, automatic logging of all movements. To meet his particular requirements, the technician had also recommended he install an electronically protected fence, though a subcontractor would have to be engaged to prepare the foundations for it. This introduced an unknown factor into the schedule for the work; that schedule would, apparently, be worked out and forwarded to him sometime tomorrow, along with the estimate. If Luca gave them the green light, they'd most likely be able to start the ground-work in calendar week twenty. So there was 'no problem', as the security guy had repeatedly assured him.

Luca tipped his head back. Not a single star was visible in the night sky, and he was resigned to the fact he'd never have answers to certain questions. For instance, why Jurij had never got back in touch with him again. They could have talked things through. But, instead, it seemed the guy had had nothing better to do than run and tell the police. Had he seriously expected that officers from any department would be called out to interrogate or even arrest him, Luca Marović? Was that what Jurij wanted? For him to be banged up for life? After all, in spite of everything, they'd been friends. Whichever way you looked at it, Jurij's attitude was about as foolish as Luca's own attempt to protect himself with alarm systems and surveillance cameras.

Maybe he was being paranoid, but he had a terrible foreboding that they were still out to make an example of him. He was afraid the men who'd eliminated Jurij would strike again, as a warning to him to keep his mouth shut in future, and that they'd hit him where it hurt most. He was fearful that they had their sights on Cecilia. His was an overpowering, irrational dread, with no basis in fact. But he knew what made his people tick. Or did his old comrades actually have nothing to do with Jurij's death? Was it the Roma who were ultimately behind it?

Ever since his run-in with that gypsy on Belgrade Street, he couldn't get that thought out of his head: namely, that the next generation of Roma – young lads bursting with strength and self-confidence – would believe they had to settle old scores. First Jurij, then him. He couldn't rule that possibility out. On the contrary, it'd be naïve of him to think that this episode from his past was now behind him and that it was all forgiven and forgotten by these people – particularly after Jurij had gone around kicking up such a fuss.

He started to walk back to the house along the public pavement beside the wall. His mind was made up. No alarm system, no cameras, no security fence. He and Cecilia would simply disappear, preferably this very evening. He'd tell her the whole truth about himself and about what had happened back then, after he'd been sent to prison. And if she still wanted to live with him after that, if she could find it in herself to forgive him, they'd settle down together somewhere on the far side of the world and wait until the whole affair had become ancient history.

He was barely thirty metres from his front gate when he saw a figure approaching him. The person appeared so suddenly that his first thought was that they could only have come out of his driveway. It was unusual for there to be any pedestrians around here, especially at this time of night. Or had they been keeping an eye on him from the other side of the street and crossed over to speak to him?

In the light of the street lamp, the vague, dark silhouette resolved first into a slight, boyish figure and then into a woman in jogging clothes – trainers and a jumper with the hood up. Her hands were buried in the pockets of her hoodie, and it looked like she was concealing something there.

The woman was armed, no question. He was certain of it, and alongside a stab of fear he was overcome by a feeling almost of relief. The threat that he'd been sensing all along had finally materialised in this person. He slowed his pace and then came to a halt; their eyes met.

The glint in her eyes wasn't one of curiosity. He saw it was born of fear and something else that was far stronger: rage, or maybe hatred. Who was this woman? Had he met her before? He needed to ask her, engage her in conversation – he had to open his mouth. If he found himself staring down the barrel of her gun, and then the bullet hit him, causing blood to flow from his lacerated veins and organs, it'd be too late. So many had died in that way on the street, in the gutter – not just the prime minister – and now it was his turn. These thoughts raced through his head, but no sound escaped from his dry throat, not so much as a gasp. He wanted to raise his hands, show her that he wasn't a danger, but he couldn't move. It was pitiful; his last thought was to hope that he'd manage to keep control of his bladder, so when they came to dispose of his body they wouldn't be able to say, with a sardonic grin, 'Look at him, the big hero – when the chips were down and he found himself staring death in the face, he pissed his pants in fear.'

The woman drew level and then walked on past him. Astonished, Luca turned to look back at her. A car was slowly approaching up the street and, backlit by its headlights, the woman changed back into the boyish figure, the dark silhouette, and was eventually swallowed by the darkness.

All at once, Luca realised what had happened. Seized by a terrible foreboding, he turned back towards the house.

Yes – the gate to his house was open, and the front door as well. He raced up the drive, cleared the steps in a single bound, and burst into the hallway.

Cecilia's suitcase was standing at the bottom of the stairs, like she'd just arrived home. Next to it were a pair of salmon-coloured court shoes.

'Cecilia?' he shouted. 'Are you there?'

No answer. He strained his ears to hear the slightest sound and moved slowly on. His heart was in his mouth. He was prepared for anything.

The first thing he noticed was the patio door: it was ajar, although he clearly remembered having left it wide open. But something else wasn't as it should be.

The oil painting had been taken down and stood propped against the wall. The safe behind it was open. He was taking a step closer, when suddenly an unknown voice rang out.

'Mr Marović?'

Luca quickly felt in the safe. All that was there was the open, empty case.

*

'Hello?' Milena called a second time. Cautiously, she followed Siniša through the doorway, though she felt deeply uneasy about the situation. The open garden gate and front door, the suitcase by the stairs, the house decked with festive lights, and a pair of shoes – expensive pumps – lying there like they'd been hastily pulled off and carelessly discarded... what did it all mean?

Silently, Siniša crossed the hall to the door beneath the staircase. 'Is anyone home?' he called out, but the dining room was shrouded in darkness.

On the other side, the hallway gave onto a living area, or at least that was what Milena assumed, since, beyond the projecting wall and a broad pillar, she could see the corner of a thick rug on the marble floor. Carefully, Milena peeked around the corner – and then instantly recoiled.

The man in the white shirt took two steps towards her. 'Who are you?' he shouted angrily. 'What the hell do you think you're doing? Marching in here like you own the place!'

'My apologies,' replied Milena. 'The door was open. We tried to get your attention. My name's Lukin.' She gestured towards Siniša. 'And this is my colleague, Mr Stojković.'

'We didn't mean to startle you, Mr Marović. I'm a lawyer,' Siniša announced, tugging down his cuffs. 'Ms Lukin is from the Institute for Criminology and Forensic Science. I'll let her explain.'

'We're looking for a woman,' said Milena. 'Her name's Anna Jovanović, and we've reason to believe that she might be here with you.'

'Anna Jovanović,' Luca repeated, shaking his head. 'What makes you think that?' he asked, tucking his shirt into the waistband of his trousers. His sparse hair was plastered to his forehead, and the wall safe behind him stood open and empty.

'She's the sister of Dušan Jovanović,' Siniša replied.

'You remember, don't you?' Milena asked, observing the man closely and trying to see if the boy's name struck a chord with him. 'The little boy who was murdered on Belgrade Street years ago.'

Luca Marović stared at Milena like he'd seen a ghost. 'The woman in the hoodie,' he murmured.

'What's that?'

'Cecilia!' he called out, and without another word, he pushed past them into the hallway and ran up the stairs.

'He means that woman we saw coming towards us on the street,' said Siniša.

'I'll call the police.' Milena opened her bag.

'And what are you going to tell them?' asked Siniša. 'She's long gone by now.' He gave Milena a startled look. 'Wait here,' he said. 'I'll go and see what's happening upstairs.'

'Be careful!' she called after him, unlocking her phone. Suddenly, her eyes lighted on the safe, the dark hole in the wall.

Inside lay an open case with a blue felt lining. It was clearly designed to hold a firearm, but the pistol was missing. Had Anna Jovanović robbed the safe?

She heard voices upstairs, including Siniša's deep bass. Then a door slammed, and thereafter came silence.

'Siniša?' Milena called out in alarm.

'Put down your phone,' a voice behind her ordered. 'Now!'

Slowly, Milena turned around.

The woman in the patio doorway was in her stockinged feet, and her once-carefully-arranged hair was dishevelled. She was holding a pistol in both hands. 'Didn't you hear me?' screamed the woman, nervously jerking her head, no doubt in an attempt to clear her hair from her face. 'Drop the phone. Just do it!'

Milena obeyed. The mobile clattered to the floor and

shattered. 'Mrs Marović,' Milena stammered. 'This is all a misunderstanding. Your husband's upstairs looking for you. He thought something had happened to you.'

'Who are you?'

'Please put the gun down,' Milena implored her.

'What's all this about? What are you doing in my house? First that other woman... are you and she together?'

'I'm guessing the person you're talking about is Anna Jovanović,' said Milena. 'Did she threaten you? What did she want?'

'Don't move!'

'Just stay calm,' said Milena, raising her hands once more. 'Anna Jovanović is the sister of little Dušan. Does that mean anything to you? The boy who was killed many years ago on Belgrade Street. Your husband and Jurij Pichler were responsible.'

'I know the story. Stop trying to distract me.'

'His sister, Anna, is in Belgrade,' Milena went on. 'We were worried she was planning something. We thought she might take revenge on your husband.'

'And what's all this got to do with you? Why are you even here?'

'We wanted to find out what had happened to Jurij Pichler.' Milena tried inching away from the wall and moving slowly in the direction of the hallway. 'The police closed the investigation,' she said, 'but we know he was murdered.'

'Stay right where you are!'

Once more, Milena complied. She kept her eyes firmly fixed on the woman and on the pistol in her trembling hands. A sudden thought struck her like an electric shock. 'Mrs Marović,' she began, 'the gun you're holding there – is it from the safe? Jurij Pichler was shot with a 6.36-millimetre weapon. Maybe you weren't aware of that.'

'What are you saying?'

'There's blood on that gun.'

'I'm warning you,' said Cecilia. 'Take one more step and I'll fire.'

'I just want to know one thing,' Milena continued, trying all the time to exude as much calm as she could. 'Why did Jurij have to die?'

Cecilia glanced wildly about her. 'Why? Because he could have ruined our life, that's why.'

'Because he knew what your husband had done?'

'I put him on the spot, this Jurij, but he wouldn't listen to me,' Cecilia said.

'*You* did?' Milena exclaimed.

'He was so self-righteous and up himself.'

'Yes,' muttered Milena and nodded. 'He certainly was.' Her heart was racing.

'You see what I was up against?'

'What happened then?' asked Milena.

'He just walked off and left me standing there! He planned to go to the police and report my husband, his best friend, who'd done time for him. He was going to throw him to the wolves. I had to do it.'

'What are you saying?' All of a sudden, Luca was there beside them in the room. His face was ashen. 'You were abroad at the time. You weren't even here!'

'Please try to understand, darling. I did it for us.'

'*You* shot Jurij?' Milena gasped in disbelief.

Luca walked slowly over to his wife. 'Don't worry', he said. 'You didn't kill Jurij. It was the gypsies.'

'I eavesdropped on your conversation with him. I wanted to know what you were discussing. I had a bad feeling right from the start – that you'd meet up with this man, that you'd start drifting, that he'd turn our life upside-down.'

'He was my friend.' He kept his gaze fixed on her, his face a frozen mask, as he cupped his hands around hers and took the pistol from her.

'I was so afraid.' Tears started rolling down her cheeks. 'And then that woman turned up here. She was standing behind the door of the dining room. *Someone's onto me*, I thought. So I got the gun from the safe and hid in the garden. I didn't know where you were.'

'Go and fetch the car.'

'Please forgive me,' she whispered.

'It's all going to be okay.'

Cecilia stared at him without a word – and then did as she was asked. Milena could feel panic rising in her. If there'd ever been a moment when she might have made her escape, she'd certainly missed it now.

'Just let us go,' she pleaded. 'Mr Stojković and me.'

'Oh, yeah, and how would that work?' Luca slipped out the magazine of the automatic pistol to check how many rounds he had left and then snapped it back into place. There was a calm and concentration about his practised movements, like he'd never done anything else.

'Where is he?'

'Your friend?' Luca lifted his eyes to the ceiling. 'He can't hear us. He's upstairs. I locked him in.' He cocked the pistol, a soft mechanical click.

Milena stared at the weapon in his hands, the pistol that his wife had used to kill Jurij Pichler. Calibre 6.36 – the same as the gun used to assassinate the prime minister. She was finding it hard to breathe, as if the oxygen in the room were growing scarcer by the second.

The patio door was open. *Just make a dash for it*, she thought, *scream for help*. But she was petrified with fear.

'Who sent you?' Luca asked, looking her up and down.

'No one sent me,' replied Milena, and the knowledge that she was at this man's mercy suddenly enraged her. 'I was stupid enough to think that you were in danger. Just imagine: I actually had to convince Mr Stojković to drive me over here.'

'I found your business card,' he said. 'I know you were in Belgrade Street.'

'I wanted to know who was leaving lilies of the valley there and keeping the memory of little Dušan alive.'

'On whose instructions?'

'There were no instructions. Believe me. Jurij Pichler was Mr Stojković's client. His story made an impression on me, and we couldn't rest until we'd got to the bottom of his death.'

Luca closed his eyes for a moment, seemingly reflecting on the situation. 'You know,' he said, 'people like you live dangerously.'

'In this country, certainly.' Milena nodded. 'Because people like you are on the loose.'

'Shut your mouth!'

'No, I won't. I want to know how many people's deaths you've got on your conscience. Little Dušan for one – and who else? Just the prime minister, or are there more?'

He didn't reply, but his jaw muscles tensed.

'Did you tell Jurij what you'd done?' Milena asked. 'Were you trying to impress him? Just like that time on Belgrade Street. You've come to the end of the road, Mr Marović. Your past has finally caught up with you. We've got Jurij Pichler to thank for that.'

Luca twisted his head like something was hurting him. 'I'm not the person you take me for,' he said.

Milena didn't answer. Just two or three paces separated her from him. Should she chance it and try to knock the pistol out of his hand? She held back.

'I was specially selected,' he went on. 'I was one of the elite. Our actions were legally sanctioned. Everyone went in fear of us. I was the best of the best.'

'You?' Milena shook her head. 'You weren't the best. If there was anyone you could truly say that of, it was the prime minister. He was a blessing for our country.'

'Just listen to me, will you?' he shouted. 'I need you to understand!'

'Please,' said Milena, 'go ahead and explain.'

'I had a lifetime of sucking up shit,' he began. 'Year after year. At home. At school. In prison. And then, out of the blue, I was selected. I still don't quite know why, to this day. I was one of just a handful who made it to the training camp, or the correctional facility – call it what you will. And I liked it there. Because I knew it'd eventually lead to something big. Finally, I had a goal in life. That objective could have been the prime minister or anyone else. It was all the same to me.'

'His death destroyed all our hopes,' said Milena. 'Our country was set back decades. All our aspirations, everything we'd believed in, shattered in an instant.'

'If I hadn't done it, someone else would have.'

'So his death was unavoidable, was it?' said Milena, edging closer to him. 'And what about Jurij?' she asked. 'He was your best friend – in fact, the only friend you ever had. Would you have killed him too if someone had ordered you to?'

'Just shut your mouth!' he hissed.

'Or would you have bottled it and wimped out like you did before?' Milena took a step back. 'Still, no matter,' she said. 'The question's irrelevant anyhow. You've lost Jurij. Your wife shot him. And why? So you'd never be brought to book for your great deed, the assassination of the prime minister.'

Luca did not reply. Milena could see every pore in his expressionless face, every bead of sweat forming on his skin.

'How many bullets have you got left?' she asked. 'Enough for two? And what then? Do you seriously think your former comrades will go on protecting you forever, after every murder you commit? Do you honestly believe that?'

From outside came the sound of car doors being slammed. Flashing blue lights filled the room.

Luca stared at her, his eyes unnaturally bright. Then he turned away, walked into the hallway with his head bowed, and disappeared around the corner.

Exhausted, Milena leant breathlessly against the wall. She was bathed in sweat and on the verge of tears.

Then a shot rang out.

31

On the left were the extension, the workshop, and the water butt, while the low door to both rooms was on the right. This corner, where no grass grew any more, smelled powerfully of urine, creating an atmosphere at total odds with the tweeting of the birds, which seemed especially loud today. And yet, Anna was only dimly aware of this as she approached the shack.

She felt like she had a fever or was close to fainting, though of course neither was the case. She found herself in quite exceptional circumstances, but then, wasn't that true of her life in general? However the situation was about to pan out, there was a taxi waiting up on the main road with her luggage in it. In two hours at the latest, she'd be sitting in the airport, and in another ten thereafter she'd be in New York. There, Steven would be waiting, and the law firm where she worked, and she'd be back in a city with a logical grid pattern of numbered streets. Her old life. She sidestepped a muddy puddle; her heart was pounding so violently it almost robbed her of breath.

For the second time in forty-eight hours, she knocked on the door, waited, and then turned the handle. She was met by a familiar mouldy smell, and her eyes took a few seconds to become accustomed to the dim light.

The bed was made, and there was even a new candle on the table. Next to it was an orange, probably one of the ones she'd left for him in the bag outside the door three days ago. The place for empty bottles was where it had always been, underneath the sink, while the clean crockery was stacked on the shelf. Everything had its proper place. Only he wasn't there.

Anna put down the bag containing the gifts she'd brought next to the bottles and the ash bucket. She couldn't decide whether she was more relieved or disappointed at not getting to meet her father after all. There'd be no joy at a happy reunion, but neither would it be a shock. No awkwardness and no questions, no 'why did you never get in touch?' She wouldn't have to explain why she was childless and unmarried. She'd never learn if he'd been waiting for her to come back all these years, or if he'd reproach her for following his instructions to the letter and never attempting to make contact with him, or if everything was just fine as it stood. And she'd never know if he was proud of her for achieving everything that her mother had wished for her, and more besides. She had enough to eat, clean clothes, and more than one roof over her head. She'd made it to a stage where no one could tell she was a gypsy just by looking at her.

She lifted the straw mats off the floor, pushed the board aside, and took out the tin box from the recess. Barely twenty-four hours had passed since she'd borrowed the gun, and here she was putting the weapon back in the box beneath the false bottom, where it belonged. She did all this mechanically, without any haste, and in the full knowledge that these were the last actions she'd undertake here.

She laid the envelope with the banknotes on top, with the photos. This injection of cash would help him stave off the worst hardships. She had decided, after her return from Belgrade, to tell Steven that she was Roma and that she'd left her father some money, anonymously, in an envelope. She already knew what he'd say: 'Do you really think you can just buy your way out?' And she'd shake her head and reply, 'No, of course not.'

Before she closed the box again, she looked once more at the photo that lay uppermost on the small pile of snaps: a crumpled colour print showing a little boy in a striped pullover and a girl standing beside him. Dušan and Anna. She slumped down on the chair and pressed the photo to her breast, this single visible piece of evidence that she'd ever had another life.

She'd left it all behind her, shrugged off her background like an old jacket and not looked back, and yet here she was again, sitting at this rickety table and sobbing uncontrollably, though she'd shed no tears after Dušan's death, or when her mother died, or when she'd said goodbye to her father. There was nothing any more, no purpose, no future, just a single question: would she have achieved all she had if Dušan had lived? Would she be the same person she now was if he hadn't died and if people hadn't organised a collection for her after his death, her fund to start a new life? Or had the life she now led only been made possible by Dušan's premature demise back then?

She tried to calm herself by taking deep breaths. As she blinked and looked up through a veil of tears, she saw silhouetted in the doorway, not three metres away, a hunched figure, the old man.

As if she'd been caught doing something wrong, she wiped her tear-stained face on her sleeve. She wanted to leap up, hug him, tell him everything, and ask endless questions – but she could find no words.

Eventually, she got to her feet. Hesitantly, she walked over to him. But, after standing there all the while rooted to the spot like some weather-beaten statue, he now recoiled from her as if she were an apparition, a ghost he was afraid of.

'Dad,' she blurted out at last, 'it's me, your daughter. Don't you recognise me? I'm Anna, Dušan's sister!'

He raised his hands as if trying to fend her off. 'Please,' he said quietly, 'please just go.'

She opened her mouth to tell him how sorry she was. She wanted to explain what had happened, and that she'd come back because one of the perpetrators had got in touch with her, and to tell him about how she'd wandered the streets for days in a state of confusion and had almost done something incredibly stupid. But her father, the old man, just kept shaking his head like he feared her words, as though every syllable she uttered was proof of her existence and a stab wound to his heart.

'Didn't you hear me?' he whispered. 'Go!'

Silently, she lowered her gaze and was turned away, confused and ashamed, but all of a sudden he held out his hand.

He stroked her cheek. 'It's good,' he said. 'It's all good.'

At the touch of his fingertips, Anna inclined her head towards him, but he looked past her like she'd vanished into thin air. He seemed to be far away, in a place where he was hearing voices, which he was listening to intently, trying to make sense of them. She gave him a searching look, studying the lines on his face and his grey eyes, and merely nodded when he said to her, 'Now go and live your life.'

She turned away, stepped over the threshold, and walked up the muddy path as if in a trance, slowly ascending the slope to the street, where her taxi was waiting.

32

Milena had imagined the fresh air might do her good and maybe even divert her thoughts onto other topics, and now she found herself battling against the fierce wind that had been gusting through the streets all afternoon. The café sunshades and the bright shop-window awnings had all been taken in, robbing the place of colour and giving the impression that a pall of melancholy and sadness had settled over the city. Unable to shake off a feeling of guilt, Milena kept asking herself if she could have prevented the tragedy – or if, worse still, she'd even precipitated it.

'You're in shock,' Siniša had said to her that lunchtime, as she sat poking at her salad with no real appetite. 'Just think about it: you were in fear for your life. Luca Marović was threatening you with a gun.' Besides, Siniša maintained, Luca's suicide had an internal logic and consistency to it. 'Believe me,' he said, 'even if he'd been charged – and the body of evidence was overwhelming – he'd never have had his day in court. His old comrades would have gunned him down somewhere, maybe on his way to the committal hearing, or would have made sure that he was hanged in his cell and it looked like suicide. Luca knew that. With his exposure and our testimonies, he was a dead man walking.'

Milena crossed the street. Number eighteen was opposite the new French designer boutique, whose opening the local television station had covered extensively. The irony that the prominent old communist and former head of the Yugoslavian secret service Vladimir Marović should be living cheek by jowl with this temple to capitalist consumerism was, of course, not mentioned. In all probability, no one was aware of it, despite the fact that his name was boldly displayed on the doorbell board.

She rang the bell and the door buzzer activated, but, as she made to enter the building, she noticed that the main door had been wedged open a crack with a folded advertising leaflet.

The flat was on the second floor, and here too the door was open. A woman's voice called out, 'Come in. Unfortunately, it's more than I thought – I've got fifteen full bin bags!'

'Excuse me,' said Milena. 'Have I got the right address? I wanted to speak to Mr Marović.'

A young woman poked her head round the corner. Her tightly knotted neckerchief in the Italian national colours struck Milena as familiar. *Meike* was written on the little name tag on her lapel. The restaurant manager from Little Italy stared at Milena like she was some kind of apparition and gasped, 'I thought it was the refuse collection...'

'We met just the day before yesterday, if you remember,' said Milena. 'In the restaurant. I showed you a picture.'

Meike's eyes suddenly filled with tears. 'Can it really be true?' she said hoarsely. 'Why did he do that? Because his wife was arrested? The police were at the restaurant this morning and turned the whole office upside-down. What a tragedy! And then I suddenly thought, *who's going to take the old man his food?*

Milena glanced down the dark hallway. 'Where is he?'

'And the kitchen's a complete tip,' Meike sniffed. 'What's going to happen now? Who's going to look after him?' She blew her nose. 'Along here. Second door on the right.'

The room was large, with high windows and heavy curtains, some of which were drawn. At the back of the room, where a small table lamp provided light, pieces of furniture and other bulky items that were evidently no longer in use stood covered in dust sheets. Plastic flowers, vases, and an old typewriter were lying amongst piles of newspapers, file folders, and old packaging. It wasn't clear whether someone had begun to tidy this room and had left the job half-finished, or whether the mess was gradually expanding and old Marović would eventually be buried under the accumulated junk.

He was sitting with his back to the door in the protective embrace of a high-backed armchair.

'Please excuse the intrusion,' said Milena, cautiously approaching him. 'I hope this isn't an inconvenient time for you. My name's Lukin. We spoke on the phone this morning.'

He jabbed his fork around in a plastic tray containing the remains of an aubergine pasta dish. Milena wasn't entirely sure he'd even heard her.

'Please accept my deepest condolences,' she said.

'Yes, I remember. You called.' He dabbed his mouth with a napkin, slowly turned his head, and fixed her with his gaze. 'You were there when it happened?' he asked.

Milena let the hand she'd tried to extend to him drop to her side. 'I'm terribly sorry,' she said. 'It all happened so quickly.' Her voice started to quaver.

'Quickly?' the old man asked. 'What was quick about it?'

'The police were already outside, and there were blue flashing lights everywhere. Mr Stojković, the lawyer who'd come to the house with me, who was locked upstairs, had called them. I only learned all this afterwards. Cecilia, your granddaughter-in-law, has confessed to killing Jurij Pichler and is now in custody.'

'That doesn't interest me,' Vladimir Marović had a stentorian voice; he spoke like he was conducting an interrogation. 'What I want to know from you is how it happened.'

'He threatened me with a gun,' Milena replied, struggling to keep control of her emotions. 'Then, all of a sudden, he disappeared.'

'Disappeared? Where?'

Milena was close to tears. 'Around the corner. And then...'

'Spit it out!'

'... then he shot himself.'

'He shot himself,' the old man repeated, leaning back in his chair and staring pensively into space.

The room was airless and stuffy. Milena would have loved to open a window, but she dared not move.

At length, he broke the silence. 'He had no backbone. He was a weakling. Always did what others ordered him to do. But at least this time he acted decisively. I'll give him that.' Vladimir Marović ran his hand slowly over the wax table-cloth. 'He made a decision before others decided for him. And that decision calls for some respect.'

'Respect?'

He looked up at her. 'What are you doing, standing there? Sit down!'

Following his instruction, Milena took a seat on the sofa, which subsided so far under her weight that the edge of the table almost reached her chin. She was forced to look up at Marović like a child. 'If you want to talk about respect,' she said, making an effort to sit up as straight as she could, 'I'd say he'd have earned that if he'd had the courage to face justice rather than taking the coward's way out.'

'Your naïve faith in the rule of law is very touching.' He pulled his face into a sarcastic grimace.

'You know what your grandson did, right?' Milena leant forward. 'All those years, you knew that Luca had been responsible for assassinating the prime minister. And you said nothing. Why? Because he was your grandson?'

Without a word, he laid his napkin down on one of the empty takeaway containers. His beard was neatly trimmed, merging down his neck into thick chest hair. Across his sunken cheeks ran a fine network of broken purple veins. Milena forced herself to stay calm. 'Did you give the order for the prime minister to be assassinated back then?' she asked. 'Were you in the background pulling the strings?'

'I won't stand for such accusations!' the old man barked. 'By killing the prime minister, Luca destroyed my life's work. That's the bitter truth of it, and the greatest sacrifice I ever made was not banishing him after that but keeping him in my life right up to the end.'

'So why didn't you prevent the assassination?' asked Milena. 'It was a contract killing, planned long ahead and meticulously organised. You must have known something. You aren't some nobody. You still had influence.'

'I'm an old man now, and I was even back then. I didn't know anything. But–' the old man was seized by a coughing fit, and a sour odour pervaded the room.

'In fact,' he continued after his cough subsided, 'I sensed something like that might happen. A politician like him who steers his own course and won't be deflected runs a constant risk of being killed – because his opponents have no counter-arguments, nothing to combat his charisma with, and they fear their privileges are about to be swept away. That's why we made a point of systematically doing away with our enemies. The prime minister didn't deem that necessary. Either he had moral scruples about it, or he underestimated the danger. He was wrong on both counts.'

'Who was behind it, then?' asked Milena. 'Who ordered the killing?'

Vladimir Marović closed his eyes and winced, seemingly in pain.

'Please tell me,' Milena implored him. 'Tell me what you know. You've nothing more to lose.'

'I have a theory,' he said, 'even if no one wants to hear it. I think Russian intelligence, the GRU, was behind it.'

'What?'

'Why do I think that? Well, the prime minister's policies were aimed at keeping the Russians from meddling in what remained of Yugoslavia at the time, especially Montenegro. He wanted to push back against Russian influence in the Balkans and reduce it to a minimum. Just like we did after the state was founded, in 1945. In that sense, his policies were a continuation of ours, and at the same time a blueprint for the Balkan countries to come together again after the catastrophe of the Yugoslav Wars, maybe even form a confederation. Why that sceptical look? The way the Russian secret service exerted its influence and used my grandson, of all people, who I loved like a son, as a tool to clear the prime minister out of their way – that's exactly how they operate.'

Milena shook her head. 'I don't know what to make of your conspiracy theories,' she said, 'but, with respect, I find it pretty sordid that you're painting yourself as the victim here. You've got people's blood on your hands; you imprisoned political opponents on the island of Goli Otok and tortured and murdered them. Your grandson is the victim of a sick system that you were responsible for creating.'

The old man looked up at the ceiling, shaking his head. When he replied, with the corners of his mouth turned down, his expression was a mask of ugly contempt. 'You're a woman, and female logic was always alien to me. Because in the end it's all about feelings with you – banal sentimentality.' He banged his fist on the table. 'But for us it was about an idea!' he shouted. 'About the unity of all the states in the Balkans, about non-alignment and independence. When we formed Yugoslavia, we were like the forerunner of a united Europe. And what are we now? A collection of little rump states that can barely thrive on their own, with their governments run by idiots – criminals who are just out to feather their own nests, who give their relatives cushy jobs and who sell their countries down the river to foreign investors. Just take a look at Kosovo. The Americans only weighed in so forcefully for its independence so they could set up the biggest NATO base in Europe there. The Russians regard Montenegro as their colony and are leaning on Serbia for all they're worth, while the Turks are working systematically for the Islamisation of Bosnia. That's what the Balkans look like today. There's no great plan, no courage, no vision. Everyone's just out for themselves, and no one's telling the world what's really happening here and what a catastrophe is looming. And you have the gall to sit there and accuse me? That's very convenient. And it's also criminal.'

With some effort, he hauled himself to his feet and groped for his stick. 'There'll be another war,' he said. 'A war in the Balkans. And I can tell you now: the world will ask itself again how that could possibly happen. Because everyone was looking the other way. Because no one read the signs and raised their voice in protest.'

Step by step, he shuffled from the room. 'Do something, why don't you? Put your people wise, tell them what's going on. What are you waiting for? Time's running away with us. Get a move on! Shake a leg!' His parting shot was accompanied by the slow, insistent rhythm of his stick thumping on the ground as he receded down the hall. Then a door slammed, and silence descended.

Milena stood up, mechanically gathered up the plastic takeaway boxes, picked up the tray, and put it in the kitchen. She strained to listen one last time, but there was no sound to be heard in the flat. She quietly pulled the front door shut behind her as she left.

It had started to rain. She turned up the collar of her jacket and thought about Cecilia Marović, who was now in custody and would in all probability be defended by Siniša. And she thought about the dead: Dušan Jovanović, Jurij Pichler, Luca Marović. At one time, they'd all been like Adam, little boys in short trousers, who imagined the world lay there for the taking, with all its possibilities. But because unscrupulousness and violence reigned, dreams like that came to nothing and families and friendships were broken. It seemed that Milena always arrived too late, and that she only ever had questions rather than answers – let alone solutions.

Moisture gradually seeped through the thin material of her jacket. She walked to the kerb and hailed a taxi.

'So,' enquired the driver once she was seated in the back of the cab, 'where to?'

She gave him an address. It was a spontaneous idea, most likely born of an unspoken yearning on her part, and she surprised herself.

Passers-by hurried along carrying umbrellas, with their shoulders hunched against the rain. Milena reclined on the upholstery, listening to the music on the radio – an American hit she used to dance to at parties – and fancied that it might gradually be brightening up.

She paid the driver and got out. She knew the house; she'd visited it once before, when his predecessor had held a reception here. But that was ages ago, when Adam had only just been born. In another lifetime.

Lights were shining behind the windows on the ground floor. She pressed the bell at the garden gate, and pangs of doubt suddenly assailed her. What if he had guests and the place was full of people?

The door at the top of the steps opened. She recognised his silhouette. Alexander strode quickly down to meet her.

She started to apologise, to explain, and to tell him what had happened, but Alexander just draped his jacket over her shoulders, took her in his arms, and embraced her – at first tentatively, and then ever tighter.

They stood there alone, in the pouring rain, though she was oblivious to it. Everything seemed to be obeying a logic and a gut instinct, and it was all right and proper.

Acknowledgements

The translator thanks her fellow translator and true wordsmith Peter Lewis for his unfailing editorial flair.

www.ingramcontent.com/pod-product-compliance
Lightning Source LLC
Chambersburg PA
CBHW050126030726
47505CB00007B/2063